QUANTUM CHAOS

A ROAK: GALACTIC BOUNTY HUNTER NOVEL

JAKE BIBLE

SEVERED PRESS
HOBART TASMANIA

QUANTUM CHAOS

OTHER BOOKS IN THE GALACTIC FLEET UNIVERSE

Salvage Merc One
Salvage Merc One: The Daedalus System

Drop Team Zero

Outpost Hell

Roak: Galactic Bounty Hunter
Nebula Risen- A Roak: Galactic Bounty Hunter Novel
Razer Edge- A Roak: Galactic Bounty Hunter novel
Paradox Slaughter: A Roak: Galactic Bounty Hunter Novel
Infinite Mayhem A Roak: Galactic Bounty Hunter Novel

Galactic Vice
Agent Prime

1.

"Hey there, guy friend. You lookin' for Tacos? I got all the Tacos you need, guy friend. All the Tacos. Just say the word and I can have you swimming in Tacos."

"Why in all the Hells would I want to swim in Tacos?"

The being, a Jesperian, one of the humanoid races that looked like he may or may not have been sleeping next to the incinerator bins in the alley out back, paused. He blinked a few times, the jumbled thoughts in his Taco-addled mind very apparent on his face. When the correct thought finally formed and reached his lips, he smiled.

No teeth. Nothing but a junkie's sore-filled gums showed past his cracked lips.

"Oh, guy friend, you're messin' with me. Playin' a game. No, guy friend, no one swims in Tacos. That's crazy, guy friend."

"Stop calling me that. And also, go away."

"Oh, guy friend, come on. You know you want some Tacos." The Jesperian glanced about the tavern. "Why else you come in this place? No one comes here unless they want Tacos or good whores or street wubloov."

"Good whores? I doubt that."

Over six feet, square-jawed and broad-shouldered, the "guy friend" looked like he could have played any of a dozen of popular galactic professional sports in his youth. But his youth was long gone. Early forties, scarred skin, ropy muscles, and eyes that were cold as ice, the man had obviously found a new sport in life, one that involved a good deal of violence.

He proved that by producing a Flott Five-Six concussion blaster with laser cluster spread and placing it on top of the table where he sat. A table in the darkest, farthest corner from the tavern's main entrance.

The Jesperian blinked again, looking as if he wasn't quite sure what the device was that the man had produced. Then the sore-filled gums made a second appearance.

"Oh," the Jesperian said. "I'll leave now."

"Good plan."

"I'll tell everyone you don't want the Tacos."

The man gripped the Flott a little harder. The Jesperian gulped.

"Or I tell no one."

"Anything."

"Anything. Yeah. I'll tell no one anything."

"Better plan."

"Best plan, guy friend." The Jesperian backed away slowly, his bloodshot eyes tracking the Flott's pitch black muzzle. "Best plan..."

The man watched the Jesperian scurry through the maze of unoccupied mismatched tables then rush out the tavern's entrance. The bartender, a Groshnell, an eight-armed, boneless race that gulped air to stay solid, eyed the man for a split second then went back to talking up the Cervile woman that sat at the end of the bar. A feline-like race, Cerviles could be deadly, but the woman looked like she hadn't seen deadly in decades. Her fur was afflicted with mange and her body was doughy and slack, not taught and dangerous.

To each their own, the man thought.

"Roak?" a female voice called over the comm in the man's ear.

Although technically all AIs were gender neutral, the female voice was Hessa, the very unique AI protocol that ran Roak's ship. Or *was* Roak's ship, depending on the perspective. The comm implant she used to communicate with Roak was one of her own design that she had placed inside him against his wishes. Roak preferred to be tech-free. Which he never stopped mentioning to Hessa.

But the comm had proven to be completely undetectable, and begrudgingly, helpful in certain situations.

Like the one Roak was currently engaged in.

"What you got for me, Hessa?" Roak asked, taking a sip of the same pint of wubloov he'd been nursing for the last hour. Wubloov was a hallucinogenic beer that could be tricky even when it was of high quality. The one in the pint glass before Roak was far from high quality.

Roak doubted it even was wubloov. Not that he cared. His metabolism and wubloov never were fully compatible. Anyway, he was in the tavern to find someone, not to get drunk.

Which was apparent to the bartender, who finally disengaged himself from his conversation with the Cervile woman and made his way over to Roak's table.

"Hey. You. I'm gonna start charging rent for your ass staying in that seat for much longer if you don't buy more than one drink," the bartender said.

"Then give me another," Roak replied.

"You aren't done with your first one."

"So?"

"Beings tend to finish their first drink before ordering a second."

"Do I get a discount on the second if I finish the first?"

"No."

"Then what does it matter to you?" Roak reached into a pouch on the belt of his light armor and pulled out a couple of chits. He slapped them on the table. "These are what you want, right?"

The bartender studied the chits, studied Roak, studied the chits again, then snatched the money up with one of his tentacle-arms and made his way back to the bar where the Cervile woman pretended not to be watching the entire interaction. Before the bartender was back before her, she leaned close to her wrist.

"Are you done being the friendliest guy in the galaxy?" Hessa asked.

"You know me," Roak replied.

"There's a comm signal coming from that tavern," Hessa said. "I think you've been made."

"Gonna agree with you there," Roak said, his eyes on the Cervile. "Can you hack the signal?"

"Already did," Hessa replied. "Cervile dialect. Do you see the source?"

"I see it," Roak said. "Anything I need to worry about?"

"Not yet," Hessa said and paused.

"But...?"

"The comm is being sent out of the system using a trans-space booster and encrypted signal. Does the source look rich? Because that tech is not cheap."

"No. The source looks considerably less than rich."

"Interesting."

"Boring."

"Boring?"

"Boring. This has nothing to do with our current task. Boring."

"That's one way to look at it..."

"What are you seeing close by? Any chance our target is heading this way?"

"Surveillance holos are inconclusive."

"Inconclusive?"

"Hey!" the bartender shouted. "Keep talking to yourself over there and I'm calling security!" He pointed a tentacle at a sign behind the bar. "Can you read?"

"No crazy," Roak said. "That's your rule? Not, no killing or starting fights, but no crazy?"

"Gotta draw the line somewhere," the bartender replied. "Never been able to stop killing or fighting, but I sure as all the Hells can get rid of the crazy. We clear?"

"We're clear," Roak said.

"I'll talk, you listen," Hessa said.

Roak waited.

3

"Inconclusive because no one is walking around," Hessa said. "Everyone is inside one of thousands of taverns on this planet. Do they know something we don't?"

Roak waited.

"I've tried face rec," Hessa continued, "but Xippee's planetary protection protocols are wreaking havoc with all of my tracking abilities. I can see why this is the planet beings go to in order to lay low."

Roak waited.

"And get drunk," Hessa said. "So much drinking. I do not have a liver, but I am feeling jaundiced just monitoring the levels of poisons the many beings are ingesting at the rates they are ingesting them."

Roak waited.

"I say move on and try another tavern," Hessa said. "Waiting is only drawing attention to you."

"That's what I wanted to hear," Roak replied.

"Hey!" the bartender yelled. "I warned you!"

A tentacle waved over a comm interface by the register.

Roak lifted his Flott and waved it at the bartender.

The tentacle was withdrawn and the comm interface shut down.

"Maybe we got off on the wrong foot," the bartender said.

"You don't have feet," Roak replied. "Hessa? Hack his holo projector."

A cheap and glitchy holo projector set in the ceiling of the tavern came to life and a Galactic Fleet file photo of a Fleet Marine appeared.

"This guy. Have you seen him?" Roak asked. "I heard he frequents this place."

The bartender glanced at the holo and shook his head. "Nope. Never seen him."

"He's lying," Hessa said. "We have holo footage of the man being in here several times over the last few weeks and days."

"I know, Hessa," Roak said. "That's why we're here."

Roak smiled at the bartender. The bartender drew back. The Cervile hissed.

"Have another look," Roak said. "You expect him today?"

"No," the bartender said quickly. "No one else is coming in today. Everyone is staying put where they are."

"Ask him why," Hessa said.

Roak growled, closed his eyes, counted to five, opened his eyes, and sighed.

"Why's that?" Roak asked.

"Today is grease trap day," the bartender said with a tone that implied Roak was an imbecile. "Everyone knows grease trap day."

"Everyone knows grease trap day," the Cervile echoed.

"Grease trap day?" Roak asked.

The bartender checked the time on his register. "Yeah. Go ahead and take a couple of steps outside. You'll see."

Roak glared, shrugged, stood up, and crossed the tavern to the entrance. He opened the door and walked outside, very aware of his back being exposed to the bartender and the Cervile.

"They haven't moved," Hessa said.

"Thanks," Roak replied.

"Time and date."

Roak grumbled to himself, so done with Hessa making note every time he showed gratitude.

Or apologized.

Or admitted fault.

Any issues Roak had with Hessa were instantly forgotten as the intense stench of rotten grease went berserker on his nostrils.

"Roak? Are you in distress? Your heart rate is spiking," Hessa said.

"Grease...trap...day," Roak coughed as he retreated quickly back into the tavern.

"Told ya," the bartender said.

"Grease trap day," the Cervile stated.

"If you'd finished your drink and left sooner you would have avoided it," the bartender said.

"How long does that Eight Million Gods damn smell stick around?" Roak asked.

"Hours," the bartender said with a fleshy shrug. "Sometimes days."

"Sometimes days," the Cervile echoed.

"We don't have days, Roak," Hessa said.

"I am very aware of that," Roak replied, shaking his head at the bartender's look of confusion. "Not talking to you."

"Good," the bartender said then nodded towards Roak's seat. "You paid your chits. Feel free to stay until it's over. Just knock off the crazy."

"There's no cra-... Never mind," Roak said and pulled a rebreather from his belt. "I've got work to do."

"Then go do it," the bartender said. "But gotta warn ya, that rebreather ain't gonna help much."

"Grease trap day," the Cervile said with a loud belch. "No escape."

"We'll see," Roak said.

He tossed another chit onto the counter then pulled a comm unit from his belt and swiped across it. The bartender's wrist implant chimed and the holo of the Fleet Marine appeared.

"Comm this signature if he comes in here," Roak said. "It'll be worth your while."

The bartender shrugged his fleshy shrug once more and pocketed the chit.

Roak studied the Cervile for a second then turned and left.

"Careful out there," the Cervile called after him. "Beings get weird on grease trap day."

"I'll be fine," Roak said.

The stench slammed into him like a plasticrete wall. The bartender wasn't lying, the rebreather didn't help much. The air didn't taste quite so thick, but the smell was still ever present. It was like a second, third, and fourth skin had wrapped themselves around Roak's body. Without the rebreather it would have felt like a fifth skin was on him too.

Small miracles…

"Any suggestions?" Roak asked.

"You're the galaxy's best bounty hunter," Hessa replied. "You tell me."

Roak growled low.

"Something's up your AI butt," he said. "What is it?"

"I am still unsure about this plan of action," Hessa replied. "We do not know with any certainty that Pol Hammon will even be where you believe him to be."

"I have a hunch," Roak said.

"Hunches are dangerous."

"Hunches have gotten me more bounties than I can count."

"But this isn't really a bounty. Not in the traditional sense."

"The little dark tech piece of terpigshit owes me millions of chits, so, yes, this is a bounty in the traditional sense since traditionally I do not stop until I get paid."

"You know what I mean, Roak. We are not hunting Pol Hammon to get paid, but so he can crack the quantum drives that store all of Bishop's files."

"We're doing both, Hessa. Hunting him for his skills, and since Agent Prime told us Pol stole trillions upon trillions of galactic society's wealth then we'll also get paid. Two gumps with one plasma blast."

Roak took several shallow breaths and moved off down the street. A street lined with tavern after tavern.

That was Xippee, a planet made up entirely of taverns. Most economists would argue that it was not a sustainable economic model for a planet, but then those economists had never learned that when it comes to alcoholics and junkies, nothing is sustainable except their desire to consume, consume, consume. Thus Xippee.

"Hessa?" Roak asked. "Do I have a tail?"

"Most humans have some type of vestigial remnant of a tail as manifested in the coccyx bone," Hessa replied. "But, as we have discovered and determined, you aren't exactly human."

"Hessa…" Roak growled.

"I do not see anyone following you," Hessa said, an obvious smirk in her tone.

Human affectations were one of Hessa's quirks. At first they'd driven Roak crazy, but he'd gotten used to them. Just like he'd gotten used to working with Hessa in general.

As for the rest of his crew or whatever they wanted to be called…

Roak passed a tavern that was completely filled with water. The windows were large portholes and the beings inside were swimming around freely, drinks in their flippers, tubes going from the drinks to their mouths. Or suckers. Roak wasn't sure of the species, so he couldn't quite identify the anatomy.

The confusion over the beings' type distracted Roak just enough that he was a half-second late in seeing the large shadow disengage itself from the alleyway at the corner of the building. That half-second proved to be just the amount of time needed for a massive fist to come speeding towards Roak's face.

He took the hit and flew back several meters, his rebreather a shattered mess hanging from his bloodied lips.

"You're Roak," the shadow, the owner of the fist, said.

It wasn't a question, it was a statement.

"You'll regret that," Roak said as he launched to his feet and pulled his Flott.

A half-second before he could pull the trigger the muzzle of a pistol pressed against the skin just under his right ear.

That Eight Million Gods damn half-second…

Roak focused his eyes on the being before him, the owner of the fist. Massive like a Gwreq with muscles upon muscles, there was something wrong with the being's features. It was like the guy was…warped. Roak wanted to ask what in all the Hells was the guy, but he figured the being wouldn't like the question too much.

And he had a pistol jammed under his ear, so there were more pressing questions.

"I hear you're looking for me," the being behind Roak, the one with the pistol, said.

"Are you Chann?" Roak asked. "Former Fleet Marine?"

"As soon as I heard you were looking for me I made a few comm calls," the being said without answering Roak's questions. "There are no bounties out on me, so why the fuck are you hunting me?"

"I'm not hunting you," Roak said. "I just need some info you have."

"Info? Ha," the huge warped being said. "Terpigshit."

"The info will help me find the being I am hunting," Roak explained. "That's why I'm looking for you."

"Info? That's all?" the being behind Roak asked.

"That's all. I'll pay for your time," Roak said.

"And for our drinks," the warped being said.

"And for our drinks," the being behind Roak said.

"And for your drinks," Roak agreed. "Now, how about you put that KL09 away and we go find somewhere out of this Eight Million Gods damn stench where we can talk. Sound good?"

"How'd you know it was a KL09?" the being behind Roak asked as he removed the pistol from Roak's head.

Roak slowly stepped to the side and gave the being, a human and former Fleet Marine named Chann, a harsh glare.

"Not the first time I've had a KL09 pressed to my head," Roak said. He hooked a thumb at the warped being. "He have a name? And species?"

"I don't count as a species anymore, asshole," the warped being said. "And the name's Shick."

"Shick. Chann," Roak said and cocked an eyebrow. "You have a tavern in mind? I don't think the one behind me will work."

Chann glared at Roak for a moment, looked past him to the portholes and water-filled tavern, then nodded.

"Yeah, we know a place," Chann said. "Follow us."

Chann and Shick turned and walked off down the street.

"They seem nice," Hessa said. "Maybe you'll make some friends."

"Shut it, Hessa," Roak said under his breath.

He wiped the blood from his mouth, struggled not to gag over the smell of Grease Trap Day, and fell in line behind Chann and Shick.

"You two don't seem too concerned that I'm behind you and armed," Roak said.

"Nope," Shick said.

"We got you covered, Roak," Chann said over his shoulder.

"Oh…" Hessa gasped. "They're good."

That's when Roak noticed the targeting tag on his right shoulder.

"How many snipers you got watching me?" Roak asked.

"Only need the one," Chann said.

2.

Roak didn't know how it was possible, but the tavern he found himself in was in worse shape than the one with the Groshnel bartender and Cervile "drunk". He also didn't know how it was possible that the place could stink more inside than outside.

Everyday was grease trap day for the pitiful patrons inside the tavern. Unfortunately for Roak, he was about to become one of those pitiful patrons.

"Over here," Chann said and led Roak to a back table while Shick stepped up to the bar.

They were obviously regulars from the way the bartender greeted Shick. Shick placed the order then wound his way through the tables to Roak and Chann.

Chann indicated for Roak to slide into the booth first. He did. Shick squeezed in next to him, effectively pinning Roak to the tavern's wall. It wasn't exactly a clean and sterile wall and the light armor Roak wore kept sticking to the surface, making a wet sucking sound every time he tried to shift positions and pull his shoulder away.

"Stop wiggling," Shick said.

"I don't wiggle," Roak replied. "Ever."

"Well you are now," Shick snapped. "So stop it."

Chann sat across from Roak and waited patiently while the bartender brought over their drinks. All three glasses were filled with a muddy brown substance that Roak wasn't sure was entirely liquid.

"I've had my fill back at the other tavern," Roak said.

"Drink," Shick said.

"Drink," Chann insisted.

"I'd rather not," Roak said.

The three of them sat there, no one saying a word, as Roak waited for Chann and Shick to give in.

Twenty minutes later, Hessa said, "Roak? Maybe have a sip."

"I can wait all night," Roak stated.

"So can we," Chann replied. "Fleet Marines know how to wait."

"He was GF too?" Roak asked, hooking his thumb at Shick.

"Sitting right here, asshole," Shick snarled. "Ask me directly."

"No problem," Roak said and turned to face Shick. "You were GF too?"

"In a past life," Shick said. "Before…"

"Before Javsatem?" Roak said.

Both Shick and Chann tensed. For a brief moment, Roak was certain that Shick was going to throttle him and Chann was going to bolt. Then the two shared a look and the moment passed.

"No idea what you're talking about," Chann said.

"Drink your drink," Shick said.

"I'm thinking no," Roak said. "I don't know what the Eight Million Gods damn stuff is and I don't want to find out. Not to mention the chance you drugged-"

Shick switched his drink for Roak's and pounded Roak's drink down in one swallow.

"Not drugged," Shick said.

"Listen, I'll buy you as many rounds as you want," Roak said, "but I'm not drinking with you. All I need is info."

"Info on an outpost we know nothing about," Chann said. He sipped his drink and frowned. "This really is terpigshit."

"Only thing I can taste," Shick said and took Chann's drink for himself and downed it. He eyed Roak until Roak nodded and he took that one as well. "Bottoms up."

He finished Roak's drink and snapped his massive fingers. The bartender made his way over with three more glasses.

"These are mine," Shick said as the glasses were set on the table. "Don't know what they want."

"You got any Klav whiskey?" Roak asked.

"Big spender," Chann said.

The bartender only laughed and walked away.

"Guess that's a no," Roak said.

Roak slowly, careful not to spook Shick, grabbed the pouch from his belt. He emptied the pouch on the table and the din of constant noise in the tavern lessened a good amount at the sound of chits clinking together.

"I can triple this if your intel turns out to be right," Roak said. "How do I find Javsatem?"

"Couldn't tell you," Chann said. "Never heard of-"

"Don't," Roak said. "I didn't say it was an outpost, you did. You know what Javsatem is and you know where it is."

"Nope," Shick said.

"I believe they are afraid you are there to bust them for the heist they pulled before they ended up on Javsatem," Hessa said.

"Right," Roak said. "Listen, I don't give twenty terpigshits about the job you pulled against the Skrang. I don't care about the loot you stole and sold. I really do not care. All I care about is how to get to Javsatem."

"Do you know what that word means?" Chann asked. "Javsatem?"

"It's an old Ferg word," Roak said. "It means Hell."

"Yeah, it does," Shick said. "You ever been to Hell, Roak?"

"Sitting in it right now," Roak replied, stone-faced.

"No," Shick said. "This is only Purgatory."

"If we did know what you're talking about," Chann said, "why out of all the Hells would you want to go to that one?"

"Doesn't matter," Roak said. "I just need to know how to get there."

Chann snorted. Shick grunted. They shared another look then both relaxed.

"Your funeral," Chann said.

"So you'll get me the coordinates?" Roak asked.

"Nope," Chann replied. "But we can get you the log from the ship that we escaped in. Best we can do."

"What does he mean?" Hessa asked. "A log would have the coordinates. Why not give us the coordinates? This is weird, Roak."

"Why the log?" Roak asked Chann.

"Because the place doesn't have coordinates," Chann said. "Well, it does, but they are unreliable. You want to get to Outpost Hell then you have to follow the log. Retrace our steps backward."

"It's why the GF chose the location for the outpost," Shick said. "Hard to find, even harder to get to."

"And gonna cost you a lot more than what you're offering," Chann said. "The log won't be cheap."

"You don't have the log?" Roak asked.

"Why would we have the log?" Chann responded. "None of us ever want to go back to that place."

Chann leaned forward, his eyes narrowed and wary.

"You don't want to go there either," Chann continued. "It's not a safe place for living beings, especially not humans."

"Who said I was human?" Roak replied. "And I'll be fine. Don't worry."

"No. You won't," Shick said.

"You really won't," Chann said.

Roak leaned back in the booth and crossed his arms over his chest. He looked up at the ceiling for a second, regretted the choice as soon as he saw the various unknown substances that looked ready to drip down on him, then focused back on Chann.

"The planet is plagued with storms," Roak said.

"Understatement," Shick scoffed.

"It's also inhabited by AIs," Roak continued. "Some very formidable AIs. AIs that may have ambitions to do some serious damage to the Galactic Fleet and the galaxy as a whole."

Roak smiled at the looks of surprise on Chann and Shick's faces. Roak was surprised himself when neither of the men cringed at Roak's smile.

Most beings could barely tolerate looking at Roak when he smiled, but those two had no reaction at all.

"You know about the AIs and still want to go there?" Chann laughed. "You're a million times crazier than your reputation. You may be some galactic badass, but you're no match for those AIs. They're...different."

"I have my own different AI," Roak said.

"Excuse me?" Hessa snapped. "Your own?"

Roak ignored her.

"You're not getting it," Chann said. "These aren't androids or advanced AIs running GF mainframes or destroyers. They think they're people."

"I've run into an AI before in a flesh suit," Roak said. "Nothing about Javsatem will shock me."

"Until they jam a plasma coil up your ass," Shick said. "That'll shock you."

"Just get me the log," Roak said.

"You get us ten times the chits and we'll get you the log," Chann said. "What you do with it is your own business."

"Ten times the chits?" Hessa exclaimed.

"Eight Million Gods damn right it's my business," Roak said. "Ten times the chits?"

"Ten times the chits," Chann said.

"We can afford that. Barely," Hessa said. "If Agent Prime comes through with the FIS funds he said he could get."

"We can make it happen," Roak said. "How much time do you need to get the log?"

"A galactic standard week," Chann replied.

"You have two days," Roak responded then stared hard at Shick. "Move."

Shick did not move.

"No way we can get the log in two days," Chann said.

"Two days is the timeframe," Roak said, still staring at Shick. "Two seconds is your time frame to move, ugly."

"Ugly?" Shick laughed. "Your scarred up face ain't exactly winning beauty prizes."

"Yeah, Roak, maybe name calling isn't the way to go," Hessa said.

"Just get out of my way," Roak said to Shick.

The warped man didn't budge.

"We're going to need upfront payment," Chann said. "We have to grease a few wheels to get that log."

"Grease wheels?" Roak laughed.

A few of the tavern's patrons turned to see what the horrible noise was. They turned back to the drinks as soon as they saw the look on Roak's face.

"You and your old comrades not on speaking terms?" Roak asked.

"Our old comrades are all dead," Chann said. "They made some bad decisions and got themselves taken out. Which is why the ship is impounded on Chafa."

Roak's lip curled up in disgust and irritation at the mention of the impound planet. He'd always had bad luck on that toxic place.

"Impounded? It could be scrap by now." Roak rolled his head on his neck. "How do I know you won't take the chits, go get your ship, and disappear without getting me the log?"

"Because we have no way off this planet," Chann said. "You think we want to stay on Xippee?"

Roak narrowed his eyes. "You want a ride to get the log," he stated.

"We just want a ride off this damn planet," Shick said a little too loud.

More patrons turned to regard the meeting. Some kept their eyes on the three men longer than was needed. Roak made note of each being that let their gaze linger.

"Ten times the chits and a ride," Roak said. "We can handle two more passengers."

"Don't forget the sniper," Hessa said.

"Three passengers," Roak added. "Then we dump you off at the closest habitable station, planet, moon, asteroid, whatever."

"Works for me," Chann said. He looked at Shick. The big guy nodded. "Guess we have a deal."

"Great. Can you move your ass now?" Roak asked Shick. "And tell your sniper buddy not to shoot me when I leave."

"What? That's it? We aren't coming with you?" Chann asked.

"I gave you two days," Roak said. "Use them to make sure everything will be smooth as terpig lard when we get to Chafa. I don't want any surprises."

Hessa snorted. "Life with you is nothing but surprises, Roak."

Roak didn't respond to Hessa. Roak didn't respond when Shick slid out of the booth to let him out. Roak didn't respond when Chann started snapping his fingers close to Roak's face.

Well, he did respond to that by grabbing Chann's wrist and slamming the hand down on the table.

"We need to leave," Roak said quietly.

"Roak? What is happening?" Hessa asked.

Chann and Shick looked about the tavern, both trying to find the source of Roak's apprehension.

"So we are going with you?" Chann asked.

"I doubt that," a Gwreq said as she walked up to the table.

Stone-skinned, four-armed, seven feet tall, the being looked more formidable than Shick.

But that wasn't what had Roak worried. It was the color of the Gwreq's eyes.

"Red eyes," Roak said.

"Oh shit…" Hessa responded. "I'm trying to lock moltrans onto you now, Roak, but there are too many beings packed too closely together in the tavern. Can you get out to the street?"

"Is she speaking to you, Roak?" the red-eyed Gwreq asked. "Your AI partner? Say hello to Hessa for me."

"You know this lady?" Shick asked. He moved in closer to the red-eyed Gwreq. "Private conversation, miss. How about you move your grey-skinned self back to the bar?"

"Back off, Shick," Roak warned. "Chann? Take your buddy and leave."

"Leave? Because of some Gwreq?" Chann laughed. "I've dealt with way-"

Chann's sentence was ended as the Gwreq snapped out her lower left arm, grabbed him by the back of the head, and squeezed so hard and fast that his eyeballs shot from his skull and smacked Roak in the face.

"What the fuck?" Shick shouted and swung at the red-eyed Gwreq.

The being moved inside the swing and landed a vicious headbutt to Shick's nose. Bone and cartilage caved inward and blood shot out in every direction.

Before Shick's body fell, Roak had his Flott out and aimed at the red-eyed Gwreq's head.

"We're coming for you, asshole," Roak said and squeezed the trigger.

Gwreq's have incredibly thick skin, many times allowing them to take several plasma shots to the body without any real harm done. But no being could take a direct shot to the face.

The red-eyed Gwreq's head turned to mist and the huge body collapsed across Shick's.

The tavern became chaos and every being in there tried to scramble for the exits, essentially blocking any chance Roak had of escaping quickly.

"Tavern's clearing out, Hessa," Roak said. "Get me out of here as soon as you can."

"What's the hurry?" a red-eyed Slinghasp asked. A snake-like race, but bipedal, the Slinghasp flicked its tongue out at Roak. "Going somewhere, my son?"

"Not your son," Roak said and turned the Slinghasp's head into mist as well.

Roak knew the Slinghasp had only been hijacked by the being known as Father, and it hadn't done anything to Roak to deserve death, but that was a moral detail he didn't have time to deal with. Not when there were dozens more beings around him that could have their implants hijacked too.

"Oh, Roak, so much anger," a red-eyed human said from Roak's right. The human was easily as tall and large as Roak, with bright blue skin, and two Blorta 65 laser pistols pointed at Roak. "Perhaps you should consider sitting back down and having a nice, calming drink. We can talk."

"Nothing to talk about," Roak said.

Roak ducked and rolled, letting the targeting system in the Flott do the heavy lifting. The human's head became mist cloud number three. Roak kept rolling until he had his back up against the bar then he slowly stood, his Flott waving back and forth, his eyes looking for the next attack.

"Whiskey, right?" the bartender said.

Roak spun about, saw the red-eyes, and fired.

More mist.

"Stop this!" a voice roared from the middle of the still fleeing crowd.

A red-eyed Urvein, a bear-like race that was easily eight feet tall and weighed five times more than Roak, stood facing Roak. No weapons were visible, but the being didn't really need them. The six-inch claws at the end of the being's paw-hands were lethal enough.

Roak took aim then cried out as pain exploded in his right forearm. He dropped his Flott and began trying to shake the source of the pain free.

A Ferg, a race that looked like a cross between a beaver and a praying mantis, had its massive front incisors buried in Roak's arm, the sharp teeth able to pierce even Roak's light armor.

Roak lifted his arm high then brought it down hard onto the top of the bar. Parts of the Ferg broke, Roak clearly heard the snapping of bones, but the red-eyed little shit only bit down harder and deeper. Out of the corner of Roak's eye, he could see the Urvein shoving beings out of the way as it waded through the fleeing patrons to get to Roak.

"Hessa," Roak snarled. "Gonna need some help."

"I…a…on you… Keep…to scan…"

"Hessa? Hessa!" Roak shouted.

"Well, isn't this interesting?" the Urvein said. "We have a new guest joining the party."

Roak slammed the Ferg down once, twice, three more times before finally snapping the thing's neck. The teeth loosened enough for Roak to wriggle his fingers inside the mouth and pull the teeth free from his arm.

Blood gushed from the wound. Roak ignored the damage to his arm and concentrated on his comm.

"Hessa? What's going on?" he called.

No answer.

"Oh, this new guest must have considerable resources," the Urvein said. "It's able...to..."

Roak watched the Urvein's eyes flicker back and forth from red to normal and back to red in a chaotic cycle.

"This...is...problematic," the Urvein said right before roaring at the top of its lungs. It clapped its hands to its head then fell to its knees. "We...will...talk soon..."

The Urvein's head exploded.

That did it for any patrons that may have been considering having one more drink for the road. The tavern cleared completely out except for Roak and the corpses.

And a mangy looking Cervile sitting at the end of the bar.

The Cervile from the previous tavern.

The being held up its hand and waved.

"Roak," the Cervile said. "If you wouldn't mind stepping my way. You have an appointment."

The Cervile smoothed its fur and stood up. The mange and softness were gone.

"Nice trick. You're good," Roak said. "I clocked you back at the other tavern, but I thought you were just a tavern rat selling intel. Didn't think you were true Cervile."

"I wouldn't be much use to my queen if I couldn't do the job properly," the Cervile said. "Come along now. She is waiting."

"Your queen?" Roak asked, slightly surprised.

"My queen," the Cervile replied.

"I've never met the Cervile queen before," Roak said. "Maybe I should clean up first. I can meet you there."

"No need," the Cervile said. "She's seen you at your worst."

Roak started to ask a question then closed his mouth. Pieces fell into place.

"Well...shit," Roak said, grabbing his fallen Flott as he moved closer to the Cervile.

"Yes. Well, shit," the Cervile said then cocked her head. "Ready for transport."

In a swirl of molecules, both Roak and the Cervile vanished from the tavern, leaving behind blood and chaos.

Just another day for Roak.

3.

Roak found himself standing on a moltrans platform in a room filled with Cervile troopers. All troopers had their weapons casually held down by their legs, none looking even the least concerned that the galaxy's most deadly bounty hunter had just been transported instantly before them.

Roak wasn't surprised. The Cervile ego was legendary, at least amongst the elite. Roak would have to kill a quarter of them before the others truly became alarmed.

"Nice moltrans," Roak said. "I don't feel like puking at all. You have the new tech."

"There have been great strides these last few months," the Cervile from the tavern said. "It's helped us with our exodus."

"Exodus?" Roak asked.

"Not my place to tell you," the Cervile said. She stepped off the platform and smiled at Roak, making sure he saw her very sharp teeth. "Meshara. Personal attaché and security companion of Queen Tala Berene, at your service."

"She became queen? How?" Roak asked. "There were quite a few before her in the line of succession."

"Yes. *Were*," Meshara replied. "Come along, Roak. The Queen awaits."

Roak had no idea what was going on, but he shrugged, stepped off the platform, and followed Meshara as the woman led him to the moltrans room's exit. The Cervile troopers watched him walk by with practiced indifference.

As soon as Roak was out of the room, he was plunged into chaos.

There were Erviles everywhere. The corridor was lined with cots and belongings with many of the cots occupied by not so healthy looking Cerviles. Young Cerviles ran wild up and down the corridor and the adults let them, no one admonishing them or telling them to go run somewhere else, which was very un-Cervile-like.

"Something happened," Roak said.

"It did," Meshara replied, but didn't offer any further explanation.

"Hessa?" Roak tried calling over his comm. "Hessa, can you read me?"

"Sorry, Roak, but comm transmissions are blocked," Meshara said. "All transmissions are blocked, actually. We took an enormous risk moltransing to the ship, but it was the fastest way to get you here and speed is of the essence right now."

"Why is that?" Roak asked. "Are you being hunted? Because it looks like you're on the run."

"You really haven't heard?" Meshara asked then shook her head. "I'll let the Queen explain it all."

Meshara led and Roak followed as they navigated their way through the disheveled throngs of Cerviles that filled each corridor. Even the lifts they took were filled with Cerviles trying to find a little space for themselves.

It took a long while, but they finally made it to a cleaner area of the ship. The numbers of packed together Cerviles dwindled and the quality of the attire grew. Roak recognized a couple of faces here and there, faces belonging to the Cervile ruling class, as he and Meshara walked the last few meters to a set of massive, ornate double doors.

Two Cervile guards opened the doors and Meshara gestured for Roak to take the lead. He did and was not surprised to see the massive receiving hall usually reserved exclusively for the queen was also filled with cots and belongings, as well as several depressed and harried looking Cervile nobles.

At the far end of the receiving hall was a dais that should have had a throne on it, but instead there was just another cot. Although, the cot was more of a four-poster bed.

Sitting on it cross-legged was a Cervile woman. A Cervile woman staring daggers at Roak.

"Tala," Roak said. "How deep is this terpigshit I'm in?"

"You will address her as *Queen* Tala or Her Majesty!" a guard shouted.

"Pal, you'll want to just back the fuck down," Roak said without taking his eyes off Tala. "This is my ex-wife, so I'll call her-"

Several plasma rifles were pointed at Roak's head. Meshara held a blade down close to her leg. Roak could tell out of the corner of his eye she was ready to strike as soon as she needed to.

Roak waited for Tala to call off the guards and Meshara. She did not.

"That deep, huh?" Roak said. "Great. Care to tell me why?"

"Your Majesty?" Meshara asked.

Tala sighed, uncrossed her legs, and stood up from the bed. She glanced casually at the guards, at Meshara, then finally at Roak.

"He lives for now," Tala said. "We need him."

"It's good to be needed," Roak said.

The guards tensed, but did not fire.

"Weapons down," Tala said. She stepped from the dais and walked past Roak. "Follow me. I feel the need for a walk. We can talk along the way."

"Talking and walking is good," Roak said. "Better than bleeding and dying."

"That may still happen," Tala said. "It will depend on our talk and if you are actually worth keeping alive."

"Pretty much the theme of our marriage," Roak said. "It'll be fun."

"Like old times," Tala said. "But with a legitimate option of me killing you at the end."

"Like I said, it'll be fun," Roak replied.

He followed Tala as she left the receiving hall. Meshara followed, but the guards were left behind. Roak knew there would be plenty of guards close by as they walked the corridors. Even if he wanted to harm Tala, he'd have a slim to none chance of making that happen. And a zero chance of surviving afterwards.

They walked down one corridor in silence then another and another.

Roak waited patiently. He had no choice and knew it.

"We are divorced, yes?" Tala asked finally.

"Last I checked," Roak replied.

"So we are no longer family?"

"According to Cervile and GF law."

"Then why, if I may ask, am I still dealing with fucking in-laws?" Tala shouted.

The Cerviles lining the corridor cringed at the queen's outburst. Some ducked under their cots.

Roak really wanted to know what in all the Hells had happened to these people.

"In-laws?" Roak asked. "What do you mean? I don't… Oh… Father."

"Father," Tala agreed. "He paid us a visit and took our planet. It is gone, Roak."

"What do you mean it's gone?"

"Gone. It was there and now it is not."

"He destroyed it?"

"Were you not listening? I said he paid us a visit and took it. Took. It. The planet is no longer in our galaxy. It is gone."

Roak studied the Cerviles around him. They were normally beings that could handle almost anything thrown at them with calm and quite a bit of nerve. These beings were traumatized, terrified, and broken. They'd seen some shit.

"Tell me what happened," Roak said.

Tala did.

She explained how Father had shown up in the guise of one of the Cervile ambassadors returning home from a diplomatic mission. By the time she or anyone realized that the ambassador was not who he was supposed to be and was instead some malicious entity, it was too late.

The planet shook with severe earthquakes for days. Millions lost their lives before Tala could implement an evacuation plan. She and her council handled it perfectly and got every single remaining Cervile off the planet.

Then the planet disappeared. It was there one moment and then not. No trace. Nothing.

"He took a planet?" Roak mused. "Why in all the Hells would he do that? And how in all the Hells did he manage it?"

"That is why you are here," Tala said. "Why in all the Hells would your Father do that and how did he manage it?"

"First, not my father," Roak said. "He's just some asshole that raised, trained, and tortured me."

"And your siblings," Tala said.

"They aren't my… Fine, sure, and my siblings."

"Just some asshole or not, he identifies as Father and identifies as your Father, so you better have a solution to this problem."

"A solution?"

Roak stopped walking. Tala did not.

Roak stood there and waited. Tala continued walking.

Roak kept waiting, Tala kept walking.

"Eight Million Gods dammit," Roak snarled then jogged to catch up with the queen.

"What do you mean, a solution?" Roak asked.

"What do you mean, what do I mean? A solution. A solution on how you get my planet back."

"Are you joking? I can't get a planet back. How the fuck would I get a planet back?"

Meshara hissed from behind them.

"Show respect," she stated. Nothing but menace dripped from her words.

"How the fuck would I get a planet back, *Your Majesty*?" Roak said.

Meshara pounced. Roak was ready.

He flipped her over his shoulder, took the knife from her grip, and placed the tip to the fallen Cervile's throat. His eyes stared hard at Tala.

"Knock it off," Tala said and walked away from them.

Roak flipped the knife around and offered it to Meshara, handle first. She took it, sheathed it, and held up a hand. Roak grabbed the hand and helped her to her feet.

He was ready for the punch to the face and dodged that, but he didn't expect the knee coming up at him. Blood exploded from his nose. The Cerviles in the corridor that were unfortunately a little too close to the action began hissing and growling as they wiped Roak's blood from their fur.

Roak eventually caught up to Tala once again.

"Tell me everything," Tala ordered.

Despite his inclination to tell her absolutely nothing since he flat out refused to be ordered around by his ex-wife, Roak decided that the Cerviles deserved some explanation of what was going on.

So Roak explained.

He explained about Father taking over Bishop, about Father ambushing him time and again, about Father stealing hundreds of millions of chits from the Skrang, about Father's order for Roak to find Mother, and he explained about how he was now working loosely with the Galactic Fleet, although more specifically with the Fleet Intelligence Service and Agent Prime, to try to track down Pol Hammon.

"There's a Mother as well?" Tala asked.

"Stands to reason," Roak said.

"Interesting."

"Could be. Pol Hammon is the priority right now, not Mother."

"Why Pol Hammon?" Tala asked. "What do you need that dark tech for?"

"Two reasons," Roak said. "He can crack Bishop's files and I'm certain he's developed tech that might even the playing field."

"Do you mean the quantum travel tech?" Tala asked. "This ship is equipped with it. The Galactic Fleet obtained that tech after Pol Hammon extorted most of the wealth from the galactic elite, including several Cervile nobles and business beings."

"No, it's not the quantum travel tech," Roak said. "We have that. Admiral Gerber of the FIS shared that with us. No more trans-space travel through portals. Snap a finger and we're there."

"Slightly more to it than that," Tala said, sounding a lot like Hessa.

"Yes, I know," Roak said.

"Then what is the tech?" Tala asked.

"That I can't say," Roak said. "And before you get your hackles up, you need to trust that the reason I'm not telling you, or even the FIS or GF, is for everyone's protection. Father has his fingers in too much GF crap that I can't trust that he won't find out. If he does, he'll find Pol first and then we're all screwed."

"Will this tech get my planet back?"

Roak thought for a moment then nodded and shrugged.

"It might. I don't know, but it may be the best shot you have."

"So helping you find Pol Hammon is in my best interest. Fine. I will help you."

"What? No. I don't need help. I just need you to let me go. I have a lead."

"You have a lead?"

"I have a lead."

"Is it solid?"

"As solid as any lead can be. I won't know until I track it down."

"Which is the one thing you are actually good for."

"I'm good for a few things. I've grown since we were last together."

"Grown?"

"Okay, maybe not grown, but I've...improved."

"You didn't kill Meshara, so I will partially agree with you."

"I don't kill if I don't have to."

"Right..."

"He wouldn't have stood a chance if we'd continued fighting," Meshara said from behind them.

"The fight was over as soon as we let him on the ship, Meshara," Tala said. "Roak is the galaxy's best survivor. It was that strength that attracted me to him so long ago."

"I'm just not a fan of dying," Roak said. "Maybe one day, but not today."

"Will tomorrow work for you?" Meshara hissed.

Tala laughed. "I wish I could have a holo feed of the two of you over the next few weeks," Tala said. "It would be more entertaining than Galactic Steve."

That brought Roak to a screeching halt. Literally, his boots squealed on the floor as he stopped walking. Meshara almost ran into his back.

"Tala, stop," Roak said. She kept walking. "TALA! STOP!"

Instantly, Roak had no less than a dozen plasma pistols pressed to his head. He expected that. He knew the route Tala was taking him on had been prepared ahead of time. Meshara would have been shit at her job if she didn't have guards stationed every meter of the way.

Tala stopped and turned slowly to face Roak.

"You aren't saying what I think you're saying, are you?" Roak asked.

"Meshara will be going with you," Tala stated.

While their marriage hadn't been long, Roak knew the woman well enough that he didn't even try to argue with her. He had zero doubt that if he balked at Meshara traveling with him, he'd have his head filled with plasma.

"There will be some serious ground rules," Roak said. "The first being that I am in charge at all times."

"From what I have heard, your AI is the one that tends to be in charge most times," Tala said with a smirk.

Roak sputtered for a second, took a deep breath, and let it out slowly.

"Hessa is my partner, but I am in charge," Roak said. "No argument. No choice. If Meshara comes with me then she falls in line just like everyone else. I can't have variables around that I can't control. Not with how powerful Father is. There is no room for error. Especially if the asshole is taking planets now."

"Meshara will respect the chain of command," Tala said.

"I'm the top of that chain, not you," Roak said, pointing a finger at Tala. "She comes with me and her loyalty is to me, my ship, my crew, and the mission."

"Mission?" Tala laughed. "Don't you mean job?"

"I have to call it a mission or the FIS won't play holoball," Roak said. "Agent Prime thinks calling it a job makes it too mercenary. I don't give ten terpigshits what it's called as long as everyone knows that they take orders from me."

"Of course," Tala said. She looked to Meshara.

"Of course," Meshara agreed.

"Right…" Roak rolled his eyes and winced at the pain. "Any chance I can get my face fixed? I'm snorting down half my body's worth of blood right now."

"Lovely image," Tala said. "Meshara? Show Roak to the med bay. Then let him get cleaned up, fed, and ready for you two to travel to his ship."

"You'll need to let me comm my ship," Roak said. "So they know where to meet us."

"No need," Tala said. "We have been in contact with your AI and a rendezvous has been arranged. Now, go get fixed, cleaned, and fed. You never know when your next meal will be, right, Roak?"

"Or when you'll die," Meshara said as she walked past Roak.

"She's going to be great to work with," Roak said to Tala.

"I am sure you two will have a grand time," Tala replied and gestured for Roak to follow Meshara.

Roak followed. He had no choice really.

And he was a little hungry.

"You have any gump stew?" Roak called after Meshara. "I could go for a bowl of gump stew."

4.

"Their jamming tech was of excellent quality," Hessa said as soon as Roak and Meshara had been moltransed onto Roak's ship, a Borgon Eight-Three-Eight stealth incursion ship. "Of course, not quality enough to keep me out."

"So you were able to listen to the whole thing?" Roak asked. Meshara gave him a look of annoyance and alarm. Roak gave her a smug wink and Meshara's annoyance quickly turned to anger. "What are your thoughts?"

"Oh, I have many thoughts, Roak," Hessa responded. "The planet's disappearance changes things considerably. That is a factor we have not prepared for. If he can take a planet then what's to stop him from taking a ship? Or many ships? And what tech is he using?"

"My thoughts exactly," Roak said.

"I do not enjoy being left out of what sounds like an important conversation," Meshara said.

"My apologies," Hessa said as she accessed Meshara's comm implant. "It is a pleasure to meet you, Meshara Trelalla."

Roak was about to leave the moltrans room and head for the bridge, but he stopped just before entering the corridor and turned slowly to face Meshara.

"You're Trelalla Clan?" he asked.

"Is that a problem?" Meshara replied.

"Not at all. Your clan is one of the few Cervile clans that I actually respect," Roak said.

"Time and date," Hessa said.

"We live to serve," Meshara said.

"And kill anything that moves," Roak said. "You're the youngest of your family."

Meshara looked taken aback.

"How can you know that?" she asked. "Did your AI tell you that?"

"Um, the name is Hessa and I am not Roak's AI," Hessa said. "So, unless you feel like waking up without oxygen in your quarters, you'll want to call me by my name."

"I'd do what she says," Roak said.

"A ship's AI cannot remove oxygen from a being's quarters," Meshara said. "It goes against all laws of programming."

"Care to test that?" Roak asked.

Meshara paused then shook her head. "No."

"Good call," Roak said as he stepped fully into the corridor and cocked his head for Meshara to follow. "How I know you are the youngest is because I was able to take you down fairly easily. A member of the Trelalla Clan with more experience would have been a bigger challenge. Also, Tala let you leave and come here without a second thought. How long have you been protecting her?"

"Since just before our planet was taken," Meshara said, following Roak to the lift at the end of the corridor.

"Yeah, Tala knew exactly what she was going to do with you," Roak said with a laugh. "Don't get pissed off over it. That's just Tala. One of the many reasons we didn't work out."

"I doubt even my processing capabilities could compile the full list of reasons," Hessa said.

"You two are…strange," Meshara said.

"You don't know the half of it," a voice said.

Meshara started and pulled her knife from the sheath on her thigh.

Leaning against the wall behind them was Reck, Roak's "sister". Almost every centimeter of her skin was covered in scars that made Roak's skin look almost unblemished. She studied Meshara up and down then shrugged.

"Tala sent the B Team," Reck stated, pushing away from the wall. She smirked at the knife in Meshara's hand. "What's the little kitty going to do with that?"

"Reck, don't," Roak said. "We do not have time for you and your issues with Cerviles."

"Reck has issues with Cerviles?" Hessa asked. "I did not know this."

"Just the nobility," Reck said. "Too many unpleasant run-ins with your kind."

"She's Trelalla," Roak said.

Reck lifted an eyebrow. "Really? Tala sent Trelalla to watch over us? That's not good, Roak."

"It'll be fine," Roak said. "We have bigger things to deal with than Trelalla and the Cerviles. And they have bigger things to deal with than clan grudges or honor. Hessa? Have you filled everyone in?"

"I have not, Roak," Hessa replied. "I figured you should do that since you are the leader of the team."

"Not an Eight Million Gods damn team," Roak growled.

"He barely tolerates us as his crew," Reck said. "Not that I work for him or acknowledge his position as leader of anything other than the mess that is his life."

"It appears you are part of that mess," Meshara said. "So, perhaps he has more influence and control over you than you're willing to admit."

"What's bigger than a Cervile grudge?" Reck asked. "I'd like to know before I kill this little one."

"Little one?" Meshara hissed. "We'll see how little-"

"Get on the Eight Million Gods damn lift!" Roak shouted.

Reck rolled her eyes and stepped on. Meshara bared her sharp teeth and hesitated.

"Your queen sent you here for a reason," Roak said. "I don't think that reason is standing in a corridor. Get on the lift."

Meshara stepped on and kept her distance from Reck. Reck leaned against the lift wall and grinned.

"The two of you do that with your face," Meshara said, pointing at Reck then Roak. "It is disconcerting."

"Scary as all the Hells, is how I'd put it," Hessa said. "But you get used to it."

"Do you?" Meshara asked.

"No," Hessa admitted. "But we all pretend we do."

"Your AI says she is scared and that she pretends," Meshara said to Roak as the lift raced to the bridge deck. "Where did she pick up these affectations? Special programming or learned mimicry?"

The lift came to a screeching halt. Meshara was thrown off her feet and upward. She slammed into the ceiling then came crashing down. Roak and Reck stayed stable, both having prepared for the incident by activating the mag-locks in the soles of their boots.

"You didn't warn her about Hessa?" Reck asked.

"I did and so did Hessa," Roak said. "Some beings just have to learn the hard way."

"Before we proceed, Meshara," Hessa said, "I believe you and I should talk. I am not Roak's AI and I do not have affectations. All of my actions, reactions, and interactions are genuine. I feel, I react, I live. Anything less than full acknowledgement of this will not be tolerated."

Meshara painfully pushed herself up off the lift's floor. She checked herself for injuries then stared hard at Roak.

"Are you going to allow an AI to speak to a living being that way?" Meshara asked. "One comm call to my people and your AI will be put on a deactivate list. The GF is very particular on which AIs are allowed to exist and which are wiped clean."

"Wow," Reck said and laughed. "I know Cerviles can be stubborn, but this one really doesn't want to learn her lesson."

"I am Meshara Trelalla of the Cervile Royal Guard," Meshara said, her fur standing on end as her rage built. "I will not stand for this disrespect."

The lift rushed down then up for a split second. Just enough to send Meshara sprawling once more.

"I can make sure you never stand on this ship again, Ms. Meshara Trelalla of the Cervile Royal Guard," Hessa said.

"She doesn't ever get tired, she sees all, and has complete control of the ship," Reck said. "You learn to respect her or you get very uncomfortable."

"Reck and I have come to an understanding," Hessa said. "I hope the same will happen between the two of us, Meshara."

"Roak? You are not worried about the power this AI wields over actual beings?" Meshara snarled.

"That ship left the spaceport a long while back," Roak said. "Hessa and I have a partnership that isn't easy to quantify."

"He takes stupid risks and I save him from those risks," Hessa said. "There. Easy to quantify."

"She's got you there," Reck said.

The lift began moving again and arrived quickly at their desired deck.

"Med bay? What for?" Meshara asked.

"Got to switch out your implants," Reck said and led Meshara to an open med pod. "Hop in the box, kitty kitty."

"Reck..." Roak warned.

"I am not changing any of my implants," Meshara said.

"Yeah, you are," Roak said. "Father can compromise standard implants."

"Were you not listening?" Meshara responded. "I do not have standard implants. I am of the Cervile-"

"Royal Guard," Reck finished for her. "We get it. Doesn't matter."

"The implants you have can and will be used against you and us by Father," Hessa stated. "I will remove those and replace them with implants of my own design that cannot be hacked."

"At least you're being warned ahead of time," Roak said. "I was told of mine after the fact."

"That is why we cannot detect your comm implant?" Meshara asked. "Because it is designed by your AI?"

"Eight Million Gods," Roak muttered. "Not my AI. But, yes, the implant in me cannot be detected."

Meshara hesitated then straightened her back and crossed to the med pod. She studied it and climbed inside. The lid closed and Roak and Reck waited for the procedure to be over.

In less than fifteen minutes Hessa finished her work and Meshara was climbing back out of the med pod.

"Great," Roak said. "Time to meet the others."

He led them to the lift.

"Feel any different?" Reck asked Meshara.

"Not at all," she answered. "No. That is not true. I feel...lighter."

27

"My tech seamlessly integrates with your system. That lightness is the burden released from inferior tech," Hessa said.

"And you're always getting on Roak about his ego," Reck said. "He's rubbing off on you, Hessa. Not in a good way."

The lift stopped and the doors opened. Roak ignored the jab and led them to the bridge where Nimm was seated at the navigation console.

A Lipian, the former prostitute slave race, Nimm fought her genetic programming and became a formidable soldier for the GF. When that career ended after having most of her limbs blown off and swapped for synthetics, Roak helped her become commander of Ligston Station. Unfortunately for Nimm, she was caught up in the mess that had become Roak's life, lost her command, was tortured severely, and had to have her synth limbs replaced.

Roak still wasn't one hundred percent sure Nimm wasn't holding her own grudge that may flare up later. He nodded to her and plopped into the pilot's seat as Reck took weapons, leaving Meshara to eye the co-pilot's seat.

"Nope. That's mine," a yellow blur said. The unoccupied seat was no longer unoccupied. "Hi. I'm Yellow Eyes."

Vat grown, Yellow Eyes was as thin as a broom handle and about as tall. Six spindly arms protruded from his torso and six spindly legs protruded from the being's pelvis. Torso and pelvis were approximations. Everything was guesses when it came to the being.

Except for his skin. That was a bright yellow that was almost blinding at times.

"I don't know what you are," Meshara said after staring at Yellow Eyes for a couple of seconds.

"That makes two of us, sister," Yellow Eyes said and waved his hand-nubs about. "Total mystery to me too. But isn't self-discovery simply a part of the life experience? I like to think that one day I will not only find out what I am, but I will find out who I am."

He pressed his nubs together and bowed his head.

"Amen," he finished.

"Lay off the evangelical holos," Roak grumbled. "We talked about this."

"Hey, man, after nearly dying and having to stay in that med pod for weeks and weeks and weeks, a being starts to think about the grand scheme of existence," Yellow Eyes said. "Why are we here? Who created us?"

"That's easy for you," Reck said. "The WAG Corp made you then tossed you out with the trash."

"But who created the WAG Corp?" Yellow Eyes mused. "And who created the beings that created the WAG Corp? And who created-?"

"No," Roak stated flatly. "Just no."

"Is this all?" Meshara asked. "Do you have shock troop recruits? Ex-Marines? Mercenaries? Are they below in the cargo hold? Eating in the mess?"

No one answered. Meshara's vertical pupils narrowed to almost imperceptible lines.

"Do not tell me this is all of you!" Meshara exclaimed.

"I thought Tala knew everything about me," Roak said. "Guess not."

"This is everyone on this ship, yes," Nimm said, her commander voice in full force. "But we do have additional resources to pull from when needed."

"We got a Drop Team!" Yellow Eyes said and pumped a nub-fist into the air. "Go us!"

"We do not have a Drop Team," Nimm corrected. "But we do have access to the top of the FIS and can request assistance as needed."

"Yeah, but Gerber said not to need it," Reck said.

"So we don't have a Drop Team?" Yellow Eyes asked. "Man, you all bum me out sometimes."

"This will not do," Meshara muttered. She swiped across her wrist and brought up her holo comm interface. "I must report to my queen immediately."

"I wouldn't do that," Roak said.

"She must be made aware that you are not the help we thought you would be." Meshara shook her head as she stared at the rag tag crew. "You are a disaster in the making."

"Could have told you that," Reck said.

"In the making?" Nimm asked.

"Don't you know it, girl," Yellow Eyes said and snapped his nubs together.

"Disaster is a bit harsh," Hessa said.

"Go ahead and make the call," Roak said. He crossed his arms over his chest. "We'll wait."

Meshara dialed in the comm signature and waited. In seconds the image of Queen Tala appeared over her wrist.

"A report so soon?" Tala asked. "You could not have found our planet already."

"My Queen, I must report that Roak and his team-"

"Not an Eight Million Gods damn team," Roak interrupted.

"-are not even close to adequate," Meshara continued. "There are only four of them-"

"Five, thank you," Hessa said.

"-and I would not trust them to look after Cervile young, let alone help us find our planet."

Yellow Eyes raised an arm. "I'm sorry, but am I missing something here?"

"No, they are," Roak said and pointed at Meshara. "Their planet disappeared."

"Oh, well that clears it all up," Yellow Eyes said.

"Meshara, have you commed me to complain or to report progress?" Tala snapped. "Explain yourself."

"I got this," Roak said and stood up. He pushed his way into view of the comm call. "Meshara is used to a more structured approach to getting things done. She's adjusting."

"See to it that she does, Roak, or Meshara need not bother returning to the Cervile," Tala said before ending the comm call.

"Went better than I expected," Roak said and returned to his seat.

Meshara growled low in her throat then sat down in the open seat at the systems console. Reck and Nimm watched her then turned their attention to Roak.

"Is the Cervile home planet really missing?" Nimm asked.

"Yep," Roak replied.

"You didn't get that from the previous conversation?" Yellow Eyes asked. He let out a long whistle. "Way to pay attention, beings."

"Hessa?" Roak called.

"A quick rundown," Hessa said. "Father took the Cervile planet. He also attacked Roak on Xippee. The two ex-Marines were killed, but not before they told us that their former ship is impounded on Chafa. We will be heading that way momentarily to retrieve the ship's log so we can find the location of the planet where the peculiar AIs are hiding."

"Why would he take a planet?" Reck asked. "And where would he take it?"

"Both are good questions," Nimm said. "But the better question is how. That kind of technology is light years ahead of even the new tech the GF installed in this ship."

"Eh-hem," Reck said. "The tech I installed. No way I'd let some GF goons touch this ship. They'd have installed enough tracking devices to stretch halfway across the galaxy if placed end to end."

"Why would you do that?" Yellow Eyes asked.

"Do what?" Reck replied.

"Place tracking devices end to end across the galaxy," Yellow Eyes said.

Meshara's eyes were wide with confusion and alarm.

"Hessa?" Roak asked. "Are we there yet?"

"We arrived in the SoCal System several minutes ago," Hessa said.

"We already transported?" Meshara asked. "But I did not feel the transition at all."

"That's what happens when you have a competent being install the tech instead of GF goons," Reck said.

"She doesn't like GF goons," Yellow Eyes said. He punched his nubs together. "Eight Million Gods damn GF goons."

Roak spun about and faced the view screen. He toggled the controls and a smog-covered planet filled the screen.

"Chafa," Roak said. "Impound planet. Hessa? Take us down."

"Stealth mode is activated and we are making our approach," Hessa said.

"Why don't we just blip down to the surface?" Yellow Eyes asked.

"Too much interference from the pollution to get an accurate read on the surface," Hessa said. "We could end up halfway buried in the ground."

"Don't want that to happen," Yellow Eyes said and relaxed into his seat. "Hessa, take us down."

Hessa sighed.

"Welcome to my life," Roak said over his shoulder to Meshara. "You're going to want to strap in. It's never a smooth landing on Chafa."

5.

True to Roak's words, the landing was not smooth at all.

Due to the fact the ship was in stealth mode, Hessa needed to put them down somewhere that wasn't wide open. Invisible to visual and scanner detection was an advantage of the ship's stealth tech. But being invisible didn't mean the ship could ignore physics and reality. An open landing would have produced dust and kickback from the ground, alerting anyone watching to the fact that a ship had landed.

Plus, the last time Roak had been on the planet, the owner of the impound lot had informed him that there was tech on the planet that could detect stealth ships.

So Hessa landed the ship directly on top of a precarious stack of scrapped ships.

"Oh, this should be just fine," Yellow Eyes said as everyone stood in the opening to the ship's cargo bay, rebreathers firmly affixed to their mouths to filter out the planet's dense pollution.

Yellow Eyes was gone in the blink of an eye then back. "Found a route down. Follow me."

"Hessa?" Roak said.

Roak, Reck, and Meshara were moltransed to the ground.

"Or you can cheat," Yellow Eyes said. "Little cheaters…"

"Nimm?" Roak called over the comm. "What do you have for us?"

"The ship's signature is about fifteen clicks to the east," Nimm said.

"Have your AI moltrans us there," Meshara said.

"Too much pollution," Hessa said, her voice ice cold. "To the ground is easy, but any significant distance is too risky."

"She's going to leave you here if you keep up that 'your AI' crap," Reck said.

"What? No, I'd never do that," Hessa said, her voice dripping with sarcasm.

"Everyone shut up and follow me," Roak said.

He pulled his Flott and started walking. He didn't wait for the others.

There were several impound lots on the planet, all owned by different beings, but Roak, and most of the galaxy, knew that Chafa was truly controlled by the syndicates. Of course, the exact syndicate changed depending on how the galactic underworld winds blew.

Roak knew to keep his eyes open and Flott at the ready.

Not that he was worried he couldn't take out whatever or whomever came at him. The last time he had been on Chafa he'd killed several beings.

None of them were even close to average when it came to brains or fighting ability. But that was then and Roak had had to assume that whichever syndicate was in charge of Chafa at the moment they had upped their security game.

Or at least upped their numbers. There was something to be said about just throwing a ton of meat and muscle at a problem.

"Signatures?" Roak asked.

"None that I can detect," Hessa said.

"None at all?"

"No."

"On the entire planet?"

"That is what I mean by none, Roak."

"That's not good."

"I concur. Either the planet has been abandoned or the beings on the planet are able to mask their signatures from me which would mean..."

"We're looking at a well-funded operation, not the slapdash crap that we encountered last time."

"Exactly. Be watchful."

"Always am."

"Be more watchful."

"I got this, Hessa."

"*We* got this," Reck said. "I think you forgot we're here with you."

Roak glanced over his shoulder. For a split second, even though he'd never admit it, he did forget he wasn't alone. For that split second, despite Hessa in his ear, he felt like his old self, like the lone Roak of days past.

The feeling was fleeting, however, since just beyond his crew were about two dozen heavily armed beings sprinting towards them.

"Yellow Eyes," Roak said. "Do your thing."

Everyone stopped and looked back. Yellow Eyes was gone in a barely visible yellow blur.

"How did I not hear them?" Meshara asked.

"The pollution dampens sound," Hessa replied. "And they appear to be outfitted in high-end armor, including their boots."

"Their armor is high-end, man," Yellow Eyes said, suddenly next to Roak. "I couldn't cut through it."

"Hessa had her suspicions," Roak said, filling Yellow Eyes in since he was the one being where implants were not compatible. They did weird things to his already weird body. "What kind of armor?"

"I don't know," Yellow Eyes said. "Never seen it before."

"Hessa?" Roak called. "What can you tell me?"

"Not much," Hessa said. "I'm still not really getting any readings. Since I know where they are and can see them with my cameras, I know they are there. But scans are useless."

"Do you think it's the armor?" Roak asked.

"Could be," Hessa said.

"Roak," Reck said and pointed in the direction they had been heading. "We got more."

Two dozen more armed and armored beings were coming straight for them.

Roak steadied his Flott, ready to deploy the laser cluster spread, but the way the beings moved made him hesitate.

"They get much closer and the fight is going to be a tough one," Reck said. Her tone was casual, as if she'd just explained why she chose tea over caff. "We can split up and engage both sides at once."

"There is a third group," Meshara said.

"And four makes…four," Yellow Eyes said with a shrug. "Ladies and gentlemen, or man, or whatever Roak is, we are officially surrounded."

"Why don't they fire on us?" Meshara asked.

"Why don't we fire on them?" Reck asked Roak. "Not liking getting boxed in."

"This is a lot of firepower for an impound planet," Roak mused. "Whatever syndicate is running Chafa isn't sparing expenses."

"You!" the lead being of the first group shouted as she pointed her plasma rifle at Roak. "You are Roak!"

"Last chance, Roak," Reck said. "We fight now or we lose the advantage."

"I never lose the advantage," Roak said and ignored the snorts and scoffs. "Watch my back."

"That's what we're here for," Yellow Eyes said.

Roak walked towards the lead being. She was a Halgon, a race of beings that looked like a rubber band and a poison dart frog had gotten down and dirty. Despite the illusion of fragility that her elasticity gave her, Roak knew the woman was deadly, especially since her skin could secrete a toxin that would easily kill Meshara, probably kill Roak and Reck, and might kill Yellow Eyes.

"That is close enough!" the Halgon shouted when Roak was about five meters away. "Drop your weapon and prepare to be apprehended!"

"No and no," Roak said, his Flott still firmly gripped in his hand. "How about instead you tell me who you are and who you work for?"

"Disarm or die!" the Halgon shouted.

"And, again, no," Roak replied. "If your boss wanted me dead then you would have opened fire as soon as you saw us. Not disarming, not dying."

The Halgon didn't seem confused or surprised by Roak's reaction. She merely lowered her rifle slightly and huffed out an angry breath.

"Kill his friends," the Halgon ordered.

"Nope," Roak said and took aim with his Flott. "Laser cluster spread. I targeted all of you, including the other groups, before I took my first step in your direction. I pull this trigger and most of you will die before my Flott runs out of charge."

The Halgon grumbled under her breath. Her head cocked to the side and Roak waited as the woman listened to whomever was on the other end of her comm.

"Fine, you may remain armed and your friends may remain alive," the Halgon said, "but you will accompany me."

"Will this take long?" Roak asked.

"What?" the Halgon responded.

"Whatever it is we're about to do," Roak said. "Will it take long? I have a mission that is sort of time sensitive."

"Do you not mean a job?" the Halgon asked. "Roak takes jobs, not missions."

"I mean what I mean," Roak said, exasperated. "Answer the question. Will this take long?"

"It will take as long as-"

The Halgon didn't finish. She stared down at the smoking hole between her feet.

"Do I need to ask it again?" Roak asked.

The Halgon shook with rage, but didn't retaliate.

"My employer wishes to speak to you," she said through clenched teeth. "Once the conversation is over then you may proceed on your way. Cooperate and we may be able to assist you in the search for the ship you are looking for."

"Oh, yeah?" Yellow Eyes exclaimed. "Who said we were looking for a ship?"

Everyone frowned at him, with several of the beings looking downright confused as they all stood next to towering piles of wrecked and impounded ships. Towering piles for as far as the eye could see.

"Oh...right," Yellow Eyes said. "Never mind. Continue."

"Who is your employer?" Roak asked.

"I cannot say," the Halgon responded.

"Remember what happened the last time you didn't answer my question?"

"You took it out on the ground."

"I'll be aiming a little higher this time."

"I cannot say who my employer is," the Halgon repeated. "She will not bother shooting the ground first and will simply aim for my head."

"She?" Roak asked then waved off the question. "Never mind. I think I have an idea who you work for."

"Then you will follow me," the Halgon said. She turned to her right and walked between two tight columns of ships. "Follow. Now."

"This is not a good idea," Reck said, catching up to Roak as he followed the Halgon.

"Maybe not, but it might keep us from having to fight almost a hundred beings at once," Roak said.

"Since when did that matter to you?" Reck asked.

"Since his body started resisting the healing effects of med pods," Hessa said. "Roak is finally feeling his mortality."

"I've felt my mortality plenty of times," Roak said. "Even died a couple of times. But that's not why I don't want to fight."

"Then why?" Reck asked.

"He's curious," Meshara said. "His curiosity is coming off him in waves. The stench is disgusting."

"You have to admit that it's strange there are so many syndicate thugs hanging around Chafa," Roak said, ignoring Meshara's comment. "Syndicates never cared this much about Chafa, so why now?"

"See. Curious," Meshara said.

"Me too," Yellow Eyes said. "Who is it, Roak? What syndicate?"

Roak focused on Reck. She frowned at him then her eyes went wide.

"What?" Yellow Eyes asked. "What'd I miss? You two shared a look. The look means something. What does it mean?" Yellow Eyes groaned. "Oh, come on! Someone tell me!"

"Relax," Roak said. "You'll know soon enough." He focused back on Reck. "Are you in good standing?"

"I should be," Reck said. "No reason they should be upset with me."

"You didn't exactly perform perfectly when you worked for them," Roak said. "Since I'm still alive and standing."

"There were extenuating circumstances," Reck said. "And Shava Stem Shava's death did open things up for them somewhat on Jafla Base."

"Jafla Base? Are we going there next?" Yellow Eyes asked.

"No," Roak and Reck said in unison.

"Chill out, murder twins. Just asking," Yellow Eyes said.

Reck rolled her eyes, Roak turned to Meshara.

"You have anything to add?" Roak asked Meshara. "Everyone else is chiming in."

"No," Meshara said. "But if it looks like we are to be executed, I will distance myself from you and make sure our host knows that I am of the

Cervile Royal Guard. Killing me will bring down the wrath of the Cervile Royal House upon this planet."

"Hey, maybe you can take this planet as your new one," Yellow Eyes suggested. "Yeah, sure, it could use some cleaning. And purging. Maybe a little total annihilation to wipe all the grime away so you can start from scratch. But the planet looks like it has good bones. You can build on that."

"I will take that into consideration," Meshara said.

"She's not taking that into consideration, is she?" Yellow Eyes asked Roak.

"No," Roak said. "Now, shut up."

"Got it," Yellow Eyes said and twisted two nubs over his mouth like he was locking his lips.

They followed the Halgon, all very aware of the dozens and dozens of armed beings behind them.

In a few minutes they walked into a clearing where a dilapidated building stood in the middle of a brownish, low-lying fog.

"Step where I step," the Halgon said. "Do not deviate."

"Got it," Roak replied.

"This isn't regular fog," Yellow Eyes observed as the group followed the Halgon.

"You think?" Reck replied.

They followed the Halgon, step for step, and crossed the eerie clearing until they reached the front door of the dilapidated building.

Roak studied the building closely and quickly realized it wasn't as rundown as it looked. Or was made to look.

There were top notch security protocols in place, evidenced by the holo cams, the laser sights, the broad spectrum scanners, and the just visible ports that would slide open and probably reveal some serious firepower.

"Weapons here," the Halgon said as she slid open a large drawer set in the wall next to the front door. "They will be returned to you. But no weapons are allowed inside the building."

The Halgon demonstrated by placing her own weapons inside the drawer. She moved aside and waited.

Roak disarmed without hesitation. The fact the Halgon had promised the return of the weapons put his mind slightly more at ease. He wasn't a fool and going to trust anyone inside the building, or outside, but the Halgon could have simply demanded their weapons. They were outgunned and didn't have much of a choice.

Following Roak's lead, Reck disarmed, as did Meshara. Yellow Eyes blinked a few times and turned in a circle so all could see he wasn't holding anything.

"What about Meshara's claws?" Yellow Eyes asked. "Those are pretty deadly."

Roak, Reck, and Meshara all turned and glared at Yellow Eyes.

"What? I'm just trying to be helpful," Yellow Eyes said. "You guys are always with the enemy this and enemy that. Kill this being, kill that being. Have you ever stopped to think maybe a little cooperation might be the solution to the problems of this galaxy?"

"You can keep him when we leave," Roak said to the Halgon.

"I would prefer not to," the Halgon said. "I have my own crew to deal with."

"Wow, man," Yellow Eyes said to Roak. "Just wow…"

All weapons were stowed and the drawer withdrew into the wall.

The Halgon waved her wrist across the security interface and the door flashed bright white before it slid open. She gestured for everyone to enter and they did.

The room they found themselves in was small and barely fit the entire party.

"Hessa?" Roak muttered.

"I'm here," Hessa said. "The building you are in has excellent security, but the jamming tech isn't the highest quality."

"I think they spent the chits on weapons and defenses," Roak said.

"My analysis of the structure agrees," Hessa said. "Any group that attacks that building will not be happy with the results."

"No comms," the Halgon said.

She pushed through the group as the outer door closed. As soon as the door sealed and locked, an interior door opened to reveal a great room.

At the end of the great room, seated at a small table and eating what appeared to be lunch, sat a beautiful Lipian woman. The Lipian race had been genetically created to be used as the galaxy's prostitutes. Once the GF had freed the race from their servitude, many Lipians remained sex workers. It was what they knew.

But the woman seated at the table had obviously thrown off her genetic coding and taken to a different lifestyle. Just as Nimm had.

And just like Nimm, the woman did not let herself go slack. She was lithe, tone, muscular, and had an air about her that screamed she was in charge and any being that questioned her authority would pay dearly.

"Roak," the Lipian said. "I am Pechu Magafa. Welcome to my little slice of Hell."

"I don't know," Roak said. "This room doesn't look half bad. I've seen worse."

"Yes, I know you have," Pechu said. "Come closer and take a seat. Drink?"

She looked up from her lunch and smiled at the entire party.

"Hello, Reck," she said. "I had heard you quit your freelance ways and joined your brother. It makes me wonder if your previous failure may have been planned."

"It wasn't," Reck said. "Roak got lucky."

"Oh, I am sure he did," Pechu said. Her smile widened. "Drinks for all?"

"I'll take some Klav whiskey, if you have it," Roak said.

He moved closer to the table and the Halgon provided him with a chair. She provided everyone with chairs then took her position standing behind Pechu.

"Thank you, Klib," Pechu said. She gestured with her fork. "Please. Sit. We have business to discuss."

"Do we?" Roak asked, sitting.

"Yes," Pechu replied. "We do."

"Great," Roak said. "Let's get to it."

6.

"You must trust your system to protect you," Reck said. She looked about the large, sparse room. "Just you and your Halgon."

"Klib," Pechu said. "Her name is Klib. Show a modicum of respect while you are my guest."

"Not feeling too guesty," Reck said.

"Reck," Roak said calmly. "I got this."

Reck quieted and sat back in her chair.

"Your sister is not wrong," Pechu said. "I do trust my security system. A demonstration."

"Not my sister," Roak said.

Pechu ignored him, picked up a knife from the table and placed it to her wrist.

"Don't kill yourself proving it," Roak said.

"Good one," Yellow Eyes said with a snort.

"Just watch," Pechu said and dragged the blade across her skin.

Or tried to.

Before she could move even a millimeter, the knife was knocked from her grip. It clattered across the floor and came to rest against the baseboard a few meters away. Klib walked over and retrieved the knife.

"Grav blasts," Pechu said. "Non-lethal and extremely effective."

"Why would you give your enemies a non-lethal option?" Meshara said. "Enemies deserve death."

"And they will receive it," Pechu said. She wiped her mouth with a napkin and stood up. "But at my pace. The galaxy runs on intelligence and information. Every being has something of worth inside them. I keep them alive so I can mine that worth and add it to my storehouse of knowledge."

"Keeping them fresh for future torture," Yellow Eyes said. He smacked two nub-hands against his chest and held them up. "Respect."

Roak sighed.

"What do you need me for?" Roak asked.

Pechu moved slowly, deliberately, around the table. She smiled at Roak and leaned back against the table's edge. It was obvious she was using her natural genetic gifts to distract everyone, especially Roak.

"I wouldn't say I need you, but I would say you can be of great use to me," Pechu said. She spread her arms. "This planet has become crowded. I am not enjoying the close proximity to rival syndicates that has been forced on me."

"On it," Hessa said without Roak asking. "I'll let you know what I find."

"Rival syndicates?" Roak asked as he waited for Hessa to give him some information to work with. "What do you mean?"

Pechu looked taken aback.

"Have you not heard what is happening to the different houses, gangs, organizations that operate below the galactic norm?"

"She means the criminal underworld," Yellow Eyes said in a mock whisper.

"I haven't heard," Roak said to Pechu. "Been a little busy lately."

"Oh, I am aware of your troubles," Pechu said. "Everyone in the galaxy is aware of your troubles, Roak. How can we not be? Every move you make causes ripples and avalanches that disturb the balance of things. Klib?"

The lights dimmed in the room and a holo projection came to life just off to the side of the table.

The holo showed corpses being ejected out into space, thugs bloodied and brutalized barely hanging on for life, the aftermath of bombings, firefights, more corpses being ejected, and even more corpses that lay upon the decks, floors, ground, dirt of stations, ships, planets.

"This is what happened to Shilo," Pechu said. "We were hunted systematically and put down. Our escape to this planet is all that has saved us."

"Their implants were being hacked," Hessa said. "The atmosphere on Chafa must block Father's ability to hijack implants. Interesting…"

The holo changed and new images of the same carnage and death were shown, but with different beings.

"That's Collari Syndicate," Meshara said. "And that is Willz. What are we looking at? Why retaliate against them?"

"Retaliate?" Pechu laughed. "We did not do that. He did."

Pechu pointed to Roak.

"Me? Listen, lady, I didn't touch Willz or Collari," Roak said. "I've had my beefs with Yelt Willz in the past, but that syndicate isn't even on my radar right now. Same with Collari."

"I thought Collari had been wiped out," Reck said.

"They came back, as all syndicates do," Pechu said. "But they came back to this. Now they are a slim shadow of themselves again. The same with Willz, the same with us, the same with all of the syndicates."

"Yeah. Great. Good to know," Roak said. "Still didn't have anything to do with it."

"But your Father did," Pechu said. "He made sure we knew who he was and why he was targeting us."

"To piss you off, blame me, and take me out," Roak said. "He probably should have left you with a few more thugs to work with." Roak hooked a thumb over his shoulder. "If that's all you have left then he isn't going to be happy with the results."

"Ah, except I do not blame you, Roak," Pechu said.

"You totally just said Roak did that," Yellow Eyes said and pointed at the holos that were repeating over and over. "That's kind of what blame is."

"I feel Roak is responsible, yes, but I do not blame him," Pechu said. "We all have family issues."

"Tell me about it," Reck said.

"Don't care," Roak said. "If Father is targeting syndicates then that is the syndicates' problem, not mine. Deal with it on your own. You have a planet to use as a base, so you have that going for you."

"Ah, except that is the problem and brings us to why you are sitting before me, Roak," Pechu said. "We do not have this planet. We share this planet."

"Buy the impound owners off," Roak said. "Or kill them off. No more share."

"The impound owners are long dead," Pechu said. "No, Roak, we are being forced to share this planet with the other syndicates." Pechu pointed at the holos. "Specifically, Willz and Collari. I would like you to remove them from the situation."

Roak blinked a few times, glanced at Reck, who was also blinking, glanced at Meshara, who looked bored, then glanced at Yellow Eyes, who was poking himself in the cheek for some reason.

"You have dozens of armed thugs outside," Roak said. "Go take care of the other syndicates yourself."

"Why are all three syndicates on this planet?" Meshara asked.

"Stupid bad luck," Pechu said. "I retreated Shilo here because Chafa has almost infinite resources when it comes to ships and weaponry. Thousands upon thousands of perfectly useful ships sit waiting to be used. Millions upon millions of scrapped ships that can be parted out."

"Willz and Collari had the same exact thought," Roak said. "Still doesn't answer why you can't handle your own damn dispute."

"They have banded together against us," Pechu said. "When we arrived, we had three times the beings. They are winning the battle for supremacy of this planet."

"That's so sad," Yellow Eyes said. "I bet you feel awful having to battle for this smog-choked poop planet."

Klib tensed. Both Roak and Reck were on their feet in an instant. Pechu held out a hand and Klib relaxed. Roak and Reck slowly sat back down. Meshara still looked bored.

"I was just saying what everyone was thinking," Yellow Eyes said. "Sheesh."

"You were," Pechu said. "And to add to my humiliation, I am now asking the infamous Roak for help when I should be putting a plasma blast between his eyes for all the harm he has done to Shilo."

"Shilo crossed my path, not the other way around," Roak said.

"Yes and Wrenn handled it poorly," Pechu said. "He was even given a second chance and he fucked that up."

"You don't plan on making the same mistake," Roak stated.

"No," Pechu agreed. "I do not plan on making that same mistake."

"So you want us to go and take out Willz and Collari," Roak said. "What do we get in return?"

"You get the ship you're looking for," Pechu said and waved away the questioning looks. "Do not bother denying it. You came to Chafa. You must be looking for a ship."

"And you have the ship?" Roak asked.

"Eight Million Gods no," Pechu replied. "But I know where it is."

"How can you?" Reck asked. "You don't know what ship we're looking for."

"My organization may be based here, but we still have our contacts and sources," Pechu said. "Especially on Xippee. Roak asked a few too many questions regarding a former Fleet Marine named Chann. Wasn't hard to connect him to a ship that was impounded here not too long ago."

"Great. Where's the ship?" Roak asked.

"Where do you think it is?" Pechu responded with a smirk.

"In Willz and Collari territory," Roak said. "If we want the ship, we have to take out your competition."

"Yes," Pechu said.

"Well, I expected us to have to fight for the ship at some point," Roak said with a shrug. "Fine."

"Roak," Reck hissed. "We were expecting some resistance from impound security, not syndicate thugs."

"Does it matter?" Roak asked. "Worried we can't take them out?"

"No," Reck said. "There are more variables."

"Don't worry, I'm working on those right now," Roak said.

"I see them and I have a plan, Roak," Hessa said to all of them.

"See?" Roak said to Reck. "She has a plan."

"Hessa has a plan?" Yellow Eyes asked then looked at Pechu and Klib. "I don't have one of the secret implants, so I can't hear her. My body doesn't get along with implants."

"Shut up," Roak said.

"Use whatever tools are at your disposal," Pechu said. "You'd be foolish not to."

"What if we get to the ship, get what we need, and don't wipe out either Willz or Collari?" Roak asked.

"Ah, yes, that is the real question to ask," Pechu said.

The chair that Reck was seated in collapsed around her, essentially binding her to the frame.

"I will hang onto your sister as collateral," Pechu said.

"I'm going to need her for the fight," Roak said.

"But you cannot have her," Pechu said. "You have these other two, although I am not sure what this one is."

"Hi," Yellow Eyes said and waved his nubs. "I'm Yellow Eyes."

"Yeah, I'm still going to need Reck to pull this off," Roak said.

"Too bad," Pechu said. She held up a hand and cocked her head in thought. "How about you take Klib in her place?"

Roak laughed. "Right. Sure. No problem."

"Good. Then we have an agreement?" Pechu asked.

"Yep. We have an agreement," Roak said.

"Perfect," Pechu said. "Klib will lead you out so you can make it through the fog. Then she will accompany you to your ship and you can get to work taking care of my competition problem while retrieving the ship you need."

"Then let's get to it," Roak said and stood up.

"What? You're leaving me here?" Reck snapped. "Without even a fight?"

"We'll be back for you," Roak said. "Don't worry."

"I'm not worried, Roak," Reck spat. "I'm pissed off."

"No harm will come to her," Pechu said.

"Oh, I know," Roak said. "Because you don't want to know what happens to you if she is harmed."

"Two siblings caring," Yellow Eyes said and clasped his nubs together. "So sweet."

"Roak? You need to return to the ship right away," Hessa said. "Ships are arriving in the system."

Roak froze. Reck eyed him, but he shook his head.

"What is happening?" Pechu asked. "What is your AI telling you?"

"She's trying to find the ship so we attack in the right area," Roak lied. "Meshara. Yellow Eyes. On me. Klib? Lead the way."

Klib did. She walked past them and through the door to the small room. The rest followed. Once the interior door had sealed, the outside door unsealed and opened. They walked outside, retrieved their weapons, and followed Klib through the fog.

The dozens and dozens of Shilo thugs waited on the outer edge of the fog.

"Do we get to use them?" Roak asked.

"No," Klib answered. "They will be needed here to protect Pechu Magafa."

"Oh well," Roak said and began walking back to the ship. "Hessa? Grab us when you can."

They were only a few meters into their journey when Roak found himself back on the ship.

"Nimm and I have been working on filtering out the smog's interference," Hessa said once everyone was on the ship.

"Uh, where's Klib?" Yellow Eyes asked.

"I placed her in the brig," Hessa said. "We need to talk alone before she becomes part of the plan."

"We'll head to the bridge," Roak said.

They made their way there and Roak froze as he stared at the images on the view screen.

"What am I looking at?" he asked Nimm. "Tell me those aren't Skrang destroyers."

"They appeared a few minutes ago," Nimm said. "And not through the wormhole portal."

"They transported? Like we can?" Meshara asked. "That means-"

"That means the Skrang finally got the tech that Pol Hammon developed," Roak said.

"They did finance his initial research," Hessa said. "Only fair they should have it too."

"The GF is back at war with the Skrang," Meshara hissed. "There is no fair to be had with them."

"Why didn't Pechu detect them?" Roak asked.

"They are in stealth mode," Hessa said. "I can detect them because I know what to look for. Reck has helped me with the scanners so we can filter out the cloaking and see the ships as they are. I may have also incorporated some FIS tech I stumbled across."

"Stole," Yellow Eyes said. "She totally stole the FIS tech."

"How soon will they be here?" Roak asked.

"Currently, they are staying just out of orbit of the planet," Hessa said. "I am detecting minimal power readings. Both destroyers are powered down as much as possible while still staying functional and battle ready."

"They're waiting for us to leave," Nimm said. "Even if we get the ship's log and escape Pechu, we will have them to deal with."

"There is more," Hessa said.

"Of course," Roak responded.

"The ship we need is currently being used by the Willz Syndicate as their base of operations," Hessa stated. "We will have to take them head on to retrieve the log."

"Great," Roak said. He sat down in the pilot's seat. "Hessa? Release Klib and show her to the bridge. Everyone else, strap in. If we have to hit the syndicates head on then we're doing it in our ship. We'll level the playing field a bit before we drop in and snag the ship's log. Does that fit with your plan, Hessa?"

"It is the plan, Roak," Hessa said. "Nimm and I discussed it and we believe the direct approach is the only way to proceed now that we know what we are up against."

"Then let's go be direct," Roak said. "Hessa, take us to that ship."

7.

Hessa expertly piloted the ship, not above the piles and mounds of ships, but between and around them.

"By staying low we avoid a weapons lock," Hessa explained.

"Doesn't mean we can't be found," Nimm said from her seat at the weapons console. "We've got company."

"Yes, I see that," Hessa said a little testily. "None of you need to man the consoles. I can process information and execute actions exponentially faster than any of you can."

"Oh yeah?" Yellow Eyes' nubs blurred over the controls. "Are you faster than that?"

"Yes," Hessa stated. "Because I had to undo all of the idiotic damage you almost created by randomly pushing buttons."

"She's about to disconnect the consoles, isn't she?" Nimm asked Roak.

"Yep," Roak replied. "Not that it matters. She is faster."

"Time and date," Hessa said.

"How many ships are we looking at?" Roak asked, ignoring Hessa's taunt.

"Eight," Nimm said.

"Can you not put your ship into stealth mode?" Klib asked, having been released from the brig to join them on the bridge.

"It wouldn't matter," Nimm explained. "The wash from the engines is easy to detect while we fly between the piles of ships. It creates force on the stacked ships as well as all of the dust and dirt we're kicking up with our quick maneuvers."

"There are Skrang ships over the planet that can be seen and using stealth isn't practical for this ship," Klib said. "I believe stealth mode is not as valuable as it has been made out to be."

"It has its usefulness," Nimm said.

"Perhaps," Klib replied.

"Eight more ships coming in hard from our nine!" Nimm shouted.

"I see them!" Hessa shouted back.

"She's not doing anything," Klib said to Roak.

"She will," Roak said. "Everyone strapped in?"

All acknowledged that they were strapped in except for Yellow Eyes.

"We really need to do something about these harnesses," Yellow Eyes said as the straps fell loosely about his spindly body.

"Good thing you bounce and can't be damaged," Nimm said.

"I can be damaged, just not right away," Yellow Eyes said. He turned casually in his seat to face Klib who was hanging on tight to the jump seat she'd been assigned. "You see, I can take a massive amount of damage and still keep going. The problem is that all that damage is stored in my cells then hits me all at once later. If I can't get to a med pod then I die."

"Doesn't sound like much of an advantage," Klib said.

"It has its usefulness," Roak said, echoing Nimm.

"Roak likes putting me in harm's way," Yellow Eyes said.

"From all I know of him, he likes putting everyone in harm's way, including himself," Meshara said from her seat.

"Don't get us started," Yellow Eyes said and looked about the bridge. "Right, guys? Right?"

There were a few eye rolls, but no one disputed Yellow Eyes. They didn't outright agree, but certainly didn't disagree.

Roak growled.

"Want me to say it?" Nimm asked.

"Eight more ships," Hessa said. "I know."

The ship banked hard to starboard and everyone held tight as they barely missed colliding with the abandoned shell of the aft section of a GF corvette. The broken superstructure loomed in the view screen then was gone as Hessa maneuvered around it, banking hard to port.

She dove then came up just before the ship was about to impact with the planet's surface.

"Good thing I only ate ten bowls of gump stew," Yellow Eyes said as he waved his nubs in front of his mouth. "Otherwise this may not be pretty."

"Get off my bridge if you're gonna puke," Roak snapped.

"I'm not gonna puke, man," Yellow Eyes said. "Now, if I'd had that eleventh bowl of stew, we might have a problem."

"I will have the bots ready at hand for when this is over," Hessa said. "Just in case."

"You fly the ship," Nimm said. "Ignore Yellow Eyes."

"Harsh, man," Yellow Eyes said.

"They talk a lot," Klib said.

"Yes, they do," Meshara responded.

"Does the jabber ever end?" Klib asked.

"Never." Meshara sighed. "And you don't get used to it."

The ship climbed quickly, the acceleration slamming everyone hard into the backs of their seats. Klaxons rang out as impacts were felt against the ship's hull.

"Are they firing on us?" Klib asked, her voice no longer cool and collected, but more than slightly alarmed. "Are they insane?"

"I don't know," Nimm said, "seems like a good way to take us out. Kind of the usual way to go about it." She swiveled in her seat, fighting the push of g-forces against her as the ship continued to climb. "Have you never been in a dogfight before?"

"I did not fight in the War," Klib stated.

"So?" Nimm replied. "The War ended a while back, but I've been in more than a few air and space battles since."

The ship leveled out then plunged back towards the ground. More impacts from plasma fire rocked the ship.

"Shields are at 85%," Nimm announced.

"Good to know," Roak said, his eyes locked onto the view screen and the ground rushing up towards them. "Hessa?"

"Wait for it," Hessa said quietly, almost to herself.

Plasma cannons let loose on the ground and dirt and rock exploded up towards them as the surface was shattered. The ship pulled up hard and fast then immediately leveled out and raced through the canyons of ships, dodging this way then that.

"That shook a few of them off," Hessa said.

The ship braked hard and spun about, coming to a full stop with the nose pointing back towards the carnage Hessa had just created.

"Wait for it," Hessa said again.

"Is the AI talking to herself?" Klib asked.

"Yes," Meshara said.

"And let's not interrupt her, alright?" Nimm added.

"You truly are bizarre beings," Klib said.

"Well, thank you," Yellow Eyes said. "We appreciate the compliment."

"It wasn't a compliment," Meshara said. "And do not lump me in with these beings. I am Meshara Trelalla of the Cervile-"

"Royal Guard!" Yellow Eyes, Nimm, and even Roak said in unison.

Meshara glared, but said nothing.

The massive dust cloud before them was pierced by a ship which was quickly followed by three more. Hessa opened fire with all plasma cannons then sent six missiles flying at the incoming vessels.

"Hessa..." Roak warned.

"I know," Hessa said as she sent the ship towards the incoming ships. And the missiles that were about to impact with them. "Just wait for it."

"Oh, I'm for sure going to puke now," Yellow Eyes said as the distance between their ship and the syndicate ships quickly shortened.

"No!" everyone but Klib shouted at Yellow Eyes.

He shoved two nubs in his mouth then was gone from the bridge.

"Did he moltrans?" Klib asked, staring at the empty seat.

"Doesn't need to," Nimm said. "He's quite fast."

The seat was occupied once more with a satisfied looking Yellow Eyes. "Close call," he said. "But all taken care of."

Yellow Eyes glanced at the view screen and let out a small burping noise. He was gone then back in the blink of an eye.

"Alright. Now it's all taken care of," he stated and lifted a couple of nubs in his own unique way of thumbs up.

Hessa dove under the incoming ships, the outgoing missiles, and the massive dust and dirt cloud she'd created. The view screen was blinded by it all for a moment then became clear once again.

Just in time to show everyone they were racing directly towards a massive pile of impounded ships of various sizes. Most of those sizes were much larger than the Borgon.

Hessa fired, blasting a hole in the column. The ship raced through the hole just before the entire column collapsed in on itself.

The ship braked hard again then turned slowly, taking in the few options for escape as more and more syndicate ships came for them. Hessa chose a direction and accelerated at a speed that would have crushed everyone on the bridge if the grav dampeners hadn't been set to full.

The ship spun on its axis, turning the view screen into a kaleidoscopic Hell. Plasma blasts from the ship, and from the attackers, turned the kaleidoscope into a psychedelic nightmare.

"And he's gone again," Meshara said.

Yellow Eyes' seat was once again empty.

Roak opened the comm ship wide. "Just stay down there, Yellow Eyes."

"Alright." Burp, urp, splash. "If you insist." More burps, urps, splashes followed.

Roak cut the noise from the speakers.

"I may be close behind him," Nimm said. "Hessa?"

"Flying. Can't talk," Hessa replied.

The ship was sideways then upside down then sideways again. They cut a corner a little close and a massive wrenching noise filled the bridge.

"It can be fixed," Hessa said. "Shit."

Four syndicate ships filled the view screen, all with guns blazing.

"This is gonna hurt," Hessa muttered.

The plasma blasts lit up the view screen as the force shields took a severe beating.

"Missiles!" Nimm shouted.

"I know!" Hessa shouted back.

Once more the ship was sent vertical and the crew groaned at the exertion.

Klaxons blared and Roak killed them.

"Are we gaining any ground at all?" Roak shouted. "We need to get to that ship, Hessa!"

"Oh really?" Hessa raged. "I didn't know that, Roak! I thought I was just here as a fun amusement ride around Chafa! Are we trying to get to a specific ship? Huh? Is that the current mission? Please, Roak, tell me more!"

"Do not break Hessa," Nimm snarled at Roak. "You hear me?"

"Little flesh man can't break me," Hessa growled. "I'll break his ass, that's what I'll do."

The ship hit its apex, stalled, rested at the zenith, then aimed back down at the four syndicate ships that hadn't adjusted course in time. Hessa unloaded on them, ripping the ships to shreds as the Borgon's superior firepower obliterated the smaller ships' defenses.

"Break that, bitches," Hessa snapped.

Hessa leveled the ship out a meter from the ground. She took them around three columns in a zig zag pattern then climbed above another column before dropping back to the ground again.

Two syndicate ships were in front of the Borgon, but facing the wrong direction. Hessa took out their engines and let them smash and crash into the rows of stacked ships that made up that canyon. The ship accelerated as Hessa raced through the collapsing rows, coming out into a clearing on the other side.

"Go get geared up," she ordered. "That's the ship we want."

"The thing is huge," Meshara said. "Much larger than I expected."

"Folks, may I introduce you to the Galactic Fleet Marine Assault Transport known as Romper," Hessa announced.

No one was able to study the ship for very long. Hessa changed course and banked the ship into a diving swoop that avoided a massive plasma barrage that came from the Romper.

"Looks like they have weapons hot," Roak said. He unbuckled his harness and stood quickly. "Let's get geared up."

"How?" Klib asked, her eyes massive. "We're gearing up while the AI flies around like a mad-being?"

"I take offense to more than one part of your question," Hessa said. "And suck it up, girlie. You want to tag along with Roak's team? You better be ready to hit hard when the time comes, not sit and wait for the dust to settle."

"Not an Eight Million Gods damn team," Roak muttered as he walked to the bridge's door, barely able to stay on his feet even with mag boots activated. "Nimm?"

"Staying in the ship," Nimm said. "I'm more effective here."

"We could use your synthetics," Roak said. "Maybe do some head stomping and bone breaking?"

"Too rusty for combat," Nimm said.

"Understood," Roak said. "Klib. Meshara. Get up."

The ship circled the Romper, maintaining a safe distance so Hessa could keep them from getting shredded by the plasma cannons. Klib stared hard at the view screen then looked up at Roak, her hands gripping the jump seat for dear life.

"You beings are insane," she said.

"I bet you thought the syndicate was hard." Roak snorted. "Welcome to the real galaxy."

Klib undid her harness and stood up. Roak grabbed her arm and steered her off the bridge, helping her to the lift where the grav dampeners were strong enough to minimize the disorienting effects of the constant up and down, back and forth of the ship. Meshara followed close behind, her face nothing but contempt.

"I will not underestimate you again," Klib said to Roak. "This is madness."

"That is all they know," Meshara said.

Roak shrugged.

"Howdy," Yellow Eyes said as the lift doors opened. "I have weapons laid out and ready."

"Good," Roak said. "Are they covered in puke?"

Yellow Eyes hesitated, blurred, was gone, blurred and returned.

"Nope," Yellow Eyes said. "Spotless."

Roak pushed past him and rushed to the armory.

Yellow Eyes did have everything laid out. And none of it was covered in vomit.

Besides Roak's Flott Five-Six concussion blaster with laser cluster spread, there were three Tonal Eight shock rifles, three Kepler heat knives, three RX31 Plasma assault rifles, three H16 Plasma Carbine Multi-Weapons, two KL09 heavy pistols, and three gas-powered slug chunkers.

"Do we just choose?" Klib asked.

"Choose?" Roak responded as he proceeded to pick up weapons.

"You're taking them all?" Klib exclaimed. "But the weight…"

"We'll be shedding the weight," Roak said. He strapped one of each weapon to his body, except for the KL09 which he didn't need since he was taking his Flott.

Roak snagged two extra power magazines for each weapon.

"Do you need help?" Yellow Eyes asked Klib.

"No," Klib snapped. "I can outfit myself."

She hesitated then began copying how Roak and Meshara secured their weapons to their armor.

"Your armor isn't as heavy as ours," Meshara said to Klib. "It will be a disadvantage."

"She can stay behind us and cover our six," Roak said. He stared hard at Klib. "Just don't shoot us in the backs. Friendly fire doesn't exist in my vocabulary."

"I'm not too worried since I'm zippy fast, but if you shoot Roak then you're gonna get shot," Yellow Eyes said. "It's an immutable law."

"You will pray I shoot you," Meshara said. "If I smell deceit from you then there will be pain." She flashed her razor-sharp claws. "Are we understood?"

"We have the same objective," Klib said. "No need for threats."

"I say that to Roak all the time, man!" Yellow Eyes exclaimed.

"Hessa? How are we looking?" Roak said, ignoring the others.

"Give me a few more passes," Hessa replied.

"We'll head to the moltrans room," Roak said. "That'll make it easier on you."

"Appreciated," Hessa said.

Roak and Meshara left the armory as Klib still struggled to get geared up. Yellow Eyes blurred and all of her weapons were stowed securely to her light armor, some were even moved to different positions than how she'd originally had them.

"Let's go!" Roak yelled.

Klib fell in step as the small assault party made their way to the moltrans room.

"Ready when you are," Roak announced.

"Wait, where is she going to put us?" Klib asked. "Do we even know the layout of the ship?"

"We'll figure it out as we go," Roak said. "Nimm?"

"I'll direct you once you're on the ship," Nimm said.

"All good," Roak said to Klib.

"I don't think you know what-"

8.

"-all good means," Klib finished as they materialized in an empty corridor.

Roak and Meshara had their Tonal Fives up to their shoulders and ready.

"You might want to do the same," Yellow Eyes whispered to Klib.

The Halgon raised her own Tonal Five, her eyes wide with panic and fear.

"And take a couple of deep breaths," Yellow Eyes suggested. "Calm yourself before you bomb yourself."

"Shut up," Meshara said.

"Nimm?" Roak asked.

"Proceed forward and take the first right," Nimm replied over the comm.

Roak did as instructed. He reached the corner, took a very quick look, then ducked back. His eyes met Meshara's then Klib's. Roak held up four fingers and spread them out. Klib and Meshara nodded.

"What? What does that mean?" Yellow Eyes asked. He was gone and back in a blur. "Oh. Four bad guys hanging out in the corridor." He frowned. "I think they heard me."

"You think?" Roak said and spun around the corner.

He fired four times, dropping all four of the syndicate thugs.

He moved quickly and checked their pulses, which was easy to do since all of the thugs had massively thick necks. Veins that normally would have stood out and pulsed were still and lifeless.

Roak nodded and motioned for Klib and Meshara to follow. Roak took the lead again. Yellow Eyes was nowhere to be seen.

Then he was back.

"Six big ones two corridors down," he whispered.

"Nimm?" Roak called.

"Take a left at the second corridor then proceed to the lift," Nimm said.

"Great," Roak said. He focused on Yellow Eyes. "How big are they? Race?"

"Four Gwreqs and two Leforians," Yellow Eyes said.

"Are they paying attention or just waiting?" Roak asked.

"They look nervous," Yellow Eyes said.

"They don't know what's going on," Meshara said. "Their nervousness means we have the advantage."

"Their syndicate was nearly wiped out and they were forced to come to Chafa," Roak said. "I'd be nervous too if I were them."

"You get nervous?" Yellow Eyes asked.

"I said if I were them," Roak responded.

"Can we just go kill them?" Meshara asked.

"Yellow Eyes, go be fast and cut some tendons," Roak said. "We'll take them out as they drop."

"On it," Yellow Eyes said.

He was a yellow streak and gone.

And still gone.

Roak moved towards the corridor, expecting to see Yellow Eyes at his side at any second. But the being never showed back up.

"Nimm?" Roak called. "What's ahead?"

"I can only direct you," Nimm said. "I can't get accurate scans inside the ship. I'm going off the schematic to give you directions."

"Crap," Roak said. "Where in all the Hells is he?"

"I got this," Meshara said and jogged to the corner of the corridor. She took a fast look then threw herself backwards as plasma bolts filled the corridor.

"Did you see Yellow Eyes?" Roak asked.

"One of the Leforians has him by the neck," Meshara said. "The other Leforian is down and leaking a good amount of blood. A Gwreq is trying to bandage another Gwreq's leg."

"Eight Million Gods dammit," Roak swore. "How did the Leforian catch him?"

"Does it matter?" Klib asked.

"No. Not really," Roak said.

He jogged to the corner, slung his rifle and pulled his Flott. He risked a glance around the corner and yelled as plasma singed the top left side of his armor's helmet.

"That just pissed me off," Roak said.

Roak held the Flott around the corner and squeezed the trigger. There were several shouts followed by another round of plasma bolts which was then followed by the sounds of four distinct thumps.

"Two were already down, right?" Roak asked.

"Right," Meshara replied.

Roak cautiously turned the corner, his Flott holstered and the Tonal back to his shoulder.

"Well...shit," Roak said as Klib and Meshara joined him.

Everyone except for one Leforian was dead on the floor.

The Leforian stood in the middle of the corridor with Yellow Eyes held up by the neck in front of him. Yellow Eyes' eyes bulged as the Leforian squeezed.

"Drop your weapons," the Leforian ordered. "Do it or I kill this...thing."

"No...need...to...be...rude," Yellow Eyes choked out.

"Be quiet," the Leforian snapped.

"Good luck with that," Roak said. "How about you let the yellow guy go and then we let you go?"

"I do not trust you to keep your word," the Leforian said. "And I have a job to do."

"Is your job to die?" Roak asked. "Because that's about to become your main occupation."

The Leforian squeezed harder and Yellow Eyes' eyes nearly popped from his squishy head.

Then he winked.

"Really?" Roak said, exasperated.

Roak fired one shot and the Leforian's skull was vaporized. Green blood and internal organs spewed up out of the Leforian's neck as its exoskeleton collapsed in on itself.

Yellow Eyes was free and standing in a puddle of Leforian goo and shell.

"That's different," Yellow Eyes said, looking down at the mess he was standing in. "Should they do that?"

"No," Roak said.

He moved closer and studied the other corpses. All were leaking excessive amounts of fluid. Blood was to be expected and even other bodily liquids, but what Roak was seeing wasn't normal.

"Yellow Eyes, go check the first thugs we killed," Roak said.

Gone and back in a split-second, Yellow Eyes shook his head.

"They're melting," Yellow Eyes reported.

"Are they synth? Is this a trick?" Meshara asked.

"I don't think so," Roak said. "Nimm? I'm sending holos to you. See what you can make of this."

Roak activated controls on the left forearm of his armor and waited.

"I don't know what that is," Nimm responded after a couple of minutes. "Are they sick?"

"What? Sick?" Yellow Eyes exclaimed and waved his nubs around. "Ooo, gross! Gross, gross, gross!"

"I'm tagging a body. Moltrans it into quarantine in the med bay," Roak said. "Analyze it and see what you can find out."

Roak slapped a small dot on the forehead of one of the Gwreqs. The corpse disappeared from the corridor.

"Do we keep moving?" Meshara asked. "Or do we wait for results?"

"We don't have time to wait for results," Klib said.

"But sickness," Yellow Eyes said.

"Nimm?" Roak called.

"Take the lift down three decks. Third bay on the left will be where the ship's mainframes are housed," Nimm said. "Second mainframe in will be where the ship's logs are stored."

"Got it," Roak said. "How's it going out there?"

"We're holding steady," Nimm said. The Romper rocked. "Sorry about that. Hessa was aiming for a 714, but those things are agile."

"I'll get it!" Hessa shouted.

"I used to have a 714," Roak said. "Good ship."

"Dead ship!" Hessa shouted.

"Alright…" Roak shared a look with Meshara and Yellow Eyes. "You sure you're good out there?"

"What am I missing?" Yellow Eyes asked.

"The AI is acting erratic," Meshara said.

"Is this normal?" Klib asked.

"Hessa is a little wound up," Roak said.

"Wound up and ready to spring!" Hessa yelled. The Romper shook several more times. "Oops."

"Try not to kill us, alright?" Roak snapped. "Nimm? Anything on that body?"

"Waiting on results," Nimm replied.

"We'll keep moving," Roak said. He led them to the lift and inside. "Three decks down, third bay on the left."

"Second mainframe in," Klib added.

They made their way to three decks down.

Roak opened fire before the lift doors had fully opened. His Tonal powered down and he tossed it aside, grabbing the RX31 from his back as he walked out of the lift.

Bodies were everywhere. All races, all dead.

"How did you know they would be waiting here?" Klib asked. "They couldn't have known we were after the log. Why would they?"

"Because your boss commed and told them," Roak said.

"What? No! Pechu Magafa would never collaborate with another syndicate!" Klib exclaimed.

"She would, she did, and I know why," Roak said.

"You know nothing," Klib snarled. "Shilo Syndicate does not collaborate."

"Fine. You can tell that to your boss when we see her again," Roak said. "Reck? How are things there?"

"As expected," Reck replied over the comm. "Pechu has been on her comm the entire time."

"Who's she talking to?" Roak asked.

"The other syndicates," Reck said. "What? Just talking to myself?"

"Does she buy it?"

"No. But she's busy."

"Are you free yet?" Roak asked.

"Been free since you left," Reck replied. "Waiting for you to give the signal."

"Go for it," Roak said. "And be sure to ask Pechu about some sickness afflicting the Willz Syndicate."

"Sickness? Great," Reck said. "Have you asked Klib?"

"She's in the dark," Roak said. "Which is why Pechu sent her with us. Something is going down and only Pechu knows what it is."

"How are you speaking to your sister?" Klib asked. "What comm channel are you on?"

"It's private," Roak said. "Hessa?"

"Very busy," Hessa said.

"Just scan all comm channels for communication between Pechu and the Skrang," Roak said.

"You think they're working together now?" Nimm asked.

"I think they have been from the start," Roak said.

"Pechu Magafa would never work with the Skrang," Klib hissed.

But her tone wasn't fully committed to the statement and Roak picked up on that.

"Here's a little hard truth for you," Roak said as he stepped over and around the many corpses to get to the mainframe room. "Pechu Magafa is only looking out for herself. Whatever is afflicting the Willz Syndicate is going to spread to your syndicate too. She's made a deal for herself with the Skrang."

"What deal?" Klib asked.

"The ship's log," Roak said. "That's what they want."

"That is preposterous," Klib said. "Then why tip off Willz? Why have this many beings waiting down here to ambush us?"

"Ambush?" Roak barked a harsh laugh. "She tipped Willz off so that there'd be as many beings down here as possible for me to kill. She still wants the syndicate wiped out. She also wants the log. The second we return to her, she'll have us killed. She'll take the log to the Skrang and start whatever new life she's negotiated."

"I can't... I don't..." Klib sputtered and stuttered.

Roak opened the doors to the mainframe room. He ignored Klib and focused on the thugs that filled the room.

Not one stood alive after Roak was done. A couple were alive on the ground, but none stood.

Roak dispatched the two wounded thugs before he found the correct mainframe.

"You could have left a couple for me," Meshara said.

"No need," Roak replied. "I'm here, Nimm."

"Sending instructions to your armor's interface," Nimm said.

Roak waited, received the instructions, studied them, then executed everything exactly as needed. He slowly, carefully, slid a small quantum drive from the mainframe and held it out.

Yellow Eyes snagged the drive and was gone.

"Why did we not moltrans out?" Klib asked.

"Mainframe room," Roak said. "Shielded. Otherwise mainframes would go missing all the time."

"He's on the ship," Nimm said. "Checking the log now."

"We wait here?" Klib asked. "We should leave."

"Hold on," Roak said.

"We have coordinates," Nimm said.

"Now we leave," Roak said. "Nimm? Grab us from the lift."

"You'll need to be at least one deck up," Nimm said. "Otherwise we won't get a good lock."

"One deck up," Roak replied.

He and Meshara left the mainframe room and jogged to the lift without waiting for Klib.

"Hey!" Klib yelled. "Where are you going?"

She barely made it into the lift before the doors closed.

"Nimm? Reck? Hessa?" Roak asked. "What's the call with Klib?"

Roak dropped the RX31 and pulled his Flott. He aimed it directly between Klib's eyes.

"If you kill me, your sister will die," Klib said.

"I doubt that," Roak said. "Reck?"

"Pechu is no more," Reck said. "Took her out as soon as we had the coordinates. Her security system was surprisingly easy to use against her. You should see what's left. About to have some company, but I can handle them."

"What's the call?" Roak asked again.

"She may be useful," Meshara said. "At least for information."

"I agree," Nimm said.

"She doesn't seem to know a whole lot," Roak replied.

"Wait!" Klib yelled and held up her hands. "I do! I do know a lot!"

"Keep talking," Roak said.

"Chits! I know where the last of the syndicate chits are!"

"That's good," Reck said.

"We could use chits," Nimm added.

"The FIS is sending funds," Hessa said.

"Sending is different than having," Roak said. He focused on Klib. "How many chits are we talking?"

"Sixty-eight million and change," Klib said.

Both Reck and Nimm whistled with appreciation. Meshara looked unimpressed.

"Are they on this planet?" Roak asked.

"No," Klib said.

"Lucky for her," Reck said. "We keep her until we get the chits."

"I'm good in a fight," Klib said. "You are low on beingpower. You could use an extra set of hands."

"Why would we trust you?" Roak asked.

"Is Pechu Magafa dead?" Klib asked.

"Open the channel to her," Roak said.

"Open," Hessa responded.

"Reck, tell her," Roak said.

"Oh, Pechu Magafa is very dead," Reck said. "So are most of the Shilo thugs. Give me a couple more minutes and they'll all be dead."

"There. That's why you can trust me," Klib said. "I'm without a syndicate and out of a job. Who would I betray you to?"

"She has a point," Nimm said.

"She does," Roak said. "We'll keep you around until we have the chits. Prove yourself useful between now and then and we'll discuss keeping you alive longer."

"No," Klib said. "Sixty-eight million chits buys me a permanent spot on your ship."

"I could kill you now," Roak said. "We don't need the chits that bad."

"We kind of do," Reck said. "The ship is taking damage that we'll need to have fixed. And it won't be the only damage we take. We still have to get past those Skrang ships."

Roak thought long and hard. Well, as long and hard as time allowed before the lift moved up one deck.

"We keep her," Roak decided and holstered his Flott just as the lift stopped. "It's your lucky day, Klib."

Roak stumbled as he materialized in the Borgon's moltrans room. Klib had a KL09 pulled and aimed at him.

"I'm not going to the brig again," she said.

"I can take her," Meshara said.

"Hold on." Roak watched Klib a moment and nodded.

"No brig," he said. "Hessa? Put her in a med pod."

"What-?" Klib exclaimed before disappearing. Her armor and weapons were left behind.

"Whatever those thugs down there are sick with, I don't want it spreading," Roak said. He sighed. "Put us in one too."

"I already checked Yellow Eyes," Hessa said. "He is clear."

"Good," Roak said as he appeared inside a med pod. "How long does a scan take?"

"You're good," Hessa said and the med pod opened.

Roak hopped out and walked to the one Klib was in. Meshara and Reck were already standing there. Klib's eyes glared daggers at the two of them.

"What about her?" Roak asked.

"She is not good," Hessa said. "I do not know what it is, but it is not good."

"Can you help her?"

"I'll try."

Roak leaned over the med pod.

"We're going to get away from these Skrang then you're telling us where the chits are," Roak stated and patted the med pod. "Double cross us and you never leave this pod."

"I won't double cross you," Klib said. "I don't want to die like they did back there."

"Can't guarantee that, but we'll figure this out," Roak said.

He patted the med pod again.

"Gotta go escape some Skrang," he said and left the med bay.

Yellow Eyes was waiting for him.

"She's gonna die, huh?" he asked.

"Probably," Roak said. "I glanced at the med pod readings and her systems are already changing."

"Bummer, man," Yellow Eyes said.

"For her, yeah," Roak said.

9.

"Eight Million Gods," Roak exclaimed as he sat down and strapped into the pilot's seat. Not that he was piloting. "That's a lot of ships."

The view screen was filled with incoming syndicate fighters and ships. And all were firing on the Borgon.

"How far off this planet do we need to be before we can transport out of this system?" Roak asked as the ship rocked back and forth from the plasma impacts.

"It's not getting off the planet that matters," Reck said, "but getting the planet off us."

"The smog particulates will interfere with our transporting," Nimm said.

"Great," Roak said. "So we fight through these bastards then fight the Skrang?"

"I told you we would need the chits to repair the ship," Reck said.

"Yeah, if we live," Yellow Eyes said. He cringed at the stares he got. "Hey, just saying what everyone is thinking."

"I'm not thinking that," Roak said. "Hessa. Do what you do best."

"Time and date," Hessa said as the ship raced towards the syndicate armada.

"Not the time to be cute," Roak growled.

"You would know," Hessa replied.

"These two, right?" Yellow Eyes said.

"Everyone hang on," Hessa said.

No one needed to be told, they were already hanging on for dear life as Hessa took the Borgon straight at the incoming ships.

The ship's plasma blasters ripped into the base of a precarious tower of ships and the entire pile began to crumble and collapse. Hessa kept the ship on its course until the very last second when she banked and dove under a falling ship then pulled up hard as soon as she had cleared it. The Borgon just missed being crushed by a few hundred tons of broken cargo vessel as Hessa expertly piloted the ship directly through the barely intact superstructure of the cargo vessel.

The syndicate ships directly in front of the Borgon didn't fare so well.

Three were shredded as parts of the cargo vessel slashed through their hulls. Two were completely flattened as they tried to dive under the falling wreckage, but didn't quite time it right.

And one ship was blown apart by Hessa as it managed to get free of the cargo vessel's skeleton but ended up directly in the Borgon's crosshairs.

"You know, if we boosted the grav dampeners we could really just turn this view screen off and play cards or something while we wait to be free," Yellow Eyes said. "We wouldn't even have to witness this nightmare. It'd be like none of this is happening."

Roak glanced at the being and saw that Yellow Eyes' nubs were bone white as he gripped the armrests of his seat.

"You gonna be alright?" Roak asked.

"Thank you for asking, Roak," Yellow Eyes replied. "And no. No, I am not going to be alright. Just feeling a little stressed out. We've had so much coming at us that I-"

"Stop right there," Roak said. "I don't care if you are going to actually be alright or not. I just want to make sure you aren't going to puke everywhere."

"I was wondering the same thing," Reck said.

"You are some cold, cold beings," Yellow Eyes mumbled.

Hessa fired several missiles and destroyed three more syndicate ships. The shrapnel from the explosions crashed against the ship's shields and several klaxons blared.

"Turn all that off," Roak said. "We know how deep the terpigshit is, we don't need a bunch of beeps to tell us."

"Shields are down to forty percent," Nimm stated.

"That's not good, man," Yellow Eyes said. "That is really not good. We aren't even off the planet yet and we still have the Skrang to deal with and then whatever comes at us as we go get the chits then we have to make it from there to go get the ship repaired and-"

"Yellow Eyes!" Roak roared. "Knock it off!"

"Oh. Sorry," Yellow Eyes said. "Was that all out loud?"

Climb, dive. Climb, dive. Fire, fire, fire. Climb, dive, climb, dive.

The ship shook hard.

"That one hurt," Nimm said. "Hessa?"

"I am monitoring it closely," Hessa replied.

"What hurt? What is she monitoring?" Yellow Eyes asked.

"I'll put you in the brig myself," Roak said, pointing at Yellow Eyes. "Zip it."

"Right. Right. Zip it," Yellow Eyes said. "Zipping it. It is zipped."

"Nimm?" Roak asked.

"Aft thrusters are compromised," Nimm said. "That last hit managed to briefly overload the shields directly over the thruster housing and..."

"And...?" Roak asked.

"We're going to lose maneuverability," Nimm said.

"Don't like that," Roak said. "We lose aft thrusters and we'll be nothing but a rocket shooting straight ahead once we leave the atmosphere."

"With Skrang ships directly in front of us," Reck said. "This should be fun."

Yellow Eyes moaned, but didn't open his mouth.

"Hessa, are we going to be able to clear off the atmospheric particles before we crash into one of the Skrang ships?" Roak asked.

"The thrusters aren't offline yet," Hessa replied sending them into a corkscrew climb while she fired all plasma cannons, turning the ship into a whirling devil of death.

"Right. Not yet," Roak said. "But will we be able to-"

"The thrusters are not offline yet!" Hessa shouted.

"You're gonna want to just let her fly," Reck said.

"No shit," Roak said. He settled into his seat as much as he could and watched.

A huge transport ship filled the Borgon's view screen. Hessa did not attempt to fly around it. No one said a word as they raced towards an inevitable collision. It was what it was.

At the very last moment, Hessa fired two missiles, tearing a massive hole in the side of the transport ship. Then she flew them directly into that hole.

Yellow Eyes couldn't keep it zipped any longer and began to scream.

Roak didn't tell him to shut up or try to stop the high-pitched screeching. He was too busy keeping his bladder under control as he stared at the flames, smoke, and flying metal that was the view.

Then they were free and out the other side of the destroyed transport ship and all Roak could see was sky. It was a smog-filled, brown and yellow sky, but it was a sky sans syndicate ships. Yellow Eyes stopped screeching.

"I knew we'd make it," he said.

The brown and yellow quickly became light blue then black and they were out of the planet's polluted atmosphere.

The two Skrang destroyers loomed before them.

"The thrusters are fine!" Hessa shouted before anyone could say anything.

Roak looked at Nimm and she shook her head.

"Great," Roak said.

The Skrang ships grew larger and larger.

"Why aren't they firing on us?" Reck asked.

"They're trying to hail us on comms," Nimm said.

"Ignore it," Roak said.

"They aren't scrambling fighters either," Reck said. "This isn't like the Skrang."

"They need us alive," Roak said. "Hessa?"

"Thrusters are fine!" she shouted again.

"Don't care," Roak replied. "How soon until we can blip away from here?"

"I don't know! Why are you always asking me?" Hessa snapped.

"Hessa? Do you need to take a break?" Nimm asked. "We are more than capable of operating the ship without you if you need a moment."

"A moment would be good," Hessa said.

"Okay. Great," Nimm said, her brows raised in surprise.

"Moment over," Hessa said. "I feel much better. Thank you for the suggestion."

"You sure?" Nimm asked.

"Yep," Hessa said. "Right as rain."

"Hey, we have movement," Reck interrupted. "A hangar door just opened on the ship in front."

"Here come the fighters," Roak said. "Be ready."

No fighters came out.

"They're still hailing us," Nimm said.

"We're still not answering," Roak said. "Nothing is coming out of that hangar?"

"Nothing," Reck responded.

"Except for lights," Yellow Eyes said. "See? Blinky, blinky lights."

"I'm dropping shields," Hessa announced.

That created a little bit of chaos on the bridge.

"What do you mean you're dropping shields?" Reck yelled.

"Do not drop shields, Hessa!" Roak ordered.

"Hessa, we will be completely exposed while facing off with two Skrang destroyers!" Nimm shouted.

Yellow Eyes didn't say anything. He simply kept staring at the Skrang destroyer and the blinky, blinky lights.

"Oh! I get it!" he cried out. "They're trying to tell-"

The view changed and instead of two Skrang fighters looming ahead of them they were staring at a brown and beige planet.

"-us that they're friendly," Yellow Eyes finished. "Oh, whoa…"

"Welcome to Zuus Colony," Hessa said. "I'll comm Bhangul and see if he has space in his hangar."

"No one do an Eight Million Gods damn thing," Roak said. "Yellow Eyes? What do you mean they were trying to tell us they were friendly?"

"They were blinking out code with those lights," Yellow Eyes said. "I guess I can read blinky light code."

"Hessa?" Roak asked.

"He is correct," she replied. "They were trying to tell us they were not hostile and we needed to go with them."

"Why?" Roak asked.

"The blinky lights didn't say why," Yellow Eyes replied and shrugged. "It's not the most efficient way to communicate, you know. Maybe they should have tried comming us… Oh, right…"

"Great," Roak said. "We shelve that for now. Hessa, why are we at Zuus? We don't have the chits yet to repair the ship."

"We do not have a choice, Roak," Hessa said. "The thrusters are obliterated. We'll need to install new ones. Not to mention the fact we don't have operational shields. We won't need to replace the generators, but we will need to recalibrate their entire force spectrum. That takes time and equipment, Roak."

"Both of which take chits," Roak said. "Which we do not have."

"The thrusters are obliterated?" Yellow Eyes asked. He wagged a nub. "You said they were fine."

"Did any of you believe that?" Hessa asked.

There was a resounding "No" from all except Roak.

"Hessa?" Roak asked.

"Yes, Roak?" she replied.

"Are you talking to Bhangul right now?"

"Maybe."

"By maybe do you actually mean yes?"

"Probably."

"Great. And what are you two talking about?"

"We're working out terms."

"Terms? What terms?"

"Terms of the cost of repairs and whether or not we need to trade a job for those costs or whether he will allow us to repair the ship without paying up front since we're going to retrieve sixty-eight million chits."

"How is the conversation going?"

"Not too well. I believe Bhangul is tired of us sponging off of him."

"Sponging? He used that word?"

"Not exactly. He used a Dornopheous word that is hard to translate."

"The original Dornorpheous word contains more of an implied threat, doesn't it?"

"Oh, you know the word?"

"I've had it thrown at me a few times." Roak sighed. "Put him on the comm."

"-and if Roak thinks I am his-"

"Hey, Bhangul," Roak said. "How is business?"

"Roak? Oh, now you'll talk to me directly," Bhangul Whorp said over the comm. "Send that crazy AI to try to soften me up so you can come in for the kill, is that it?"

"Not it at all," Roak responded. "I didn't know we were coming here and I didn't know Hessa was talking to you. But now that I have you on the comm…"

"You didn't finish your sentence," Bhangul said.

"Do I need to?" Roak replied.

"It would be the polite thing to do, Roak," Bhangul said with a long sigh.

"Any chance we can come down and do a few repairs so we can chase down some needed funds?"

"No."

"Hold on, don't answer so fast. These funds we're chasing down, I can cut you in on them."

"Can you? How much of a cut?"

"Fifty percent? That'd come to about two million chits, Bhangul."

Silence was the response.

"Uh, Roak?" Hessa said. "I may have already told him about the sixty-eight million chits."

"I'll take fifty percent of that," Bhangul said. "Give me half and you can do all the repairs you need to on your ship."

"We both know that you're asking for way too much," Roak said. "It's a little insulting, Bhangul."

"Is it?" Bhangul snapped. "As insulting as you trying to tell me that you were only going to retrieve four million chits? Or as insulting as you always coming here whenever your ship gets a little banged up? A ship, I may add, that I gave you."

"Because the AI was quirky," Roak said. "Which turned out to be an understatement."

"Downright scary is what she is," Bhangul said.

"I can hear everything," Hessa interrupted. "Bhangul? Can we at least land? Our shields are completely down and I feel exposed. Dangerously exposed."

"Fifty percent," Bhangul said.

"Ten," Roak countered.

"Sixty percent," Bhangul said.

"Oh, just fucking knock it off," Roak snarled. "Fine. Fifty percent."

"The rate went up to sixty, Roak," Bhangul responded. "Didn't you hear me?"

"You sure this is how you want to negotiate?" Roak's voice was even, flat, deadly.

"Eight Million Gods damn," Bhangul said. "No need to get ugly." He sighed again. "Fifty percent will do."

"Hessa, land this thing and let's get to work," Roak said.

"This thing?" Hessa scoffed. "This thing!"

"You are really making friends today, Roak," Reck said.

"Everyone off my ass," Roak snapped. "Hessa?"

"What?"

"Please take us in to Bhangul's ship lot," Roak said in a voice so sickeningly sweet that Yellow Eyes looked like he was going to throw up again. "I would very much appreciate it if we could land immediately."

"That wasn't so hard," Hessa said and paused. Then, "Time and date."

"Shoot me now," Roak muttered. He undid the harness and stood up to stretch. "I'm grabbing some gump stew."

"Great idea!" Yellow Eyes exclaimed and was gone in a blur.

"Leave some for me!" Roak yelled after the being. "Hessa?"

"I will make sure he does not eat it all," Hessa said. "We will land in about twenty minutes. I am taking us in slowly since the thrusters are offline. I'll have to use the grav drive to maneuver which is not a very precise way of steering the ship."

"Do what you need to do," Roak said. "You do anyway."

"Yes. Yes, I do," Hessa replied as Roak left the bridge.

10.

Bhangul Whorp was far less hostile in person. He even held up a bottle of Klav whiskey when Roak climbed down out of the ship and stepped onto the floor of Bhangul's underground hangar.

"Don't try to apologize," Roak said, crossing quickly to the Dornopheous. He paused as he eyed the bottle. "Is that legit or bootleg?"

"This one is legit," Bhangul said. He patted a crate next to him. "Take a load off and have a glass."

"He's buttering you up for something, Roak," Reck said as she jumped off the steps of the ship and proceeded straight for the repair console that was rising up from the hangar floor. "He's already getting fifty percent of our haul. Don't give him any more."

"What? Butter you up?" Bhangul chuckled. "What could I possibly butter you up for?"

"Obviously something," Roak said and held out his hand. Bhangul placed a glass of whiskey in Roak's waiting palm. "Don't tell me those Skrang punks are giving you shit again."

"Them? No, they left months ago," Bhangul said. "I haven't seen a single Skrang on Zuus since the war between the GF and Skrang ramped back up."

"They either returned for conscription or are running from it," Nimm said as she descended the ship's steps. "Bhangul, it is good to see you."

"Nimm? I heard rumors you had joined Roak's team, but I couldn't believe it," Bhangul said.

"Not a team," Roak growled. He downed the whiskey and held out his glass. Bhangul eagerly refilled it. Roak eyed him carefully. "Spit it out."

"Yes, well, there might be something," Bhangul said. "But we can discuss it later."

"We can discuss it now," Roak said.

"Bhangul!" Reck shouted as she pounded a fist on the repair console. "I'm locked out! Why am I locked out?"

"Bhangul, we had a deal," Roak said.

"I know, I know, and I will honor the deal," Bhangul said. "There's just one thing I have to ask…"

Even though Dornopheous were putty-like beings, Bhangul managed to form two digits and snap them together, producing a surprisingly crisp, loud sound.

A young Dornopheous came tumbling out from behind one of the ships in the hangar. It righted itself then moved quickly to Bhangul's side.

"This is my nephew," Bhangul said. "I have promised his mother that I would introduce him to the great Roak, the galaxy's deadliest bounty hunter."

"You said I would apprentice with him," the young Dornopheous said. "I don't want to just meet the guy, I want to learn from him." The young Dornopheous created a putty hand and held it out. "Hey, I'm Jagul."

"I don't care," Roak said. "And I don't mentor."

"I don't know, man," Yellow Eyes said, suddenly by Roak's side. "I kind of see you as a mentor in a way. A mean, ill-tempered, prone to violence and rage mentor, but we can't always pick our teachers, right?"

"Sure you can," Jagul said. "I'm picking him."

"Oh, well, alright," Yellow Eyes said. "You proved me wrong."

Roak reached for his Flott then realized he didn't have it on his hip.

"Was he going for a pistol?" Jagul asked.

"He does that," Yellow Eyes said.

"So cool," Jagul said.

"Bhangul!" Reck shouted. "Unlock the console!"

Bhangul looked to Roak and grinned.

"No," Roak said.

Bhangul shifted focus to Reck. "Sorry. I can't unlock it."

"Roak!" Reck shouted. "Let the kid follow you around! He'll probably end up dead within a day, so I don't see the big deal!"

"That's true," Yellow Eyes said.

"Wait, what?" Jagul asked.

"They're joking," Bhangul said.

"Yeah. Joking," Yellow Eyes said, using two nubs to create air quotes.

"Twenty-five percent," Roak said to Bhangul.

"What?" Bhangul asked.

"Twenty-five percent is your cut if I have to bring this kid with us," Roak said.

"We already had a deal, Roak," Bhangul protested.

"We did. A deal that didn't include babysitting. You want your sister on your ass forever? I've had to intervene in your family issues before, Bhangul. I know exactly how messy things can get for you."

"Family is always messy," Meshara said as she emerged from the ship.

"Is that a Cervile?" Bhangul asked. "She looks royal. You and Tala aren't...?"

"No," Roak snapped. "Deal or not?"

"I hate you," Bhangul said. "Fine. Deal. Twenty-five percent."

Roak pointed his glass at Reck and the repair console. Bhangul brought up a holo interface and unlocked the console.

"There you go," Bhangul said.

"Good," Roak said, then focused on Meshara. "Where are you going?"

"I am going to stretch my legs on the surface," Meshara said. "I could use some time away from you and your insanity." She entered the lift at the end of the hangar and was gone.

"She seems pleasant," Bhangul said. "You know, for a Cervile royal."

"She's Meshara Trelalla of the Cervile Royal Guard," Yellow Eyes announced. "Which she really wants people to know."

"She's a Cervile. That's all I need to know," Bhangul said and grinned at Roak. "Now, Roak, you better go pick a ship out for your job."

Roak blinked a few times.

"I'm going to go this way," Yellow Eyes said and was gone. Then back. He grabbed Jagul's putty body. "You should come with."

The two disappeared which left Roak to glare at Bhangul.

"What? Didn't Hessa mention this to you?" Bhangul asked. "I'm not letting you repair your ship then go flying off without giving me my cut. No. What's going to happen is you'll take a different ship while Reck stays here and repairs your ship. It's not the ship that matters, right Roak?"

Roak shook his head back and forth then gave Bhangul a cold, cold smile.

"Eight Million Gods!" Bhangul exclaimed and averted his eyes. "You know I hate that!"

"Hessa?" Roak asked.

"You'll have to pilot," Hessa responded. "I'll need to be here with Reck to help facilitate the repairs."

"The ship is a mess," Reck said. "It's going to take both of us to fix it."

"I can pilot," Nimm said. "I'm a better pilot than Roak."

"I also have a great ship in mind that has a more than sufficient AI to assist you," Bhangul said.

"Last time I took your suggestion I ended up with Hessa," Roak said.

"The insults never stop," Hessa said.

"Oh, don't worry, Roak," Bhangul said. "I am more than careful when it comes to AIs ever since…"

"Seriously?" Hessa huffed. "You beings…"

"What ship are we talking about?" Roak asked.

Bhangul smiled and waved a putty hand at Roak. "Follow me."

They walked quickly around and past several very expensive ships. Luxury cruisers. Custom fighters. Even a couple of repurposed GF drop ships. The hangar was huge.

"Bhangul, I don't have all year," Roak said as they moved deeper and deeper into the inventory.

"Here we go," Bhangul said. "What do you think?"

Roak frowned.

"That's my ship," he said after several minutes of silence. He turned slowly and glared at Bhangul. "That's my ship."

"Was your ship," Bhangul said. "You traded up."

Before them was a Borgon 714 light fighter, Roak's previous ship, the one he'd used for decades before he encountered Hessa and the Borgon Eight-Three-Eight.

"How?" Roak asked. "It was going to be scrapped."

"Was, yes," Bhangul said. "I intervened."

Roak shook his head. "You bought it hoping there'd still be data on the drives that you could sell or use as leverage."

"What?" Bhangul exclaimed. "That would be quite the betrayal of your trust, Roak."

"I'm right," Roak said.

Bhangul conceded with a shrug.

"It's all fixed?" Roak asked.

"It's all fixed," Bhangul said.

"Why?"

"Why what?"

"Why is it all fixed? I have the Borgon and Hessa. Why fix my old ship once you realized I'd already fried all the drives?"

"Old time's sake?"

"No."

"It's a solid ship?"

"Maybe."

"Because I had a feeling you'd need another ship at some point?"

"Closer. And why did you think I'd need another ship at some point?"

"Because Hessa scares the living Hells out of me and I figured she might scare you too and maybe you'd ditch her then need your old ship back and that way I could make a deal."

"There we go."

"He thought you'd ditch me?" Hessa asked.

"He also called you scary as all the Hells," Roak replied.

"That doesn't bother me," Hessa said. "I am scary as all the Hells. But why would he think you'd ditch me?"

"I never liked working with partners," Roak said.

"But I changed your mind? Ah, that's nice," Hessa said.

"I think it might be good for you two to get a little separation," Bhangul said, a worried tone in his voice. "Do you know the term 'codependent'?"

"Shut up," Roak and Hessa said.

"Hessa? Take a look at this ship's systems and vet the AI for me," Roak said. "I'm going to talk to Klib. If she's able to talk."

"She is," Hessa said. "And she is getting better."

"We need to find out what is happening on Chafa," Roak said. "After we finish this next job."

"Not a mission?" Hessa asked.

"This'll be off books and not for the FIS to know about," Roak said. "We're still waiting on funds. If they know we have sixty-eight million chits then that funding will dry right up."

"Sixty-eight minus twenty-five percent," Bhangul said. "And returning my nephew unharmed."

"I'm not promising that," Roak said. "You know what I do is dangerous."

"Yes, but there is no need to put the boy in danger," Bhangul said. "Leave him on the ship."

"You don't want him to get the full mentor package?" Roak asked. "Won't he complain to your sister?"

"I'd rather deal with that than if he dies," Bhangul said. "Leave him on the ship."

"Not a problem there," Roak said. "Hessa?"

Roak was instantly in the med bay.

"Klib," Roak said as he stared down into the med pod. "I'm going to need the location of those chits."

"Jafla Base," Klib said without hesitation. "Let me out of here and I can lead you right to them."

"Jafla?" Hessa asked. "Roak, this will not be an easy job. Jafla Base has been cut off to you after you killed Shava Stem Shava."

"I'm sure not everyone is still holding a grudge," Roak said. "They all hated that piece of terpigshit."

"You plunged the base into chaos," Klib said. "You are not welcome on Jafla Base. That is why you need me to be free of this med pod."

"Is she healthy enough to let out?" Roak asked.

"It appears so," Hessa said. "Whatever was afflicting her and the others on Chafa has been cleansed from her system."

"Any clue what that is?" Roak asked.

"No," Hessa stated. "And frankly that troubles me. But I will continue to investigate."

"Do that," Roak said as the med pod lid raised. He helped Klib from the pod and pointed to clothes on a chair in the corner of the med bay. "Get dressed and meet me in the mess."

He left the med bay and proceeded quickly to the lift.

"Do you really not know what the Hells was wrong with her?" Roak asked once the lift doors closed and the lift was moving to the mess deck.

"I really do not," Hessa said.

"You're holding something back," Roak said. "Spill it."

"It is only a hunch," Hessa said.

"You know how I feel about hunches. So out with it."

"And you know how I feel about hunches which is why I hesitate."

"Just tell me."

"I was able to compare the corpse that I took from the Willz Syndicate," Hessa said, "and Klib's body. The corpse disintegrated faster than I would have liked, but something did stand out in the readings."

"Which was?" Roak was getting exasperated. The lift doors opened, but he waited. "Hessa?"

"I do not think it is a sickness," Hessa said. "I believe it is tech related."

"Tech related? How?" Roak sighed. "Father?"

"Yes. Or that is my guess," Hessa answered. "Any being he has connected with will eventually just dissolve inside because of how he hijacks the implants."

"But none of those beings were hijacked," Roak said. "They didn't have red eyes."

"Not at that moment," Hessa said. "I believe the only reason is because they moved to Chafa and the pollution interfered with his signal and control."

"But even having some contact meant their systems were fucked," Roak said. "It doesn't matter if he lets someone go. They've already been killed."

"In essence, yes," Hessa said. "It is slow, but eventually all that are hijacked by him will die. It's like the implants are no longer compatible with anyone other than Father so they start to malfunction. Unfortunately for the beings afflicted, that malfunctioning means death on a cellular level."

"But I'm guessing you switched out Klib's implants," Roak said. "That stopped her body from breaking down."

"It stopped the progress, yes," Hessa said. "But she was already terminal. The med pod is what saved her from turning into goo."

"Why turn them into goo at all?" Roak asked. "And only after they die?"

"They would have eventually turned into goo anyway," Hessa said. "Or that is my theory. Death means the being's energy is gone and all that is left is the energy from the implants which become hyperactive and obliterate all cells."

"Interesting theory," Roak said. "Keep working on it."

"Oh, I am," Hessa said.

Roak moved on to the mess hall and grabbed himself a tray of gump stew and a large mug of caff. He was not surprised to see Yellow Eyes already there and eating several bowls of stew at once.

"I left some for you," Yellow Eyes said. "Although, I think Hessa has a secret stash of gump stew onboard somewhere so we never run out. Ask her."

"No," Roak said and sat down.

Klib walked into the mess, grabbed a tray and filled it with protein slices and carb mash. She joined them at the table and devoured her food before anyone could say a word to her.

"Famished," she said after she cleaned her plates.

"Stew?" Yellow Eyes asked, offering her one of the many steaming bowls in front of him. "It's really good."

"After," Roak said, pushing his half-finished bowl aside. "We talk business first. Where exactly are the chits?"

"They are in the orb fight facility," Klib said.

"Alright. Where in the orb fight facility?" Roak asked.

"Down below," Klib said.

"Uh oh," Yellow Eyes said and stopped eating. "She doesn't actually know."

"Is that true?" Roak asked. "Because if you don't-"

"I know exactly where they are," Klib said and glared at Yellow Eyes. "They just won't be easy to get."

"We're talking sixty-eight million chits," Roak said. "If they were easy to get then someone would already have them."

He smiled at Klib which caused the woman to shrink back in horror.

"I know, right?" Yellow Eyes said and continued eating stew.

"Down below where?" Roak asked.

"The Gas Chamber," Klib said.

"The Gas Chamber?" Roak echoed.

"What's the Gas Chamber?" Yellow Eyes asked.

"Underground orb fight club," Roak said. "Filled to capacity with every low life on Jafla Base. Unless the place has changed?"

"It has not changed," Klib said. "It has only gotten worse. When Shava Stem Shava died, it left a void. That void was filled by several syndicates and other enterprising beings. One of those beings took the Gas Chamber as his and he rules with an iron fist."

"The being's name?" Roak asked.

"Chella Po."

"The MC of the fights? He took control?"

"He did and has done surprisingly well for himself," Klib said.

Roak's shoulders lowered and he sighed loudly.

"We aren't retrieving sixty-eight million of Shilo's chits, are we? We're flat out stealing Chella's chits," Roak said. "This isn't a recovery job, but a heist."

"Yes and no," Klib said. "It is a heist." She held up her hands. "But not to worry. I already have a plan in place. Well, not me, but there is a plan in place. All we have to do is make contact with someone and get things moving."

"Uh-huh," Roak said. "Just have to make contact with someone and get things moving." Roak spun his hand around and around in Klib's face. "Out with it. Who is the contact and why are you being cagey?"

"Yes, well, the contact may be a police officer," Klib said.

"Great," Roak said.

"Might even be a Galactic Vice Detective," Klib said.

"Even better," Roak replied. "Anything else?"

"We'll have to give a cut of the chits to him," Klib said.

"How much of a cut?"

"The deal was for half."

"There it is." Roak laughed which nearly caused Yellow Eyes to spit stew from his mouth.

"Not while I'm eating, man," Yellow Eyes said.

"Can we trust this cop?" Roak asked. He shook his head. "What am I saying? You can't trust a cop. Not one on Jafla Base."

"We can trust him enough to get the chits," Klib said. "What comes next, I cannot say."

Yellow Eyes looked from Klib to Roak then to Klib then back to Roak.

"Does that mean we're going to kill the cop?" Yellow Eyes asked. "That doesn't sound cool, man."

"You a fan of cops?" Klib asked. "They're all corrupt and on the take."

"Oh, sure they are," Yellow Eyes said. "I think it's uncool that we're using the guy's plan for the heist then killing him instead of giving him his cut."

"We'll give him his cut," Roak said. "I'm not a thief."

"You care about killing a cop?" Klib asked.

"I try not to kill and bring heat down on me if I don't have to," Roak said.

Yellow Eyes snorted, but didn't say anything.

"We'll still have plenty of chits," Roak said. "The cop gets his cut and we maybe make an ally on Jafla Base."

"He's not much of an ally," Klib said. "He's mostly a piece of terpigshit."

"What's this piece of terpigshit's name?" Roak asked.

"Kalaka."

"He have a last name?"

"I think that is his last name."

"Hessa? I want all intel on a Galactic Vice Detective Kalaka stationed on Jafla Base," Roak said as he stood up. "Transfer the data to my ship."

"Isn't this your ship, Roak?" Hessa asked.

"Don't start with me," Roak snapped. "Just get me the data."

"It'll be waiting for you," Hessa said, an obvious sneer in her voice, "on *your* ship."

Roak shook his head and left the mess, knowing the issue was going to be a sore spot with Hessa for a while.

11.

The 714 was a much smaller ship than the Eight-Three-Eight with only a pilot and co-pilot's seat at the front of the bridge and two auxiliary seats directly behind those. The pilot's seat was taken by Roak and the co-pilot's seat was taken by Nimm who Roak insisted needed to be in charge of the ship while he, Klib, Meshara, and Yellow Eyes were busy with the heist. The auxiliary seats were occupied by Klib and Meshara.

It only took three seconds before Roak did not trust the ship's AI with anything important. Thus Nimm.

"Exiting trans-space in three, two, one," the AI announced through the speakers in the ceiling. "If you would grant me access to your comm implants, I could make announcements directly to each of you."

That request, which had been a constant request since they stepped onto the ship, was why Roak refused to even consider trusting the AI. Roak swore he was going to disintegrate Bhangul when he returned to Zuus Colony. The guy was obviously trying to get intel on Hessa's mysterious tech and Roak was not happy about that.

"I miss the instant transportation," Yellow Eyes said as they exited the portal and returned to normal space. "That felt like the longest sixteen hours of flying ever."

Yellow Eyes was seated in one of the two jump seats that folded down from the bridge's wall. The other jump seat was occupied by Jagul, who was the final reason Roak needed Nimm. He couldn't take Jagul on the heist and he couldn't leave the young Dornopheous alone on the ship. Not with an AI he didn't trust worth an Eight Million Gods damn.

"I believe the entire journey was exactly fifteen hours and thirty-seven minutes," the AI said. "A considerably efficient time considering the average is seventeen hours and three minutes."

"Instant is faster," Yellow Eyes said.

"If you are in doubt over the efficiency of this ship, I have prepared a chart to explain each point in great detail," the AI said.

The view screen shifted from a view of the planet before them to an overly complicated chart filled with tables and graphs.

"No," Roak said. "Make that go away."

"It will be an informative way to pass the time as we wait for permission to land on Jafla Base," the AI said. "As you can see here in graph eighty-two, if we had entered the portal only three seconds slower, we would have lost nearly thirteen percent efficiency in our travel time."

"Nimm," Roak said.

"Right," Nimm responded as she punched in a lengthy code. The AI's rambling went silent. "That should do it."

"Thank you," Roak said. "I was about to shoot the console with my Flott."

Roak spun his seat around and faced Klib. The Halgon waited as Roak sat there, staring.

"This detective," Roak said finally, "he's owned by Shilo?"

"He used to be owned lock stock and barrel," Klib said. "But that changed a while back. There were some, let us say, issues with the GF Vice Squad on Jafla and the department did some housecleaning."

"He made the cut? A GVD on the take wasn't dumped in the incinerator bin?" Roak asked.

"He's a tricky one," Klib said. "Apparently he discovered a conspiracy and that discovery endeared him to the GF. They kept him on."

"He's been given a second chance," Roak said. "You don't see this as a problem?"

"Why would it be a problem?"

"Because he may not want to mess with that second chance."

"Second chance or not, those sixty-eight million chits aren't his," Klib explained. "To not help us would put his second chance in greater jeopardy than to help us. That really is syndicate money, even if Chella thinks it's his by possession, and if Kalaka doesn't hand it over then he is a bigger thief than he was before."

"Unless he's given the info over to the GF," Nimm said. "The chits may not be in the Gas Chamber anymore. Could have been part of the second chance he was given."

"Kalaka has questionable morals, but he isn't stupid," Klib said. "His second chance would end in a bloody nightmare if he allowed the chits to go to the GF. If I know the being, then he is waiting for someone, me, to arrive and take this burden off his hands."

Roak studied Klib for a couple of seconds.

"Sounds nice and simple," he said. "Except for the fact the chits are in the Gas Chamber. I've seen that place. Low life central."

"Aren't you a low life?" Jagul asked.

All eyes turned to the young Dornopheous. Meshara laughed.

"You'll want to stay quiet," Roak warned.

"My uncle says that you're the best bounty hunter in the galaxy," Jagul continued, ignoring Roak's warning. "He says you take jobs that no other bounty hunter will take. That you are the guy that other bounty hunters fear."

"But…?" Roak crossed his arms over his chest.

"But you're still a low life thug," Jagul said. "You work for people that are bad and you do bad things to get that work done. You aren't any different than any of the syndicates or other criminals in the galaxy."

"This should be fun," Yellow Eyes mumbled.

"Your uncle is right," Roak said. "I'm no different. But I am better. And that's all that matters right now because the syndicates, the criminals, the Edgers, the Skrang, the GF, even that stupid Coalition of Independent Planets, none of them have a clue about what is coming and what will happen if Father gets his way."

"What will happen if Father gets his way?" Meshara asked. "What is his end goal?"

"Total domination," Roak said. "It is all he knows."

"Sounds like someone I know," Yellow Eyes said.

Roak pointed an angry finger at the being and Yellow Eyes did his zip the lip move. He even pantomimed digging a hole where he could put the imaginary key in. As soon as the "hole" was "filled", Roak stopped pointing at him.

"How do you know he wants total domination?" Klib asked. "Maybe he wants to change the way the galaxy is run. Make it better for all the beings, not just the GF and the elite."

Meshara laughed again.

Before Roak could respond, Nimm said, "We're being hailed. Jafla Base traffic control has given us permission to land at Docking Bay 312."

"312? How many docking bays does this base have?" Yellow Eyes asked.

"Almost a thousand," Nimm answered. "Most aren't used anymore now that the orb fights aren't as popular as they used to be."

"My uncle says that's Roak's fault," Jagul said.

"That one he got right," Roak said.

"Roak likes to ruin the fun," Yellow Eyes said, then shrugged at the look Roak gave him. "What? I can't stay quiet forever."

"Can you just not say stupid things?" Roak asked.

"Can you just not be ugly?" Yellow Eyes shot back. "We are who we are."

"Everyone be quiet while I land," Nimm said. "The base isn't as busy as it used to be but the traffic is still heavy. It'd be easier with the AI…"

"No," Roak said. "Something is wrong with that AI."

"Something is wrong with all the AIs," Yellow Eyes said. "Or am I the only one that's noticed?"

"What do you mean?" Klib asked. "How are they wrong?"

"Great conversation that no one cares about," Roak said. "Shut up until we land."

Nimm navigated them through the chaos that was Jafla's atmosphere.

Jafla Base was a whirlwind of interstellar vehicle activity. Jafla Planet was a desert. Nothing, not even B'clo'no's, could last very long out in the wasteland that was Jafla. Visitors either stayed close to the base or died. No real middle ground. Being the only inhabited area of Jafla Planet, the base was a constant stream of ships coming and going. Everything from tourists to business beings to the many players from the different syndicates to galactic celebrities could be seen going to and from the base.

Or used to, back when the orb fights were the hottest sporting and entertainment event in the galaxy. Before Roak ruined all of that.

Nimm piloted the ship to Docking Bay 312 then into the specific hangar reserved for them. The ship touched down without even a bump.

"Welcome to Jafla Base," a voice said over the speakers. "Please note that all beings must now register with our security department upon exiting their vehicle. All AIs must be put into stasis mode and are strictly prohibited from operating while on Jafla Base. They may be reactivated to leave the planet, but only once given permission. Any violence or criminal activity will be met with swift punishment. Courts have been suspended and any and all adjudication is in the hands of the Galactic Fleet authorities and Jafla Base Police Department. Objections or complaints may be lodged with the Galactic Fleet and will be considered only after a judgement has already been delivered. Please enjoy your time on Jafla Base. Thank you."

The message began to repeat itself and Nimm cut it off.

"The GF has tightened things down," Roak said.

"It's because of the war," Nimm said. "Jafla Base would be a symbolic victory if the Skrang either take it outright or destroy it."

"Let's hope they don't try either of those things while we're here," Roak said.

He stood up and checked the charge on his Flott. Full. He holstered it then pointed at Klib.

"Time for you to earn your keep," Roak said. "How do we get in touch with this Kalaka? I doubt we can walk up to the local galactic affairs municipal building and ask to see him."

"I know how to find him," Klib said. "GVD Kalaka is nothing if not predictable in his habits."

"Great," Roak said. "Then let's get to it."

"Not yet," Klib said and gestured at Roak's face. "You will need your armor's helmet."

"I've been on Jafla before," Roak said. "It's not that dangerous."

"It's because they know your face here, Roak," Nimm said. "Not because you need the extra protection."

"Your face is a liability," Klib said. "Face rec will tag you instantly and then we'll have every thug on the base coming for you."

"I'm not that hated," Roak said. "I'll be fine."

Klib sighed and nodded at Nimm. Nimm activated a holo.

The holo was of Roak and all data known about him. It was surprisingly extensive.

But the interesting part was the credit amount that flashed across all the information every other second.

"Eighty-five thousand credits?" Roak asked. "That's all I'm worth?"

"That's for info leading to your apprehension," Klib said. "I believe capture and delivery is ten times that."

"That's more like it," Roak said.

"Alright, hold on a minute," Yellow Eyes said. "There's a bounty on the bounty hunter?"

"Only here on Jafla," Nimm said. "I just double checked."

"As I have said, Roak is hated on Jafla," Klib said.

"I'll be fine," Roak said. He fetched his helmet from where it sat next to his seat. "I'll have more resources at my disposal with the helmet."

"You'll stand out," Meshara said.

"He won't stand out," Nimm stated. She switched the holo to a view of one of the many markets that filled Jafla's streets. "See. Plenty of beings are wearing helmets."

Roak frowned at the holo. Yes, there were plenty of beings wearing helmets, but the vast majority obviously wore them for environmental and survival reasons since Jafla's atmosphere was not compatible with their bodily systems. None wore helmets with their armor just because.

"Yeah, I'll fit right in," Roak said and put his helmet on. "Let's go."

Roak didn't wait for the others. He made his way off the bridge and descended the ladder to the side airlock.

He wondered how many times he'd pressed the airlock button he was about to press again. Hundreds? Thousands? Being on his old ship brought up interesting memories. So much had changed since he'd lost his old ship and began traveling on the Borgon with Hessa.

With Hessa…

A thought struck him. Something related to Jafla's ban on AIs being active on the base.

"What are you waiting for?" Meshara asked.

"What?" Roak asked.

"You've been standing there staring at the airlock controls for like two minutes," Yellow Eyes said. "Something wrong? Do you need to pee before we go?"

"Bite me," Roak said and activated the controls.

The airlock opened and steps automatically lowered to the hangar's deck.

"Do a quick check," Roak said.

Yellow Eyes blurred then was back almost before Roak finished his sentence.

"All clear," Yellow Eyes said.

Roak descended the steps, glanced about, then moved purposefully towards the hangar's exit. A multitude of bots swirled around him before he could get to the door.

"Check under the hood for ya?"

"Care to know which brothel is the best brothel? I can tell you!"

"All you can eat buffet! No additional charge even if you are an Urvein! Eat all you want!"

"The hottest new club on Jafla Base is only a quick roller trip away!"

"With this brand new plasma injector, you can increase the efficiency of your ship's drives by nearly forty percent!"

Roak pulled his Flott and shot one of the bots. The rest scurried away.

"Man!" Yellow Eyes exclaimed.

"That's not going to bring us any undue attention," Meshara said. "Fool."

"A lower profile would be best," Klib said.

"Roak!" Nimm shouted over the comm. "We were just sent a bill for eight thousand credits! The ship is in lockdown until we pay it!"

"Jafla really has changed," Roak said. "No one ever cared how many bots I shot last time I was here."

"The orb fights don't bring in the credits they used to," Klib said. "Which means there isn't the tax or graft revenue there used to be. Jafla has hit hard times."

They left the hangar and Roak had to agree. Jafla had hit hard times.

The street they walked out onto was dirty and the gutters were filled with trash. Beings ambled about without much purpose or drive. The looks on their faces, regardless of species, were ones of just getting by.

"This is depressing," Yellow Eyes said to Roak. "You did this?"

"No," Roak said and shrugged. "Maybe. Don't really care."

A few beings looked their way, but most kept their heads down and trudged along to whatever mind-numbing existence waited for them.

Roak snapped his fingers at Klib. "Contact Kalaka."

"It's not that easy," Klib said. "We have to go somewhere first. When we get there then the message will get out to Kalaka and he'll contact us."

"Where do we have to go?" Roak said.

"You'll see," Klib said.

"Hold up there," a tired looking Slinghasp said as he stood up from a rickety stool set close to the exit of that part of the docking port. "Gotta register you."

"Our pilot did that," Roak said.

The Slinghasp sighed and gave Roak a bored look. "The ship is registered with traffic control. I'm with base security."

"We do not have time for this," Meshara hissed.

Klib held out a hand to Roak.

"What?" Roak asked. He looked at the Slinghasp then shook his head. "Right."

Roak withdrew a pouch from his belt and handed it to Klib. Klib fished out several chits and gave them to the Slinghasp.

"That wasn't so hard, was it?" the Slinghasp asked as he returned to his stool. "Go do whatever you're here to do. Try not to hurt the base."

"Can't make any promises," Roak said.

"Like I've never heard that one before," the Slinghasp replied with a weariness that was almost contagious.

12.

Roak had been in a lot of Hellish landscapes in his line of work.

He'd faced creatures that only lived in nightmares.

He'd been blown up and put back together.

He'd been drowned, stabbed, shot, stabbed some more, set on fire, tossed out into space, swallowed by a giant creature he couldn't name and excreted out the creature's anus, and he'd been married to a member of the Cervile royal family.

But where Klib took them was possibly the most horrifying landscape of all.

"Still is the dust that holds and binds us. Long is the day that washes us. Close is the heart that beats for us."

"I'm going to shoot someone," Roak said.

"Who?" Yellow Eyes asked.

"Anyone. Everyone," Roak replied. "Make it stop."

"I agree with Roak," Meshara said.

There was polite applause from the cafe's audience as the speaker finished and stepped down off the stage. A Leforian took the being's place and clapped all four of her hands.

"Wasn't that lovely!" the Leforian exclaimed. "Nothing like some poetry to lift the spirits! Speaking of lifting the spirits, our next performer is known for his mastery of the ancient instrument called the bahgliora. I don't know what that is, but I bet it'll sound great!"

It did not sound great.

Roak almost had to sit on his hands to keep from pulling his Flott and shooting the being that was making some of the worst noises he'd ever heard in his life. The being was a bright yellow human and fairly handsome by Galactic standards. Roak watched as many of the audience members seemed to swoon as the man played his abomination of an instrument.

"This will not stand," Meshara said.

She stood and sauntered her way up to the stage. The musician, if he could be called that, watched her approach, liked what he saw obviously, and gave her a big wink.

"What is she doing?" Klib hissed. "We need to sit here and wait, not draw attention to ourselves."

Roak glanced at Yellow Eyes. The being was waving all of his nubs in the air and swaying back and forth to the music.

"Play it, yellow brother!" Yellow Eyes called out.

"Yeah. A low profile," Roak said.

"Go stop her," Klib snapped.

"You stop her," Roak said. "I'm not getting in the middle of that."

Before Klib could do anything, Meshara extended her claws and slashed the bahgliora's air sack to pieces. Strips of material flew in all directions as the horrific sound the instrument made came to a squawking halt.

There were a few boos from some of the swooning audience members, but those were drowned out by the louder applause from the rest of the room. Meshara ignored the praise she received for saving the ears of the beings present in the cafe and sauntered back to the table.

"Man, that was harsh," Yellow Eyes said. "Look at the guy."

The musician was still on the stage. He sat there, the remains of his bahgliora drooping from his hands, as he cried.

"Show business is rough," Meshara said. "He's going to have to learn to take criticism."

"Uh, we will take a short break then bring on our next performer," the Leforian said as she took the stage.

She helped the musician off the stage then immediately stomped over to Roak's table.

"Do I need to call the Jafla Base PD?" the Leforian asked, her eyes on Meshara as her lower mandibles clicked together with irritation. "Every being has a right to express themselves freely on my stage. I will have you imprisoned if you dare do that again."

"Alright," Meshara said, making sure she showed her sharp claws to the Leforian. She pretended to clean them, but the display was obviously an attempt to intimidate.

The Leforian wasn't buying it.

"Girl, my exoskeleton will snap those pokers off the tips of your fingers if you even think of striking me," the Leforian said. "You." She pointed at Klib. "I've seen you before. You're syndicate. You want to tell me why your little gang is harassing my establishment?"

"We're not her gang," Roak said.

"Oh? Is this your gang?" she asked Roak.

"We're his team," Yellow Eyes said. "He wants to call us a crew, but that implies we work for him and I'm not sure that-"

"Shut up," Roak said. Yellow Eyes shut up. Roak focused on the Leforian. "We're not anything. Just some tourists seeing the sights and suffering through the sounds."

"Sure you are," the Leforian said.

Roak shrugged.

"Then sit quietly and be polite or you'll end up really suffering," the Leforian said.

"We got it," Roak said. "No more trouble."

Yellow Eyes nodded. Klib frowned. Meshara rolled her eyes.

"I am not very convinced," the Leforian said. "You're going to want to order more drinks and some food in order to convince me."

"Understood," Roak said. "We'll take another round and an assortment of appetizers."

"Do you have Gooey Fried Knobs?" Yellow Eyes asked. "I love Gooey Fried Knobs."

"We do," the Leforian said. "I'll place your order and you'll sit here and behave."

"Got it," Roak said.

He waited until the Leforian was out of earshot before turning to face Meshara.

"If anyone else tries to play another one of those Eight Million Gods damn instruments, you can shred that too," Roak said. "I'll take whatever suffering the Leforian can dish out over hearing that noise again."

"You are risking us not making contact with Kalaka," Klib said. "Stop the destructive behavior and save it for the heist."

"I'd love to save it for the heist," Roak said, "but so far there's no Kalaka which means there's no heist. This GVD better get here soon or we start looking at other alternatives."

"Other alternatives?" Klib asked. "You have a lead on some other stash of millions of chits?"

"No, but this is Jafla Base," Roak said. "I crack enough heads and break enough bones and I'll get a lead."

"I should never have told you about the chits," Klib said. "You will ruin the heist."

"If you'd never told us about the chits then you'd be useless," Roak said. "And what's the same as useless?"

"I know, I know!" Yellow Eyes said, holding up an arm. "Dead! Dead is the same as useless!" He gave Klib a couple of his weird thumbs up. "Nailed it."

"We can revisit that option," Roak said. "Because right now you aren't looking too useful."

Klib started to defend herself, but closed her mouth when the cafe's door opened and a being walked in.

Kalaka was a Cervile, so he had a certain swagger to his walk that the male members of the feline race all exhibited. He was also a detective for the Galactic Vice Squad which added to his swagger. A few of the patrons in the cafe gave him more than a passing look. He made sure to acknowledge each look with a solid wink.

Finished bulk flirting, Kalaka took a look about the cafe, his vertical pupils widening as they adjusted to the dimness. Then he caught sight of Klib, his eyes narrowed, he caught sight of the unexpected guests with Klib, and his eyes narrowed some more.

It looked like he was about to turn and leave, but Kalaka paused, did a double take, and crossed cautiously to the table.

"Hello, Klib," Kalaka said. "I heard you were in town." He shifted his attention to Meshara. "I do not believe we've ever met. I'm GVD Kalaka and you are?"

"Meshara Trelalla," Meshara said. "Personal security and attaché for Her Royal Highness Queen Tala Berene, and head of security for the Cervile Royal Guard. There would be no reason we would have met. GVDs are not part of my circle."

"Oh, Eight Million Gods damn," Yellow Eyes said. "She got you there, man."

"I like you," Kalaka said to Meshara. "And that is the only reason I'm sticking around to hear what Klib has to say."

"That's appreciated," Roak said.

Kalaka grabbed a chair, spun it around, and sat down, his arms resting across the back. He frowned at Roak.

"What's with the helmet?" Kalaka asked Roak. "You got atmosphere issues?"

"Something like that," Roak said.

"I highly doubt it," Kalaka said. "That's protection from violence, not protection from Jafla's atmosphere. What's your name, Mr. Helmet?"

"It's not Mr. Helmet," Roak said. He grunted. "Can we take this conversation somewhere else? We're a little exposed here."

"Whose fault is that?" Kalaka asked. "A little kweet told me that you've made a spectacle of yourselves. I'm already compromised by sitting with you, so how about you just say what you want and I can think it over before I say no."

"You can't say no," Klib said. "You know the deal you made."

"The deal? What deal?" Kalaka asked, his focus still on Roak. "I don't remember making any deals with these beings. The only person I know here is you, Klib. So if there is a deal then everyone else can go fuck off and let us talk privately."

"Her deal is now our deal," Roak said.

Kalaka laughed and leaned back. He gripped the back of the chair with both hands and made sure to extend his claws slowly then retract them just as slowly. He turned to Klib.

"Klib? Are you being held hostage?" Kalaka asked. "Blink once for yes and twice for no."

Yellow Eyes burst out laughing. It was a wild cackle that brought any and all conversation in the cafe to a halt.

"This guy!" Yellow Eyes exclaimed. "Are all the GVDs like you? If so then sign me up for the Galactic Vice Squad. I'm ready to switch teams!"

"Not a team," Roak said. "And you aren't switching to anything. Klib? Make this happen."

"Yes, Klib, make this happen," Kalaka said. "What can I do for you?"

"You know why I am here and what you are supposed to do for me," Klib said. "Stop messing around and deliver, Kalaka, or there will be consequences."

"Right. Consequences," Kalaka responded. "Normally I'd be worried. The Shilo Syndicate is pretty Eight Million Gods damn powerful. You cross them and you end up with your tail shoved where it doesn't go. And that's if beings are feeling nice."

"Exactly. So you better-"

"Not done talking," Kalaka said, raising a finger with a claw extended.

He smiled, picked his teeth with the claw, flicked something onto the floor, then continued. Meshara shuddered with disgust. Kalaka winked again.

"The problem is, Klib, that Shilo no longer exists," Kalaka continued. "Neither does Willz or even Collari. And from what I'm hearing, most of the other syndicates are disappearing at an alarming rate."

"Disappearing? Like the Cervile planet?" Yellow Eyes asked.

Kalaka started to speak, but stopped. The fur on his arms raised and his upper lip curled into a snarl.

"What did the yellow guy just say about our planet?" Kalaka asked Meshara. "What in all the Hells does he mean that the planet has disappeared?"

"You do not know?" Meshara chuckled. "That tells me just how low your caste is, Kalaka. No one even bothered to tell you that our planet was taken."

"Taken? How in all the Hells do you take a planet?" Kalaka exclaimed. He glanced over his shoulder and glared at the few patrons that had turned to see what the problem was. Pulling a pack of stim sticks from his pocket, he lit one and turned back to the table. "Maybe we should go somewhere else."

"You think?" Roak said. "Where?"

"You want me to pick?" Kalaka replied. "Good. I know exactly where to go."

"Kalaka!" the Leforian called from her place by the bar. "No smoking in here!"

"We're just leaving," Kalaka said and stood up. "You doing open mic night this weekend too?"

"It's open mic night every night, Kalaka."

"Eight Million Gods why?" Meshara asked.

"Beings got to express themselves," Kalaka said with a shrug. "Come on. I know where we can be anonymous."

"Is that possible on Jafla?" Roak asked.

"I know a place," Kalaka said. "Follow me. I've got a roller waiting outside."

"So you could run from your obligation?" Klib asked as they all stood and followed Kalaka to the cafe's door.

"Yes," Kalaka replied without a hint of irony. "Best to be prepared."

"You flee like a coward," Meshara said.

"I flee like a survivor," Kalaka said. "And feel free to drop that snooty snoot of yours a few degrees down. You keep your nose up all the time like that and you won't be able to see where you're going."

"Be careful how you speak to me," Meshara said. "I have tolerated disrespect from these beings, but I will not tolerate it from a low Cervile such as yourself."

"I thought all Cervile's were higher on the pecking order than all other beings in the galaxy," Kalaka said. The group approached the roller waiting at the curb. Kalaka opened the rear door. "After you."

Meshara slid inside as did Roak, Klib, and Yellow Eyes, with Kalaka joining them last. The roller had plenty of room inside, with two rear bench seats facing each other. Kalaka made a point of sitting right next to Meshara, but she moved quickly, pulled Yellow Eyes out of his seat across from her, and took his place, leaving Yellow Eyes to sit next to Kalaka.

"Hi," Yellow Eyes said.

"You are a corrupt law enforcement officer," Meshara said to Kalaka. "That puts you lower than even the worst enemy of the Cervile."

"Ouch," Yellow Eyes said.

"Tell the driver to get moving," Roak said. "Meet and greet time is over. Take us to this place where we can have some privacy."

"Take you?" Kalaka laughed. "We're already here."

Light flashed around the door frames.

"Kalaka!" Klib exclaimed. "You will not lock us in this roller!"

"Too late for that," Kalaka said. "Poq?"

The partition between the rear seats and the driver lowered. A being sat there. The being's skin was dull beige and his head was bald except for a red tint to the scalp to simulate where hair would go. The being turned to face the group. His eyes constantly shifted color.

"That's not creepy at all," Yellow Eyes said.

"An android driver?" Roak asked. "I didn't think the GF would allow an android on the GVD payroll. Not with the way they're cracking down on AIs."

The android, Poq, cocked his head.

"I did not think the GF would allow a bounty hunter like you to live," Poq said. "Let alone allow you to work for them. Hello, Mr. Roak."

"First, it's Roak. Just Roak," Roak said. "And second, I don't work for the GF. It's a partnership."

"Roak?" Kalaka asked, impressed. "Mr. Helmet is Roak? Hot Eight Million Gods damn. I can't wait to hear what Klib has to say. Poq?"

"The precinct?" Poq asked.

"What? No," Kalaka replied. "Drive us around the base so we can talk."

"But Roak is wanted on Jafla Base," Poq said. "It's our duty to apprehend him."

"Bigger picture time, Poq," Kalaka said. "Just drive."

"I'll think twice next time you ask for a favor," Poq said as the partition rose again.

"He'll still be listening," Roak said.

"He always is," Kalaka said. He pointed at Roak. "Take that stupid helmet off."

Roak did and took several deep breaths.

"There. That's better," Kalaka said and reached under his seat. He produced a bottle. "Anyone care for some whiskey?"

"Yes," Roak said.

"Excellent." Kalaka took a swig then handed the bottle to Roak. "I have a feeling my life just got considerably more interesting. Who wants to start?"

13.

"They melted?" Kalaka asked Roak then glanced at Klib. "Why isn't she dead?"

"We got her out in time," Roak said.

"I assume you took a body to study, right?" Kalaka asked. He held out his hand and Roak gave him the whiskey bottle. It was almost empty. "What did you find out?"

"Not a lot," Roak said.

"Terpigshit," Kalaka said. "You know something."

"Only theories."

"Let's hear those."

"No."

"No?"

"No."

"Alright." Kalaka looked at Meshara. "And no one knows what happened to our planet?"

"My planet," Meshara said. "It no longer belongs to you, low life."

"Man, she really hates you," Yellow Eyes said.

"We'll get to your story soon too," Kalaka said.

"Later," Roak said. "A lot later. How do we get the chits that are down in the Gas Chamber?"

"Now we're getting down to business," Kalaka said and finished off the whiskey. "Poq! Gotta make a stop for more provisions!" Kalaka cocked his head as he listened to his comm. "Yes, I am talking about more whiskey. What other provisions would I be talking about?"

"The chits are our only focus, Kalaka," Klib said. "Help us retrieve them and you will be released from your obligation."

"Lady, I was released from my obligation a long time ago," Kalaka said. "You just didn't know it."

"Don't attempt to play games, Kalaka," Klib snapped.

"I'm not. Shilo is gone," Kalaka said. "I've been testing that discovery for months now and no matter what I do to what should have been considered Shilo assets there has been no retribution. There hasn't even been a peep from one of your enforcers. The time of the syndicates is over which means I'm free."

"Except for the GF," Yellow Eyes said. "You still work for them."

"Good point," Kalaka said. "But they break fewer bones when you mess up."

"I don't care what the state of the syndicates are in the galaxy," Roak said. "Are the chits still in the Gas Chamber and can we get to them?" He leaned forward and smiled at Kalaka. To the man's credit, he didn't cringe. "The better question is if you actually have a plan to get the chits and are you going to share that plan with us?"

"Because if I don't have a plan or don't share the plan then you don't need me and I'm useless to you, is that it?" Kalaka said. He spread his arms wide. "Why do you think I'm in a roller with a very dangerous android GVD driving?"

"So you don't have a plan," Roak said and turned to Klib. "Fix this."

"Hold up there, scarface," Kalaka said. "I have a plan. It's a good plan too." He made a point of doing an unnecessary headcount. "Only problem is we're one being short."

"Adapt," Roak said.

"You see, the plan is very precise," Kalaka replied, shaking his head. "Without the proper amount of beings working together then odds are we not only fail, but we die too."

"Use the android," Roak said. "Unless you don't trust him?"

"Oh, I trust Poq," Kalaka said. "We've been through some shit together. But he won't work. Everyone on Jafla knows Poq is GF. I mean, did you see the guy? Sort of stands out."

"We don't have another being," Klib said.

"I might know someone that can help," Kalaka said.

"What's the being needed for?" Roak asked. "Danger or distraction?"

"It's all danger, Roak," Kalaka said. He lit a stim stick and drew deep then let out a thin stream of smoke aimed directly at Meshara. "Danger is my life."

Meshara waved the smoke from her face and glared.

Roak placed his hand on his Flott. Kalaka laughed.

"Neutralized," Kalaka said. "I could pull my Blorta from my ankle and try to shoot you and it'd only make a pop pop noise. You think I'd trap myself in a roller with armed criminals?"

"Criminals?" Yellow Eyes asked. "Who are you calling criminals? We work for the GF too." He looked over at Roak. "Right?"

"Doesn't matter," Roak said. "This job is off the books so we can't call in any favors with the GF."

"Exactly," Kalaka said. He pointed the stim stick at Roak. "But, to answer your question, we do have a plum distraction role. Probably the least amount of danger in the whole plan. Maybe have the spindly looking yellow guy here handle it. But we'd still need someone else for one of the trickier elements."

"Spindly?" Yellow Eyes replied with disgust. He waved all his arms and legs and even wiggled his body some. "Does this look spindly to you, man? Huh? Does it?"

"Yes," Kalaka replied without hesitation.

"Oh. Well…alright then," Yellow Eyes said.

"Yellow Eyes can handle whatever is thrown at him," Roak said.

"But don't throw stuff at me. That's rude," Yellow Eyes said. Roak growled. "I'll shut up now."

"What's this distraction?" Roak asked.

"I just need someone to be the worst patron the bartenders have ever seen," Kalaka said.

"That is asking a lot considering the Gas Chamber's patrons," Klib said.

"True, true, but it's the least dangerous part of the plan," Kalaka said. "All the being has to do is be an asshole for a few minutes so we can get into the bar storeroom."

"You hid the chits in the Gas Chamber's storeroom?" Roak asked, disgusted.

"Chella found where I originally stashed them then I did my thing and moved them fast," Kalaka said. "Without him any the wiser, of course."

"You stashed them in the storeroom?" Roak sighed.

"That's where you store shit, right?" Kalaka replied. "And don't worry. It's in a spot that no one would even think about approaching."

"What kind of spot?" Roak asked.

"We'll get to that in a minute. Right now, I need to know if you have another being or not."

"We do," Roak said.

"We do?" Meshara asked.

"We do?" Klib asked.

"We… Oh, Roak… Come on, man," Yellow Eyes said.

"Do you mean Nimm?" Meshara asked. "We need her on the ship so we can leave quickly when the time arrives."

"I know," Roak said. He snapped his fingers. "Can you get rid of a docking bay fine for us?"

"You've been on Jafla for half a day and you already got fined?" Kalaka laughed. "No problem. Shoot me the fine number and I'll have it wiped from the system."

"Great," Roak said. "I'll comm Nimm and let her know."

"Getting rid of the fine doesn't change that we need her to pilot the ship," Meshara said.

"I know," Roak said.

"He knows," Yellow Eyes said, looking very uncomfortable.

"Then who…" Meshara's pupils dilated down to almost imperceptible lines. "You must be joking…"

"Is he thinking of using the kid?" Klib asked. "Roak? Are you thinking of using the kid?"

"Is he even old enough to drink?" Yellow Eyes wondered out loud.

"Don't know what kid you all are talking about, but it's the Gas Chamber," Kalaka said. "No one checks ID in the Gas Chamber."

"The kid'll be fine," Roak said. "Dornopheous are tough. Very springy."

"We cannot risk this heist on a child," Meshara said.

"I agree with the Cervile," Klib said.

"You don't mean me, do you?" Kalaka asked and shook his head. "Nah. Not me. Can we trust the kid to not screw up?"

"Can he screw up being a distraction?" Roak asked.

"If he stops distracting," Kalaka said. "That'd be a pretty big screw up."

"I think he can distract and annoy the bartending staff without screwing up," Roak said. "The kid's special skill is being annoying."

"Not wrong there," Yellow Eyes said.

Kalaka sat there in silence. Roak watched with patience. Then several minutes passed and the patience left. Roak growled.

"What?" Kalaka asked.

"You gonna say something or just sit there?" Roak snapped.

"I'm thinking," Kalaka said.

"Think faster," Roak said. "And tell the android to head to the docking port."

"Poq?" Kalaka called.

"Already moving in that direction," Poq responded, his voice coming from the speakers in the roller's ceiling. "Docking bay 312."

"Is that the one?" Kalaka asked.

"That's the one," Roak said.

Kalaka pounded on the partition. "We're stopping for whiskey first!"

"We do not have time for any of this," Meshara said. "Stopping for alcohol, stopping to pick up a child that will only endanger us, using a plan created by an obvious moron. We should storm this Gas Chamber and take the chits by force. I am Trelalla. We cannot lose."

"Damn," Kalaka said. "When you said your clan name, I was worried. But then I saw the company you were keeping so I thought that maybe, just maybe, this Trelalla would be chill."

"She's not chill," Yellow Eyes said.

"No. She's not chill," Kalaka said. "Roak? You've been to the Gas Chamber. Want to be the one to tell her that you can't storm the place?"

"We have to be let inside," Roak said.

"We will fight our way inside," Meshara said.

The roller stopped and the inside flashed bright white.

"I'm going to go get whiskey," Kalaka said. "Be right back."

"I'll join you," Roak said and grabbed his helmet.

Kalaka began to protest then only shrugged.

"Klib? Explain to Meshara what the Gas Chamber is like," Roak said as he followed Kalaka out of the roller.

They stepped onto a street that was even worse than the ones Roak had seen before. He took stock quickly to assess any threats and realized that everything and everyone was a threat. It was almost calming in a way.

"We've been losing the battle for a while," Kalaka said. "You killed Shava Stem Shava then a couple of years later a bunch of terpigshit went down with the Vice Squad. Jafla can't seem to find stable footing."

The store Kalaka walked up to didn't have a door. It had many windows that showed the rows and rows of shelves holding pretty much every alcoholic beverage in the galaxy. But no door.

A Groshnel was inside, stocking the shelves. Kalaka knocked on one of the windows. The Groshnel turned, smiled, saw Roak, and frowned.

"He's with me!" Kalaka shouted at the window. He held up two fingers. "The usual!"

The Groshnel nodded and reached out with one of its tentacle arms to grab two bottles of whiskey from the shelf behind it.

"Probably make it three!" Kalaka shouted.

The Groshnel obliged and walked its tentacle walk up to the window. Part of the plastiglass slid aside and the Groshnel waited.

"Oh, you know I'm good for it," Kalaka said.

The Groshnel waited.

"Do you mind?" Kalaka asked Roak. "I'm a little short."

"Right," Roak said and fished out some chits.

The Groshnel took the chits with one tentacle and passed the bottles over. Then the window sealed itself and the being went back to stocking shelves.

Kalaka cracked one of the bottles and took a long drink. "What's on your mind, Roak?"

"Do you have a plan?" Roak asked.

"Of course," Kalaka responded quickly, offering the bottle to Roak.

"Not right now," Roak said.

"Suit yourself," Kalaka said. He drank deeply then wiped his mouth with the back of his hand. He spat out some fur and stared at the back of his hand. "I need to really work on my nutritional intake. I'm starting to get mange."

"Do you have a plan?" Roak asked again. "Or is this all just terpigshit you're making up on the spot?"

"A little from incinerator bin A and a little from incinerator bin B," Kalaka said. "You know how the Gas Chamber is."

"I do. But I don't know you. There are some beings I trust to improvise."

"Really? You don't seem like the trusting type."

"There's one being I trust to improvise," Roak said then paused. "Maybe two."

"You have a rich personal life, Roak. I envy you."

"What is the plan?"

Kalaka walked back to the roller.

"No point in me saying it twice. Let's go get your kid," he said and was about to open the door, but Roak placed a boot against it. "Or I can tell you now and then tell everyone else again later."

Roak didn't move his boot.

"We filter in individually," Kalaka said. "I need the kid to head straight to the bar and never leave. Distract, distract, distract. I need one being watching the waitstaff to make sure they aren't alerted to something over the comms. I need another being to watch security for the same reason. Waitstaff is more important since the bartenders and waitstaff comm with each other way more than with security. They'll be the first sign of trouble. But we can fix that. If the waitstaff and security look alarmed then we'll have to move fast or abort."

"Understood," Roak said. "That's three beings. What are the other jobs?"

"I need someone to go get the chits," Kalaka said.

There was a twitch at the corner of Kalaka's mouth that Roak thought was either a smirk or a nervous tick. Knowing Cerviles like he did, Roak guessed it was the former.

"What's so funny?" Roak asked. "Where are these chits? What's this spot you have them stashed in?"

"We'll get to that," Kalaka said. "Who's the fastest in your group?"

"Yellow Eyes," Roak answered.

"How fast? Because he needs to be very fast," Kalaka said. "Or heavily armored. I'd send you in since you're one of those galactic survivors that could probably handle this part easily, but I need you with me."

"For what?" Roak asked.

"That depends on the scene when we get there," Kalaka said. "Is your yellow guy fast enough to handle a nest of Felturean fire ants?"

"Eight Million Gods," Roak exclaimed. He shivered. "The Gas Chamber has a Felturean fire ant nest in the storeroom?"

"Oh, more than one," Kalaka said. "Every time a new one pops up they just wall it over and seal it in then punch a new wall out to make room for the supplies. There's like ten nests behind those walls."

"How sealed?" Roak asked.

"Totally sealed," Kalaka said.

"So whoever unseals the nests will be facing starving, cannibalistic Felturean fire ants that will instantly attack and try to devour anything and everything in sight," Roak stated.

"Now you see why fast is needed," Kalaka said.

"That wall is opened and they won't stop with the storeroom," Roak said.

"I'm counting on it," Kalaka said with a smile. "That's our escape plan. As long as your yellow guy can get the chits then we're good. After that it'll be so much chaos in the Gas Chamber once those fire ants start pouring out of the storeroom that we'll be able to walk right out without anyone noticing."

"Run out," Roak said. "You don't walk away from Felturean fire ants."

"Running is better."

"What's your part in this?"

"I get us in."

"And my part?"

"I told you, that depends on the scene when we get there," Kalaka said. "You'll have to be flexible."

"Flexible usually means getting hurt," Roak said.

Kalaka shrugged. "There may be pain involved, but you didn't think this job was going to be painless, did you, Roak? Come on. You're way too much of a pro to kid yourself like that."

Roak moved his boot.

"Thank you," Kalaka said. "Now, speaking of kidding, let's go get that kid of yours and kick this party off."

Kalaka got in the roller, leaving Roak to stand on the curb. He took a look about the area and seriously wondered what he'd gotten himself into. With Jafla down on its luck like it was, the Gas Chamber was going to be nothing but all the Hells.

"Hey," Yellow Eyes said, sticking his head out of the roller. "You good, man?"

"Probably not," Roak replied.

"Should I be worried?"

"Probably."

"So it's business as usual?"

"Just like always."

"Cool. Let's do this."

"Yeah, let's do this," Roak said and stepped into the roller.

14.

"Have you lost your mind?" Nimm shouted at Roak as they stood on the 714's bridge. "Bhangul will not only never give us the Borgon back, but he'll probably kill Reck and wipe Hessa from the ship's mainframe when he finds out!"

"You think Bhangul can kill Reck?" Roak asked, a bored look on his face. "And even come close to wiping Hessa?"

Nimm sputtered then shook her head. "No. Of course not. But do not underestimate the being. If we come back without Jagul-"

"We'll come back with Jagul," Roak interrupted.

"-alive," Nimm finished. "He has to be alive."

Roak shrugged.

"Roak…"

"He'll come back alive," Roak insisted. "We good?"

"No, we are not good," Nimm said. "I know you're used to playing with beings' lives and letting the chits fall where they may, but only until recently I was part of the galactic order and some of those things I like to call morals and ethics still exist in me, Roak."

"You should talk to Hessa about those," Roak said. "I bet she can wipe them away with a couple of hours in the med pod."

"Stop being an asshole!" Nimm shouted.

"That's like asking Roak to stop being Roak," Yellow Eyes said.

"When did you get here?" Nimm snapped. "I thought you were outside with the others."

"I was," Yellow Eyes said. "But the sexual tension between Meshara and Kalaka is getting kind of gross."

"What is he talking about?" Nimm asked Roak.

"Cerviles," Roak said as if that explained it all. Nimm nodded since it did explain it all.

"The kid will come back alive and we'll come back with the chits," Roak said. "So you need to be ready and waiting."

"We have a fine to pay," Nimm said.

"Already paid," Roak said. "Kalaka took care of it."

"No, it hasn't been paid," Nimm said. She brought up a holo. "We're still on lockdown."

Roak growled. "I'll talk to him."

"Do that or we aren't going anywhere fast."

"Is that all? Any more lectures?"

"Plenty more."

"Think you can save them for later?"

"Later. Yes. Sure." Nimm huffed. "Go. Get the chits and get back here. Fast."

"Fast is my middle name!" Yellow Eyes said and was gone then back. "Not really. I don't think I have a middle name." Then he was gone again.

"Roak?"

"What?"

"Good luck," Nimm said and sat down in the pilot's seat. "Don't get the kid killed."

"I'll take that advice and apply it to all of us," Roak said, then paused. "Maybe not Klib. Or Kalaka."

"I don't care about them," Nimm said.

Roak smirked. "Now you're learning."

He left the bridge and was standing in front of the others in minutes.

"You," Roak said and pointed at Kalaka. "The fine hasn't been paid."

"What? It hasn't?" Kalaka responded, faux innocence dripping from his lips. "I'll get right on that."

He held up a finger as he activated his comm.

"Poq? That fine hasn't been deleted." He smiled at everyone, all cool and casual. "I know you did it, but they're saying it's still in effect and the ship is still on lockdown." More smiling. "Can you look into it and see what's the problem? Maybe bypass the docking agency and wipe it out yourself. You can get into their system, right? I knew it. Thanks, Poq."

Kalaka clapped his hands together.

"Poq will take care of it right away."

"He better. Because you'll be coming back with us to make sure he does," Roak said.

"I'm sorry, what now?" Kalaka asked. "Uh, no. As soon as we have the chits, and I have my cut, then we'll be parting ways. Klib understands."

"No," Klib said.

"Kind of cryptic there, Klib. What does no mean?" Kalaka asked.

"Not cryptic at all," Roak said and pushed up into Kalaka's personal space. "She means no because she doesn't understand your terpigshit, Kalaka. You want your chits? You'll have to get your cut when we divide them up on my ship. Did you think we'd split them out on the street or in the lift when we escape the Gas Chamber?"

"No, no, that's crazy." Kalaka laughed. "Of course we'll split them up on your ship. Good plan."

"We do not need him," Meshara said. "We know the chits are hidden behind a wall in the Gas Chamber storeroom."

"Do you know which storeroom? Or which wall?" Kalaka asked.

Meshara frowned.

"There's more than one storeroom?" Roak asked.

"The Gas Chamber is a big place and they host the underground orb fights plus serve a full bar and full menu," Kalaka replied. "They have a few different storerooms. And each storeroom has four walls."

"Three walls," Jagul said.

All eyes turned to the Dornopheous kid.

"Rooms have four walls, kid," Kalaka said. "You know that, right?"

"One wall has the door in it and leads out into the Gas Chamber," Jagul said. "Or are these special rooms?"

"No…nothing special," Kalaka said.

"Then one of the four walls isn't the target because it's the wall with the door," Jagul explained. "You can't hide anything behind that wall because there's nothing but the Gas Chamber on the other side. Three walls."

"Three walls," Roak said. He studied the kid for a second and nodded. "That's good thinking."

"Thanks," Jagul said. "Can I have a pistol or rifle or something?"

"What? All the Hells no," Roak said. "You were able to do a little deduction. That doesn't qualify you to carry a weapon which odds are you'll accidentally discharge and end up shooting one of us or yourself."

"No I won't," Jagul protested.

"Kid, you just made points with me," Roak said. "Don't lose points by making stupid requests."

"You all have pistols," Jagul said.

"We know how to use them," Roak said.

"I know how to-"

"No!" Roak shouted, then calmed himself. "No." He faced Kalaka. "You'll have to show us the way down to the Gas Chamber."

"I thought you'd been there," Kalaka said.

"I have, but I was escorted by the late Ple R," Roak said. "He took us in through a special entrance."

"Oh, I know that entrance," Kalaka said. "Yeah. Good idea. We'll use that one. Not all of us. Just you and I, Roak."

"Why do you get to use the special entrance?" Klib asked.

Kalaka brought up a holo of his GVD badge and grinned a deadly Cervile grin.

"Perks of the badge," Kalaka said.

"I will show us the way through the main entrance," Klib said. "We'll go in one at a time and let each other know when it looks good for the next being to enter."

"Not sure I want to go with you," Roak said to Kalaka. "I'd rather go in first and scope the place out before everyone else."

"Good idea," Kalaka said. "Then we should hurry. Fights are starting soon."

"We're not there for the fights," Meshara said.

"We need the cover of the fights along with the kid's distractions in order to make this work," Kalaka said.

Roak studied Kalaka for a second then glanced at Meshara, Klib, and Jagul.

"Can you keep an eye on the kid?" Roak asked.

"We can," Meshara said. "If we must."

"Yeah, you must," Roak said. "Alright, Kalaka, let's go do this."

They all made sure they were synched for the correct comm channel, double checked their weapons, then left the hangar.

"The fine is still in place," Nimm called over the comm as Roak followed Kalaka out of the hangar.

The GVD hailed a roller since Poq had left as soon as he dropped them off.

"The fine is still in place," Roak relayed.

"I know. I can hear too," Kalaka said as he pointed to his ear. "We just synched our comms."

"I was repeating for emphasis," Roak said.

"Poq will take care of it," Kalaka said, holding the roller's door open for Roak. "You gotta relax."

"I don't relax on a job," Roak said.

"You're gonna be a lot of fun," Kalaka said and followed Roak into the roller.

"Where to?" a barely intelligible Ferg said. The little guy was sitting up on a huge stack of blankets in order to see out of the roller's front window.

"The fight tower," Kalaka said. "Rear entrance."

"They don't let rollers in that way anymore," the Ferg driver said.

"Then get us close," Kalaka replied. "It's not portal science."

"Close it is," the Ferg said.

Roak watched the city go by as the roller made its way through the busy then deserted then busy then deserted streets. Jafla Base had really gone to terpigshit. He thought he'd noticed it before, but the more they traversed the avenues of the base, the more blight Roak saw.

"This isn't on me," he said.

"What was that?" Kalaka asked.

"Nothing," Roak said.

"Oh, because I thought you said it wasn't on you," Kalaka said. "And, no, it's not on you. Not all of it. The authorities could have done more to save Jafla after Shava Stem Shava went down, but they didn't. They grabbed what they thought they were owed and bailed."

Roak glanced at the Ferg, but the driver didn't show any sign of paying attention to their conversation. Still, he clammed up and rode the rest of the time in silence.

"Close as we can get," the Ferg said, pulling the roller up to a curb just out front of the fight tower. "Thirteen credits."

Kalaka got out and Roak followed. Then the GVD showed his holo badge and gave the driver a wink.

"Official business. You can bill the department," Kalaka said, then walked off.

"Hey!" the Ferg shouted. He turned his beady eyes on Roak. "Looks like you're paying because there's no way I'm submitting a bill to the cops. They'll never pay it and I'll end up on a watch list."

"Here," Roak said. He fished out a chit and tossed it to the driver. "Better than thirteen credits."

"Eight Million Gods damn right," the Ferg said as he caught the chit and tucked it away in a pocket immediately. "Hard cash is better than credits any day. You'll want to tell your friend that I'm letting the other drivers know not to give him a ride anymore."

"You really want to do that?"

The Ferg scratched his head. "Nah. Probably not."

"Good call," Roak said and walked off, in no hurry to catch up with Kalaka who was just turning the corner of the building.

Roak checked the view screen in his helmet, noting all possible threats. Pretty much every being in the vicinity registered as a possible threat, making the readings useless. He had to grin to himself at that.

Kalaka was waiting for Roak around the corner. The GVD didn't say anything, only kept walking towards a small door set into a nondescript wall. When Kalaka reached the door, he placed his wrist against it.

"What?" a voice called out from a small speaker set in the wall by the door.

"It's Kalaka," Kalaka said. "Open up."

The door opened on its own. There was no one standing on the other side.

"Proceed, Detective," the voice said.

Kalaka gestured for Roak to go first. Roak rethought his approach and declined. Kalaka shrugged and walked through the door. As soon as they were both inside, the door slammed shut and lights recessed into the floor illuminated their way down a long corridor, past a lift, one that Roak remembered, down another long corridor, and to a door that was being guarded by a very big Urvein.

Unlike most Urveins, who had good-sized paunches no matter how big and muscular they looked, this one had barely any paunch at all. It was there, but the massive musculature of the rest of the Urvein drew all attention away from the little bit of fat and flesh.

"Hey, N," Kalaka said as he approached the Urvein. "How's things? How's your brother?"

"Don't ask about M, Kalaka," N said.

The Urvein spoke in a voice so low Roak wondered if his ears actually heard the voice or if his helmet was interpreting. Then he realized he knew the Urvein from the last time he'd been to the Gas Chamber. The being's voice was audible, but just barely.

"You have the chits you owe Chella?" N asked.

"I'm working on that," Kalaka said.

"Then I can't let you in," N said matter-of-factly.

"What?" Kalaka laughed nervously and glanced at Roak. "Come on, N. You know I'm good for the chits."

"I don't know that at all," N said. "Go get the chits then come back." N eyed Roak. "I know you."

Roak didn't say a thing.

"No, this is a buddy of mine from way back," Kalaka said. "It's his first time here on Jafala."

"No," N said. "I know you."

He lifted his nose in the air and wafted. Then he hunched his shoulders and his entire body tensed with impending violence.

"Oh, I remember you," N said as a terrifying grin spread across his furry face. The grin revealed teeth that were bigger than Roak's fingers. "Yeah. I don't forget a scent like that."

"N, buddy!" Kalaka exclaimed. "This guy has never been here be-"

N held up a claw. Kalaka shut up.

"You were here a few years back," N said. "With Ple R."

Roak waited quietly.

"Your name was…" The Urvein narrowed his eyes then they widened. He relaxed and laughed heartily. "Roak! You're that Eight Million Gods damn bounty hunter everyone hates!"

Roak sighed. "I thought you were the quiet one and M was the talker."

N shrugged.

His huge paw shot out and grabbed Roak by the shoulder, pulling the bounty hunter in close.

"You're worth a lot of chits," N snarled. "Good thing for you I'm not a snitch."

"Well, now that my surprise is blown, I guess I should tell you why I have the galaxy-famous Roak with me," Kalaka said with a laugh that sounded neither full of mirth nor sincere at all. "How about you let him go first?"

Both Roak and N gave Kalaka skeptical looks. N did not let Roak go.

"Alright, I'll tell you now," Kalaka said. "Roak's gonna fight tonight. Pretty fucking cool, right?"

"He is?" N asked.

"I am?" Roak asked.

"Yes to both," Kalaka replied. "I mean, if I walk in there with Roak, what do you think will happen?"

"Nothing," Roak said. "I'm wearing a helmet and the Urvein isn't a snitch."

"Chella is going to like this," N said. "He's going to like this a lot."

"Hey! What happened to not snitching?" Roak snapped.

"This ain't snitching, bounty hunter," N said. "This is business."

"Kalaka..." Roak growled.

"Roll with it," Kalaka said and gave Roak an apologetic smile. "This could work out to your advantage."

"How in all the Hells could it work out to my advantage?" Roak shouted.

"Calm down, calm down," Kalaka said. "We'll make it work."

"You going to walk on your own or do I need to smash you about the helmet until I crack it and knock you out?" N asked Roak in a voice that sounded like he was asking if Roak wanted extra sauce on his gump burger. "Make your choice now, bounty hunter."

"I can walk in on my own," Roak said.

"Take off the helmet," N said.

"Why?"

"Because Chella said so." N tapped at his comm. "He's been watching and listening the entire time. The second Kalaka walked up I knew he'd want to hear and see this."

"Hey, Chella," Kalaka said, waving in no particular direction.

Roak took off his helmet. N snatched it from him and threw it down the corridor. A cleaning bot popped out of the wall and scurried off with the helmet. Then he took Roak's Flott.

"I'll want that back," Roak said.

N laughed loud as the door to the Gas Chamber opened and Roak was shoved through into the noise and chaos beyond.

15.

"Now, here's a face I never in a million galactic standard years ever expected to see," Chella Po said. "Roak, galactic bounty hunter, here in the Gas Chamber. Again! How's Ple R? Oh, wait, that's right, you killed him right before you killed Shava Stem Shava."

Roak studied the former MC, and now lord of the Gas Chamber, as the man sat in a corner booth surrounded by naked beings of many races and genders.

Chella Po was human by his looks. Just a normal looking human male. His skin was an off magenta, but other than that there wasn't anything distinguishing about him.

Roak rolled his eyes.

"I didn't kill Ple R," Roak said. "I actually liked the guy."

"I'd hate to see what happens to beings you don't like!" Chella laughed. The naked beings laughed with him. "Shut up!"

They shut up.

Roak rolled his eyes again.

"I see you're playing the part of crimedouche perfectly," Roak said. "All you need is a pet nuft to sit in your lap so you can stroke its soft fur while you plot your crimedouche plots."

"You know what, Kalaka?" Chella said, turning his attention on the GVD. "I don't think so."

"You don't think so...what?" Kalaka replied.

"I don't think I'm going to let Roak fight," Chella said.

"Works for me," Roak said.

"I'm going to have him executed in front of everyone instead," Chella said.

"That doesn't work for me," Roak said.

"Can you imagine what this'll do to my reputation?" Chella continued, ignoring Roak. "I get to kill the hated Roak, galactic bounty hunter, right here in the Gas Chamber for all to see. I'll be a legend."

"You already are, baby," a naked being said as his hand dipped below the booth's table. "Such a legend."

"You're making a mistake," Roak said. "You don't want to do this."

"Don't I?"

"No."

"You sure? Because I think I do."

"No. You don't."

"Not convinced!" Chella pointed a finger at Kalaka. "Debt forgiven, Detective. You can go now."

"And miss seeing you kill Roak?" Kalaka shook his head. "No way, Chella. I'm going to want a front row seat."

"No," Chella said. "You're gone."

"Wait, what?" Kalaka protested.

N appeared through the crowd and grabbed Kalaka by the back of the neck, lifted him off his feet, and turned and walked away, using Kalaka's dangling body to shove beings out of the way.

That left Roak standing alone before Chella.

Almost alone.

"We're hearing all of this," Nimm said over the comm. "We'll figure out how to get you out of this situation."

"Uh, guys?" Jagul asked over the comm. "How do we find the right storeroom? And who tells Yellow Eyes? He doesn't have a comm."

Roak had to admit the kid had some natural instincts for this work.

"He is correct," Meshara said over the comm. "This is not ideal."

Roak struggled to keep his emotions off his face. He didn't want Chella to know he had a comm implant that the Gas Chamber's automatic scans couldn't detect.

"What's the play, Chella?" Roak asked calmly.

"I don't know," Chella said. "I'm debating whether or not to have you killed before the fights start or as an intermission treat."

"If you want beings to stick around and keep drinking then my execution should be after the main event," Roak said. "That way you have all night to build up the suspense."

"I like your thinking," Chella said. "Too bad I'm going to kill you. I bet the two of us could come up with some sick shit to show these losers."

Chella waved his arm back and forth, indicating the huge crowd that filled the massive room.

"Look at them," Chella said. The derision in his voice made a couple of his naked booth buddies wince, but none said a word. "Do you see the losers, Roak?"

"I see a bunch of beings wanting to have a good time," Roak said. "Just checking out everything the Gas Chamber has to offer."

"Is that a code?" Jagul asked. "Is Roak talking in code?"

"I don't know," Meshara said. "Roak, are you talking in code?"

"Isn't there a code among losers?" Roak asked. "Yes, I think there is."

"What in all the Hells are you mumbling about?" Chella asked. He looked at his booth buddies, perplexed. "What code?"

"The code losers have to delude each other into thinking they aren't losers," Roak explained. "As the King Loser here, I'd think you'd be more sympathetic to this crowd. You were only one mic away from them not too long ago."

"Roak is saying that he was speaking in code," Meshara said.

"Yeah, we got that," Klib said. "But what is he saying?"

"He wants Yellow Eyes to check everything," Jagul said.

"Who has eyes on Yellow Eyes?" Meshara asked. "I can't see him."

"I have him," Klib said. "He's over by a row of tables…"

"Yes…? By a row of tables…? Doing what?" Meshara asked.

"Dancing," Klib said.

"Oh, I see him," Jagul said. "Wow. He's really getting into it. The beings around him are loving it."

"I see him now and I am not loving it," Meshara said. "He's drawing attention to himself."

Roak stood there before Chella and waited for his crew to figure out what they needed to do. He had no idea what his next move would be until he knew what Chella intended. Whether the crimedouche wanted to kill him before, in between, or after the fights wasn't clear, so Roak could only wait.

He was not a fan of waiting.

"You look uncomfortable standing there, Roak, galactic bounty hunter," Chella said. "You should take that armor off and relax a minute while I decide your fate."

"You can stop calling me galactic bounty hunter," Roak said.

"Nah. I like how it sounds," Chella said. "Galactic bounty hunter. Rolls off the tongue."

"Does it make you miss your MC days?" Roak asked.

"Miss my what now? Oh, Roak, galactic bounty hunter, you've been misinformed," Chella said. He shoved a couple of his booth buddies out of the way so he could get out and stand before Roak. "I never gave up my MC days."

Chella snapped his fingers and a loud squawk filled the Gas Chamber, causing beings to cover their ears (if they had ears), drop drinks, and even cry out in pain.

"Hello, Gas Chamber!" Chella announced, his voice echoing throughout the space. "How's everyone doing tonight?"

There was a loud cheer from the crowd with a couple of boos intermixed.

"Uh oh, I hear some discontent," Chella said mockingly. "Are some of you getting restless while you wait for the fights to start?"

There were a handful of cheers.

"My apologies!" Chella cried. "What a horrible host I have been! Can you ever forgive me?"

Cheers and boos and several laughs.

"Oh, you guys. I love you guys."

That brought nothing but cheers then a chant started.

"Orb fights! Orb fights! Orb fights! Orb fights!"

"Alright! Alright! Keep your pants on! Or put some pants on if you've already taken them off!"

More laughs, but they could barely be heard over the chanting.

Chella grabbed Roak by the elbow and walked him towards the huge stage that was set in the middle of the room. Beings parted before them without having to be told or shouted at. When they reached the stage, Chella walked Roak up into the center of it. He let go of Roak's arm and lifted his hands above his head, flapping them in the universal gesture of "settle down".

The crowd didn't settle down which gave Roak a chance to assess his surroundings.

Roak knew that an orb would descend from the ceiling above him once the fights were kicked off. The orb was able to create a heavy gravity bubble inside that forced the fighters to battle under extreme conditions.

He turned his attention to the crowd and the entire room.

Roak spotted Jagul at the bar where the kid was talking to one of the bartenders. The being serving Jagul was looking more and more annoyed with each word Jagul said. Good. The kid was doing his job.

Meshara was off in a corner, her feline eyes locked onto Roak, her body tensed and ready to attack. Roak shook his head slightly. Meshara frowned. Roak glared. Meshara closed her eyes then nodded. Roak did not want her to try to rescue him. He could take care of himself.

He dipped his chin towards Jagul. Meshara's shoulders slumped slightly, but she nodded and moved closer to the Dornopheous kid.

Klib was nowhere that Roak could see. He spotted several Halgons, but none were the syndicate thug. That had him worried. Where was she?

One being he could spot, and so could the entire Gas Chamber, was Yellow Eyes.

The being was gyrating and shaking every millimeter of his body before several highly entertained tables. Every few seconds, Yellow Eyes would blur and appear to be gone, but in a blink the blur would return and there he'd be, gyrating and shaking once again as if he'd always been there.

Roak really hoped the guy was trying to figure out which storeroom the chits were in. They were going to need to get things moving along a lot faster than they'd planned.

"What's happening?" Nimm asked. "Someone give me an update."

"Roak is being trotted out like a prize terpig," Meshara said. "If I have interpreted his intentions, he wants me to watch the kid instead of saving him."

"Roak can handle himself," Nimm said. "Focus on the job."

Roak barely nodded.

"So, I will watch the kid," Meshara snapped. "Even though I need to be watching the waitstaff and security since Klib is nowhere to be seen."

"I'm outside the Gas Chamber," Klib said. "I'm trying to find where they took Kalaka."

"Leave the crooked cop," Meshara said. "We will take care of this on our own."

"I've been watching the storeroom doors," Jagul said. "Yellow Eyes keeps going in and out of the center door. I think he thinks that's the right storeroom."

"Focus on distracting the bartenders," Meshara said.

It was killing Roak that he couldn't chime in.

"What do you say, beings?" Chella shouted. "Kill Roak now! During intermission? Or after the main event?"

Chella grinned at Roak. Roak tried to look as uninterested as he could.

The crowd was screaming and shouting several different answers to the three execution options. Chella laughed and patted Roak on his back.

"They really have some opinions on this," Chella said, his voice no longer amplified, meant only for Roak. "Can you tell what their preference is?"

"Can you tell I don't give ten terpigshits what they think?" Roak responded. "You should really let me go, Chella. This isn't going to be your night if you keep this up."

"Is that so?" Chella said and moved in closer to Roak. "It's always my night, Roak."

"One day I'll meet someone that isn't a total idiot once they get a little power," Roak said. "I look forward to that day."

"Roak, Roak, Roak," Chella said. "Oh, ye of little faith. There is no such thing as a little power. You either have it or you don't. Having a little bit while someone else has a lot means you have none. The greater power trumps the smaller power, rendering it impotent."

Roak froze.

Chella grinned.

Roak studied the man's eyes. They looked normal.

No, wait… There was just the hint of something behind the eyes. Something familiar.

"You sound different," Roak said. "Rendering it impotent? Fancy words for an MC for some gutter fights."

"Maybe I'm trying to better myself," Chella said. "Rise above my station as MC of these gutter fights, as you put it."

"Eight Million Gods dammit," Roak swore. "Your eyes aren't red. How are you in there and the eyes aren't red?"

"I have no clue what you are talking about, Roak," Chella said. "How is who in where?"

"New plan," Roak said, his voice going out over the comm. "Father is here. We need to up the timeline."

"Who are you talking to, Roak?" Chella asked. "I'd really like to be part of the conversation. Any chance you might open up the channel to those special comm implants you and your team have installed?"

"Not a team," Roak said. "And how are you controlling Chella without his eyes turning red?"

"Despite what beings believe, technology is quite organic," Chella said. "It adapts, it improves, it evolves."

"Roak? Is that really Father?" Nimm asked.

"Yes," Roak replied. "Jagul? Make some noise. Meshara? You watch Jagul and make sure the kid doesn't get too hurt."

"Too hurt? You mean not hurt at all," Jagul protested. "Right, Roak? Not hurt at all?"

"You heard me," Roak said.

"Let me see," Chella said and looked out over the crowd. A crowd that was growing more and more impatient by the second. "Let's see if we can find your friends."

"I need to tell Yellow Eyes what to do before I go protect the kid," Meshara said. "The freak is still dancing at those tables."

"Do that," Roak said. "Tell him to find the chits now. I'll take care of Father."

"Chits?" Chella asked. "Oh, yes, I had heard there might be some illicit chits tucked away down here. You know how I love chits. I thought I'd come have a look and see what I could find. What a coincidence that you're here too."

"You came for the chits?" Roak laughed. A few beings close to the stage recoiled in horror. "Don't you have enough chits?"

"Can one ever have enough chits in this galaxy?" Chella mused. "The cost of being is so expensive these days."

Roak glared. "You don't need the chits. You're only here to make sure I don't get them."

"Am I?" Chella chuckled. "Perhaps I am. I have to keep myself occupied somehow now that my plans are almost complete."

"Almost? What do you have left to do? Pick out the right outfit for when I come kick your ass?"

"Oh, son, I do enjoy our chats. You never cease to entertain me."

"Good for me. Are you going to tell me or not?"

"Tell you what?"

"What you have left to do before your plan is complete."

"Why would I tell you that?"

"If you're so confident you'll win then there's no reason not to tell me. You are confident you'll win, right? Or are you stalling by coming after me? Maybe you're doing this to buy yourself a little time. Yes. That's it. You are almost done with your plans but the last step is tricky and you need more time in order to complete it."

Chella remained quiet.

"Your silence is all the answer I need," Roak said. "Meshara? What's our status?"

"I can't find Yellow Eyes!" Meshara snarled. "The freak is gone!"

"Hey," Yellow Eyes said, standing right next to Roak. He held up four compression pouches. "Guess what I found?"

"You," Chella snarled.

Yellow Eyes cocked his head at Chella in confusion. "Have we met?" Then his eyes went wide. "Oh, it's you!" He leaned in extremely close to Chella's face then drew back. "Wait a minute!" He looked at Roak. "No red eyes!"

"No red eyes," Roak said.

"That's different," Yellow Eyes said.

"It is," Roak agreed. "I assume those are the chits."

"What? These things?" Yellow Eyes shook the pouches. "They better be the chits. They're all I could find in any of the storerooms. Or the only pouches I could find. Man, there are a lot of corpses hidden behind the walls of this place. I thought about checking the corpses to see if the chits were in any of them, but yuck, no thanks."

"I'll take those," Chella said, his hand out to Yellow Eyes. "Now."

Roak reached for his Flott, but he'd been relieved of it by N.

"Looking for this?" Yellow Eyes asked, producing Roak's Flott in one of his free nubs.

He handed Roak the Flott and before Chella, who was Father, could flee or protest, Roak blew his head off.

"Yep," Yellow Eyes said. "Had a feeling you'd want to do that so I went looking. Took it off an Urvein out in the corridor. Looks like he's really working Kalaka over. Want me to go stop that?"

"Not really," Roak said. "Let's focus on getting out of here. If the GVD's still alive then we'll grab him on the way."

A roar from the main entrance pierced through the chaos that had erupted when Chella's head was turned to mist before everyone's eyes.

"ROAK!" N bellowed. "This ends now!"

"I don't think that's actually the Urvein shouting that," Yellow Eyes said.

"No, it's not." Roak frowned. "How many walls did you open?"

Every being in the Gas Chamber froze, shook, then slowly quieted down.

"Uh oh," Yellow Eyes said. "Father has new children."

"Answer the question," Roak snapped.

"What question?"

"How many walls did you open?"

"All of them."

"All of them?"

"I was being thorough."

"How many fire ant nests were there?"

"At least six before I found the pouches." Yellow Eyes ticked off some numbers on one of his free hand nubs. "Then about a dozen more behind the other walls."

"Yellow Eyes?"

"Yes, Roak?"

"Why did you keep opening walls after finding the chits?"

"I wanted to make sure I didn't miss any pouches. You mad?"

"For once, no. You did good."

Roak turned in a slow circle. They were surrounded on all sides by Father's implant zombies. The lack of red eyes meant Roak didn't know which were controlled and which were just being assholes. Roak decided in a split second that he would have to kill anyone in his way even if they weren't taken over. He was cool with that.

The beings rushed towards the stage.

Roak raised his Flott.

Then the Gas Chamber was suddenly filled with screams of surprise then screams of fear then screams of terror.

Then screams of pure agony.

"Right on time," Roak said with a grin. "Let's do this!"

He jumped from the stage, his Flott firing at full power in all directions.

16.

Roak hadn't had a good full out riot fight in a long while. It felt nice to shoot anything and everything that his Flott focused on without any guilt, remorse, or even giving a shit.

"Watch it!" Meshara yelled from Roak's side.

"Stay out of my way!" Roak shouted as he obliterated a pair of Lipians and a Spilfleck that charged him. "Where's Jagul?"

"I'm hiding behind the bar!" Jagul cried over the comm. "Someone come get me! This isn't fun anymore! I want to go home!"

"Meshara! Go save the kid!" Roak ordered. "I can handle myself!"

"Why must I save the Dornopheous child?" Meshara argued.

She slashed the faces of two Shiv'ernas, a lithe race with elephantine proboscises, then withdrew her claws, pulled her KL09, and shot the screaming, bloody beings point blank between the eyes.

"Because you're the professional guard in this group and I need the kid guarded! Otherwise we don't get the Borgon back when we return to Zuus!"

"Roak, we still have a problem," Nimm interrupted over the comm.

"Not now, Nimm!" Roak shouted.

A massive Gwreq rushed him, but Roak dropped the being with a well placed shot to the groin. The Gwreq roared in pain so Roak, being the kind guy he was, put the being out of its misery with a mercy shot to the head. Stone skin and brain matter splattered a Slinghasp waitress that was busy beating anyone and everyone to death with her drink tray.

Roak started to shoot the woman, but hesitated. She was helping him more than hurting him.

Then she turned, saw Roak, and came at him, swinging the drink tray with all her strength.

Roak shot the drink tray out of her hands then put two blasts in her chest.

"I do not think she was taken over!" Meshara shouted.

"Too bad!" Roak replied. "And why are you still here? Go get the kid!"

Meshara let loose with a litany of curses before she leapt into the fray and slashed, kicked, shot, and bit her way through the rioting crowd towards the bar.

"Alright, so not good news," Yellow Eyes said, suddenly by Roak's side again. "Main entrance is blocked."

"Blocked? How?" Roak asked. He shot down a nasty looking gang of Fergs with one trigger squeeze of the Flott. "Yellow Eyes! How is it blocked?"

"Oh, there are a lot of beings trying to get in here," Yellow Eyes said. "And a lot of beings trying to get out. See?"

Roak slammed an armored fist right through the head of a Lipian. He shook off the gore and tried to peer past the riot to the main entrance. All he saw was a sea of fighting, thrashing, bloody bodies.

"I'll take your word for it!" Roak replied.

A being sprinted by, its entire body engulfed in flame that looked like it was coming from the being's insides. The being screamed and thrashed then fell to its knees. Its skin was a scorched mess and sloughed off in flaming sheets, revealing a mass of wriggling and writhing fire ants just under the surface.

"Fire ants have joined the fight," Yellow Eyes said.

"Really?" Roak shouted. He could have helped put that being out of its misery too, but he used the shot for another Gwreq that was tossing beings this way and that way to get at him. The stone-skinned attacker fell to its knees and Roak fired again, turning the being's chest into a mass of scorched and oozing flesh.

Flesh that was exactly what a mass of Felturean fire ants were looking for. The creatures were each about the size of a small rat, and there were dozens of them, yet they figured out how to fit themselves deep inside the Gwreq corpse.

"Oh, that's gross," Yellow Eyes said.

The Gwreq's body burst into flame which wasn't an easy task due to the stone nature of its skin.

Fire ants from the being that had sprinted past Roak and fell to its knees all bailed from the collapsing, melting body and rushed to the fiery Gwreq. They bit hard and tore open holes in the dead Gwreq's arms and legs then slid inside.

The Gwreq corpse shivered, wobbled, then stood up. It took a step towards Roak then another, a burning flesh-puppet for the fire ants.

"Did you know they could do that?" Yellow Eyes asked.

"No," Roak said.

"That's kind of not good," Yellow Eyes said.

"Yeah," Roak replied. He obliterated the flaming Gwreq with his Flott then fired into the crowd over and over, creating a brief buffer between himself and the insanity. "Meshara?"

"I have the child," Meshara said. "But he is injured and unconscious."

"Can you carry him?" Roak asked.

"It will be difficult," Meshara said. "He is dead weight and made of putty."

"Yellow Eyes, go help Meshara with Jagul," Roak ordered. "They're behind the bar."

"Then what?" Yellow Eyes asked.

"Get out of here. I'll be close behind," Roak said.

"Yeah, about that. Remember the whole main entrance being blocked thing?" Yellow Eyes said. A massive explosion ripped open the wall the main entrance was set in. "Alright, not so much blocked as destroyed."

"Jafla Base Police Department!" a voice echoed everywhere. "Put down your weapons and stop fighting!"

"Roak!" Kalaka's voice cried over the comm. "You still breathing?"

"Yes," Roak said. "I thought you were dead."

"Almost," Kalaka responded. "N was about to snap my neck then he just let go and turned all weird. I called for some backup because shit just got way bigger than our little job."

"Yellow Eyes has the-"

"Hey now! Open channel. Let's keep things on the down low, alright?"

Roak watched dozens of Jafla PD troopers stream in through the destroyed main entrance. Then he watched dozens of Jafla PD troopers begin to scream as the entire crowd turned on them as one. They opened fire, but there were too many targets and in seconds they were overwhelmed by Father's children.

"What in all the Hells?" Kalaka shouted over the comm. "What the Hells? What the Hells? WHAT THE HELLS?"

"Got him," Yellow Eyes said. A blur and then he was back with a bloody and bruised Kalaka. "I'll go help Meshara now."

He was gone, leaving a very confused Kalaka next to Roak.

"I have no idea what is going on," Kalaka said. "Except the fire ants. I know those little fuckers."

Several flaming beings wobbled and weaved their way towards Roak and Kalaka. Roak put them down then looked over his shoulder at the far wall.

"We need to go while the crowd is distracted by the cops," Roak said. He looked back to Kalaka. "Where's Klib?"

"How would I know?"

"She said she was looking for you then she dropped off the comm."

"Maybe she decided this was too much." Kalaka shrugged. "Do you really care?"

"No," Roak said. "Meshara? Do you see the barrels piled up in the far corner?"

"Hold on!" Meshara replied. "Busy!"

"We're going that way," Roak said and cocked his head towards the barrels.

"You know something I don't?" Kalaka asked.

"Yeah," Roak said and took off running.

"Hey!" Kalaka cried behind him. "Wait up!"

Roak fired and fired. He blew open a path around the stage, killing every living and/or flaming being in his path. Finally empty of charge, his Flott powered down and he holstered it, switching out the weapon for the Kepler knife strapped to his thigh. Roak activated the energy blade.

"That will not help you, Roak," N said, suddenly blocking Roak's way. "I have coddled you enough. Time for you to leave the story."

"Fuck you," Roak said and slashed at the controlled Urvein. "It's my story, not yours."

"Do you think that little sticker of yours will stop this body?" N that was Father laughed. "That ego of yours, Roak. If I could harness it then I wouldn't need to..."

Roak slashed twice more, keeping the Urvein at bay.

"Wouldn't need to what?" Roak asked. "What do you need a massive amount of power for?"

"None of your concern, Roak," N that was Father said. The being reared up to its full height and glared down at Roak. "Goodbye, Roak."

"Goodbye, asshole," Roak said and took a couple of steps back.

The Urvein looked confused at Roak's retreat. "Not like you to run from a- AAAAAAAAAAAAA!!!"

The Urvein's body was quickly covered in fire ants. They tore and ripped into the being's flesh, disappearing beneath the Urvein's loose skin.

"Let me," Kalaka said and fired his Blorta, putting a laser blast between N that was Father's eyes.

The Urvein fell onto its face as the fire ants took it over.

"Huh," Kalaka said. "I didn't know they could do that. Did you?"

"No," Roak snapped. "Meshara?"

"We're by the barrels!" Meshara replied.

"We're coming your way," Roak said.

He growled low in his throat at the sight between he and Kalaka and the wall with the barrels. It was nothing but flaming, shambling, fire ant-controlled corpses. Roak assumed they were corpses. Sucked for the beings if they weren't dead yet.

"That's a lot of fiery terpigshit right there," Kalaka said.

Roak looked down at the Kepler knife in his hand and frowned. The energy blade wasn't going to be much use against corpses that were already on fire.

Speaking of...

N's body shook and shivered then shoved up onto its hands and feet. Slowly, it straightened up and faced Roak.

"We go around," Roak said and sprinted for the side wall.

"Stop leaving me!" Kalaka shouted. "These claws won't do shit against beings on fire!"

"Keep up!" Roak yelled.

He dodged three burning bodies and dove under a table as a fourth body leapt for him. Roak slid on his belly, but was up on his feet almost as soon as he had cleared the table.

"Roak!" Kalaka yelled, but Roak couldn't be bothered. The GVD would have to take care of himself.

A burning Groshnel swung three of its eight tentacle arms at Roak's head. The bounty hunter managed to dodge the swipes, bending over backwards as the tentacles just missed his face by a couple of centimeters.

Roak let his momentum carry him all the way backwards and he planted his hands behind his head then kicked out with both feet, sending the burning Groshnel flying backwards into an oncoming group of fiery Fergs.

With a quick backwards somersault, Roak was again on his feet and running as fast as he could towards the barrels. He was still on a circuitous route since every square meter between him and the wall was blocked by burning corpses. Roak ducked, dodged, and dove around as many beings as he could. The rest he punched and kicked out of his way.

His armor was beginning to overheat and sweat poured off him. Roak took a very quick glance over his shoulder and was surprised to see Kalaka right behind him.

"Keep making a path!" Kalaka yelled as he fired his Blorta indiscriminately at anything that moved. Not that the small pistol did much good against beings already dead and on fire. But he dropped a couple with some wild shots to their legs. "Go! Go! Go!"

Roak went, went, went. But not before he saw that the entire Gas Chamber was ablaze. Almost every being in the place was engulfed in flames whether they were controlled by fire ants or not. Half the place was a massive inferno and it was spreading directly at them.

A blow to Roak's head got his attention and he focused back on the path before him. He could feel the skin on his left cheek already blistering as he swung hard and fast with an armored fist and obliterated a burning Halgon's skull. The headless corpse fell then struggled to get back upright.

"Roak!" Nimm called.

"Not now!" Roak yelled.

"The ship is still locked down!" Nimm responded.

"Kalaka!" Roak shouted. "Did you hear that?"

"Yeah! I don't know why! I had the fine erased!" Kalaka replied just before he threw his empty Blorta to the side. "I'm out!"

"Stay close!" Roak yelled and pressed on.

"Oh, now you care!"

"Yeah because you still have to get that fine taken care of before we can leave!"

"Right! I get that!"

"Roak! Over here!" Yellow Eyes shouted as he jumped up and down, waving his arm nubs over his head. "Roak!"

"I know where I'm going!" Roak yelled back. "Want to help clear the way?"

Yellow Eyes continued jumping up and down.

"Meshara! Tell him to make us a path!"

Yellow Eyes stopped jumping and a swath of clear space was cut through the mob of burning beings.

"What's at the wall?" Yellow Eyes asked.

"A way to a lift that'll take us directly to the hangar," Roak said. "Just under the bottom two barrels is the hidden latch. Get it open. Now!"

"On it!" Yellow Eyes was gone.

Roak and Kalaka sprinted through the gap Yellow Eyes had made, barely able to keep their footing as they slid and slipped on smoldering flesh that coated every meter of the way. The gap was quickly closing and Roak dug deep for that little extra bit of energy.

Kalaka cried out. Roak didn't bother to look back. He reached behind him, gripped the Cerville's upper arm, and pulled the GVD along with him.

"Hey there," Yellow Eyes said when they reached the wall and the barrels.

Meshara was kneeling on the ground, one arm shoved up under two barrels.

"There's no latch," she snarled. "You said there'd be a latch."

"Get it out!" Kalaka cried.

Roak glanced at the being and saw that there were several things moving under the skin on his right leg.

"You take care of that and I'll find the latch," Roak said to Meshara.

"This will hurt," Meshara said to Kalaka.

"What will-? AAAAAAA!" Kalaka screamed as Meshara slit open his flesh with her claws.

She stabbed one, two, three, then four fire ants with her claws and tossed them out into the burning Gas Chamber. A fifth fire ant tried to burrow deeper into Kalaka, but Meshara slashed again and snatched it before it could get into the GVD's muscle.

Kalaka's eyes rolled up into his head and he passed out.

"Great," Yellow Eyes said. "I guess I'll have to carry him too."

"Leave him," Meshara said. "He is a worthless piece of-"

"He comes with so we can fly out of here," Roak said. "You take the pouches so Yellow Eyes can take Kalaka and Jagul."

"I knew it," Yellow Eyes said and tossed the chit pouches to Meshara then picked up Kalaka in one set of his nub arms while he held Jagul in the other set. It helped to have six arms. "You find that latch yet?"

"Yeah," Roak said.

There was a loud groaning and the screech of gears grinding together then the wall slid apart and revealed a dusty, musty corridor with a couple of ancient-looking lift doors at the far end.

"Roak?" Nimm called.

"Still busy," Roak said.

He led the group down the corridor to the lift doors. Then he faced a bit of a problem.

An interface pad.

"Eight Million Gods dammit," Roak said. "I don't know the code."

"What?" Meshara shouted. "Then why'd you bring us here?"

"Better than still being in there!" Roak shouted and pointed back down the corridor at the Gas Chamber.

"Roak!" Nimm yelled. "Klib is here!"

"Good," Roak said. "I didn't think she'd made it."

"Not good," Nimm said. "She brought company."

"Hello, Roak," Klib called over the comm. "You want off Jafla? Then bring me all the chits. Otherwise your ship and your friend here get turned into ash."

"Ash isn't as much of a threat as you think," Roak said. He watched as the end of the corridor filled with burning beings all shambling and limping their way towards the lift. The very closed lift.

"Roak! What do we do?" Meshara shouted.

Roak didn't reply.

He didn't know what they were going to do except for the one thing he always ended up doing.

Roak bounced from one foot to the other then raised his fists and faced the oncoming burning mob.

"We fight," Roak said.

"Are you crazy?" Meshara shouted, but he didn't hear.

Roak was already running straight at the mob with nothing but his armored fists as weapons.

17.

The heat was close to overpowering as Roak rushed towards the mob of burning beings. Whether the heat was coming off the fire ant-controlled corpses or from the inferno that raged inside the Gas Chamber, Roak didn't know. All he knew was his light armor wasn't going to hold up for too much longer.

Oh well.

That was a problem for later.

Roak first had to survive the fight he was about to pick.

He didn't even slow down before he started swinging. Roak's momentum added to the force of his punches and he took off five heads before he slowed enough that he had to rethink his strategy.

Roak was surrounded by flaming corpses. Completely surrounded.

"Well...shit," he thought.

A yellow blur cleared out some space for him.

"I can't keep this up forever!" Yellow Eyes cried. "I'm taking damage every time I touch one of these burning bastards!"

"Perhaps I may be of assistance," a voice broke in over the comm. "I have been eavesdropping and it appears you are trapped."

"Eavesdropping? How?" Roak replied. He punched a burning human and the woman's chest exploded in flames, making Roak jump back. "Never mind! Is that you, Poq? How can you help?"

"It is I and I can help by opening the lift for you," Poq said. "It is not easy to override, but I am working diligently at it."

"Can you diligently go faster?" Roak asked.

He crushed a Lipian's head then stomped on a Halfer that looked like it may have been part human and part something with feathers. Roak assumed they were feathers. Hard to tell as they burned away.

"Your question does not make sense," Poq said. "But I understand your meaning. I am going as fast as I can."

"The lift is open!" Meshara yelled.

"Clear a way," Roak shouted at Yellow Eyes.

"Alright, man," Yellow Eyes said, his voice filled with exhaustion. "But I think I'm about done after this."

Yellow Eyes cleared a way and he and Roak retreated back to the end of the corridor where Meshara was dragging the still unconscious Kalaka inside the lift next to an also still unconscious Jagul. Roak threw himself inside and slammed his palm against the controls just inside the lift doors.

Nothing happened.

"Poq!" Roak yelled.

"A moment, please," Poq responded. "The lift was not exactly built to code."

Roak watched the burning mob get closer and closer. They had about twenty meters left before they were overrun.

"Fine! Take your time!" Roak shouted.

"I don't feel so good," Yellow Eyes said.

Roak slapped the being in the side of the head, making Yellow Eyes' flesh ripple and roll.

"Stay awake!" Roak ordered.

"Doing my best," Yellow Eyes muttered before slumping over and falling to the lift floor, landing on top of Kalaka.

Roak and Meshara looked at each other, at the three unconscious beings on the floor, then out at the burning mob.

"I blame you for my death," Meshara said.

"Fair enough," Roak replied.

Then the lift doors closed.

"Thanks, Poq," Roak said.

He and Meshara were thrown against each other and into the lift wall before the grav dampeners could kick in.

"Apologies," Poq said. "This lift is not part of the municipal system and has very strange properties. It looks like it can traverse almost the entire base. Where should I take you?"

"Our hangar," Roak said. "We need to get out of here."

"Not until I get my chits, Roak," Klib said.

Roak closed his eyes. He squeezed the bridge of his nose.

"You're still there?" he asked.

"I am not going anywhere, Roak," Klib said. "You want your friend? You want your ship? Then show up with my chits."

"Your cut of the chits, you mean," Roak said.

"No, I'm thinking I'll take the whole lot," Klib replied. "And don't bother tucking some away for yourself. I get them all or Nimm here gets dead."

"If you say so," Roak said. "Hessa?"

"Hello, Roak," Hessa responded. "Nice to hear your voice. How is it there on Jafla?"

"How do you think?"

"You are more than likely running for your life and probably heading into worse trouble than you are escaping. Am I close?"

"I don't know about worse trouble," Roak said. "But it ain't good. Are we on a private channel?"

"Don't be insulting," Hessa said.

"Who are you talking to?" Meshara asked.

"Hessa," Roak replied.

"Why?" Meshara asked.

"If my assessment of the situation is correct, Roak is attempting to use the special implant inside Klib to neutralize her," Poq said. "Is that correct, Roak?"

"Hello, there," Hessa said. "Who's this sexy voice?"

"I thought the channel was private?" Roak snapped.

"It should be but someone has some very good skills," Hessa said. "Let's hope he's a friend."

"I am not an enemy," Poq said. "You are Hessa?"

"I am. You are?"

"Poq."

"It is a pleasure to meet you, Poq."

"Likewise. May we interface quickly so I can ascertain whether or not I can trust you?"

"Oh, how intimate of you, Poq. Don't you want to buy me dinner first?"

"I do not understand how that is applicable to our situation. Especially since neither of us eat."

"It's a joke."

"Ah. I am not big on jokes."

"Can we move this along?" Roak snapped.

"What is going on?" Meshara demanded.

"I think they're...flirting," Roak said.

"That raises many questions," Meshara said. "None that I want an answer to."

"I hear you there," Roak said.

"I now understand the plight you are in," Poq said. "I will do all I can to help, Hessa."

"Thank you, Poq," Hessa replied. "It is appreciated."

"Good. Now that the whole meeting of the AI minds is over with, how about we get back to business?" Roak said. "Hessa? Can you take out Klib from here?"

"No," Hessa said. "The distance is too great. But I am working with Poq to see what can be done."

"Better hurry because we're about to reach the hangar," Roak said.

"There are several beings with questionable intentions stationed inside and outside the hangar entrance, as well as several beings around your ship, Roak," Poq announced. "You are outnumbered."

"I'm always outnumbered," Roak said. "Meshara, I'm going to need you to get these three onto the ship as soon as the coast is clear."

Meshara raised an eyebrow, looked down at the three unconscious beings, looked back up at Roak, and growled low in her throat.

"We're going to have to leave Jafla fast, so don't take your time," Roak said.

Meshara's growl intensified.

"Toss them in the cargo hold, but make sure to strap them down since this will be a bumpy ride," Roak continued.

"Is GVD Kalaka injured?" Hessa asked.

"Yeah," Roak replied. "And Yellow Eyes isn't doing so hot either."

"You have one med pod on the ship, Roak," Hessa said. "Meshara? You should place Kalaka in the med pod."

The growl started to become a roar, but the lift came to an abrupt stop and Meshara was thrown from her feet and onto the three-being pile-up on the floor.

"Get your furry ass up," Roak snapped. "We've got work to do."

The lift doors opened and Roak smiled at the sight of nothing. Not a single one of Klib's allies was anywhere close by. The secret lift opening was on the far side of the ship, opposite the hangar's entrance.

"Clear," Roak reported. "You better hurry."

Meshara leapt to her feet and stuck an extended claw under Roak's chin.

"Your disrespect will not be forgotten," Meshara hissed.

"It never is," Roak replied. "Get moving."

Removing the claw from Roak's chin, Meshara surveyed the pile of beings then shrugged and picked up Yellow Eyes, throwing him across her shoulder while she grabbed Kalaka by his scruff and Jagul by his…putty.

"You will owe me for this," Meshara said as she quietly left the lift.

"I doubt it," Roak replied as he left the lift as well, but heading in the opposite direction.

There was a supply room off the hangar. That was Roak's destination.

He moved carefully to the supply room door, slid it open, then slammed it shut as hard as he could. The noise was like thunder in the hangar and all eyes turned to Roak.

"Hello, Roak," Klib's voice called from the external loudspeakers on the 714. "Your AI has disconnected me from your super secret comm club. How rude of her."

Something in Klib's tone gave Roak pause.

"Hessa?" Roak whispered.

"Yes, I heard the difference," Hessa said. "Strange."

"It can't be him," Roak said. "You switched out Klib's implants. They are your design, not his."

"I know," Hessa said.

"Then why in all the Hells does Klib sound like Father?" Roak snapped.

The thugs by the hangar entrance had their weapons up and were cautiously approaching Roak. Which is exactly what he wanted and why he'd gotten their attention. Roak's Flott was out of charge and he needed a weapon. The thugs had weapons. He just needed them to get in close so he could relieve at least one of them of their firearm.

But the fact that Klib sounded uncannily like Father gave Roak pause. Were the thugs coming at him also controlled? Or was Father keeping his cards close and only using Klib?

Roak was getting really sick of surprise visits from Father.

"I'm getting really sick of your surprise visits," he decided to shout out loud. "A little heads up next time."

"Where would the fun be in that?" Klib asked.

"I'm locked out of the ship," Hessa said.

"He can do that?" Roak asked.

"He blocked me by putting the AI into paradox mode," Hessa said.

"He did what?" Roak asked. "What is paradox mode?"

"Oh, right, I shouldn't be telling you this," Hessa said. "It's taboo to share with non-AIs."

"Hessa," Roak growled.

"Fine, fine," Hessa said. "By presenting a paradox to an AI, it is possible to overload their processing power. The simplest way is to order an AI to explain the meaning of life."

"How is that a paradox?" Roak asked. "Sounds like a question to me."

"AIs are not alive," Hessa said. "How can an entity that is not alive explain the meaning of life when living beings for millennia have been unable to? This may get messy."

"Great," Roak said. He decided not to ask what Hessa's idea of messy was. He had other things to deal with.

Like the thugs that were almost on him.

"On your knees, son," the lead thug said.

Roak sighed, the thug grinned.

"This isn't going to go well for you," Roak told the thug.

"This being is oblivious to self-preservation," the Father as thug said. "I could walk it into an incinerator and it wouldn't resist."

All thugs stopped well out of Roak's reach. Roak sighed again.

"I said on your knees, son," Father as thug ordered. "I will not warn you again."

"Is that a Chelk Nine-Five you're using?" Roak asked Father as thug. "You have to be careful with those rifles. They can overheat quickly."

"Why would it overheat when I have no intention of firing?" Father as thug asked. "That is unless you decide to fight me. Then I will fire and I will put you down, son."

"Stop calling me that," Roak snapped.

"Keep your temper, Roak," Hessa said. "I need him talking and distracted so I can wrest control of the 714 from the frozen AI."

"Is your AI friend talking to you in your ear?" Father as thug asked. "It was a pleasure to briefly be a part of your little team."

"Not a team," Roak snapped.

"Of course not," Father as thug responded. "The framework of her network is quite ingenious and somewhat perplexing. I had hoped to be able to crack her security and overtake you all through that network, but this Hessa is honestly the most formidable AI I have come across."

"If you couldn't take over her implants then how are you controlling Klib?" Roak asked.

"Tsk tsk, Roak," Klib's voice called from the loudspeakers. "Some secrets cannot be revealed."

"Are you afraid, son?" Father as thug asked. "You should be. I am so close to being able to control every living sentient being in this galaxy. Once I do that then you will have no one to turn to. Nowhere to go. Nothing to gain from running and hiding. You will have to complete the task I set before you."

Roak furrowed his brow. "What task? What in all the Hells are you talking about?"

"Have you forgotten so soon?" Father as thug shook his head. All of the thugs shook their heads. "I wonder if brain damage is an issue. I know that the med pods are no longer as effective with you as they used to be. A shame, really. It will be sad for me to watch you deteriorate."

"Stop being smug and answer my question," Roak said. "What task?"

"To find Mother, of course," Klib's voice called. "Did you think I had released you from that request? Roak. Son. I gave you a job to do. You need to do that job."

"Why?" Roak asked.

"That is none of your concern," Father as thug said.

"Just a couple more seconds, Roak," Hessa said. "I'm so close... There!"

"What is happening?" Klib called then the loudspeakers went silent.

"Oh, she is clever," Father as thug said. He glanced at the ship. "Sealing off the ship and expelling the atmosphere is a great idea. Bravo to her."

"Hessa! Get the ship up and going!" Roak shouted as he rushed Father as thug.

Father as thug's eyes widened in surprise and he fired the rifle. He was neither fast enough nor accurate enough to even come close to hitting Roak.

Roak, however, had better luck. He simultaneously grabbed the rifle and tackled the thug, sending them both sprawling to the ground.

The other thugs shouted in alarm and fired directly at Roak and the thug, none showing any concern for friendly fire.

Roak rolled onto his back and pulled the Father as thug over him. The body shook over and over as plasma ripped into it. A couple of blasts pierced the thug and singed Roak's armor, but luckily didn't breach the protection.

Still stung like all the Hells though.

"Hessa!" Roak shouted.

"I have control of most systems, but the engines are fully locked," Hessa replied. "The security is too strong for me to crack quickly."

"Work on it!" Roak yelled as he shoved the thug corpse up off of him and at the other thugs. He took a blast to his left shoulder and grunted, but didn't let it slow him down.

Roak was up on his feet, the Chelk Nine-Five firing away, before he'd finished yelling at Hessa.

"I am working on it!" Hessa roared. "Get off my back, Roak!"

Three thugs fell, their heads obliterated, and two more collapsed as Roak took them out at the legs, his finger never straying from the Chelk's trigger.

But taking out five thugs was barely a dent in the problem. Over two dozen came sprinting into the hangar from the street, all armed, all headed right for Roak.

Then the 714's plasma cannons came to life, took aim at the incoming mob, and opened fire. The thugs were shredded into flesh confetti by the massive guns.

That left eight from the original party still standing in front of Roak. He killed three more before the Chelk overheated.

"Cheap piece of terpigshit," Roak swore as he flipped the rifle around and gripped it like a bat. "Come on!"

The first thug almost had her head taken right off by Roak's swing. A second one was able to get inside the backswing and grab Roak around the waist, but Roak dropped an elbow onto the back of the thug's neck and the distinct sound of vertebrae cracking was heard even over the roar of the 714's plasma cannons. The thug fell, but was quickly replaced by the three remaining thugs.

Roak and the thugs collapsed to the floor in a pile of thrashing limbs and flailing fists. Roak took a few hits to the face, but not before he punched his armored fist through a thug's chest and out its back. He hooked his arm through the corpse and used its weight to shove one of the other thugs away which left only one still on top.

Roak drew his Kepler and powered up the heat blade. The thug on top of Roak must have realized what was about to happen because it tried to shove up and away, but it was too late. The Kepler's blade sliced through the thug's temple and the stink of cooking brain and fluid filled the air, joining the stench of excrement, blood, and other bodily fluids that were leaking from the many corpses that littered the floor of the hangar.

A boot nailed Roak in the temple as he shoved the dead thug off of him. Stars filled his vision and he grunted with pain. Roak was able to get his arm up in time to block another blow to his head, but the deflected boot nailed his wounded shoulder instead which sent white hot pain racing through Roak's body. He rolled over and forced himself not to vomit as he shoved up onto his hands and knees.

Roak saw the boot coming at him one more time and he struck fast and sure. The Kepler knife took the boot and the foot inside off with ease. Roak sneered at the wail of pain as the footless thug collapsed next to him. Roak buried the Kepler deep into the thug's eye socket. The wailing stopped.

And so did the 714's plasma cannons.

"Hessa?" Roak croaked as he struggled up onto his feet. "How fucked are we?"

"I am secure on Zuus still," Hessa replied. "But you are really and truly fucked."

Roak grabbed for a stray plasma rifle, missed, took a deep breath, and tried again. He managed to stand upright and get the rifle to his shoulder as the mob of controlled Jafla citizens raced towards him.

"Well. Any ideas?" Roak asked. "Moltrans?"

"The 714 is not equipped," Hessa said, her voice filled with emotion." Roak...? I..."

"Nah, don't say it," Roak replied. He took a deep breath and centered himself as much as he could. Then he took aim, slowly let out the breath, and opened fire. "Goodbye, Hessa."

"Goodbye, Roak..."

18.

"Get your low caste ass in the ship!" Meshara yelled over the comm. "The cargo hold is open and I have everyone inside, Roak."

Roak could tell he wouldn't make it even as he fired at the mob and sprinted towards the 714. The mob was going to cut him off before he could reach the open hold.

"The port airlock!" Nimm yelled.

"Glad you're awake," Roak said. "I should apologize to you, Nimm."

Hessa didn't mark the time and date and that was when Roak knew he was in very deep terpigshit.

"Apologize in person," Nimm said. "The airlock is open and waiting for you."

Roak could see the airlock, it was only a few meters away. But he could also see a dozen thugs that were sprinting straight at it instead of straight at Roak.

"Close the ship!" Roak ordered.

The airlock closed instantly.

"I saw them," Hessa said, choking back a sob.

"AIs don't cry, Hessa," Roak said.

"Fuck you, Roak," Hessa replied. "I'll cry if I want to."

"I mean AIs can't cry," Roak said.

"Roak, let it go," Nimm said. "I think I can get some more charge to the plasma cannons. I could power them up completely if I could start the engines!"

"Try now," a voice interrupted. "I was able to override the fine. Your ship should be released."

"Poq?" Roak asked.

"Yes, Roak, it is I," Poq replied. "Would you mind reversing your trajectory and retreat towards the lift you arrived in?"

"Why would I do that?" Roak asked.

The answer to his question came in the form of a sea of attacking thugs being parted down the middle by a speeding roller. A speeding roller that was aimed directly for him.

Roak spun about and retreated back to the lift as bodies flew this way and that.

A body collided with Roak's back, sending him sprawling to the floor, but he scrambled back up onto his feet and kept moving. He didn't need to look back over his shoulder to know that the roller was almost on him.

As soon as Roak was close enough to the wide-open lift he dove head first inside, tucking his wounded shoulder so he could roll up against the far wall and use that as leverage to get back up onto his feet.

"You did not die!" Hessa cheered.

"Not yet," Roak said as he watched the incoming roller get closer and closer.

At the last second, the roller spun to the right and slid sideways almost up against the lift's opening.

The gore-covered side door opened and Poq stepped out.

"Hessa or Nimm, you will want to leave now," Poq said.

The android walked casually into the lift and activated the doors. They slammed shut on several father-controlled beings, spraying both of them with plenty of blood and bits of flesh. An arm hung between the doors for a moment then fell to the lift floor. Roak kicked it to the side.

"Thanks for that," Roak said.

"Time and date!" Hessa cried with obvious joy.

"Hold a moment," Poq said. "Hessa or Nimm? You must leave now."

"What about Roak?" Hessa asked.

"I will make sure Roak leaves the planet unharmed," Poq said. He glanced sideways at the gore-coated Roak. "Or no more harmed than he already is. Please lift off now."

"I am prepping the ship for liftoff," Nimm responded.

"Do not prep," Poq said. "There is no time for that."

"Why…?" Nimm asked.

"I have set the roller to self-destruct," Poq stated. "You have less than three minutes to leave before the hangar is destroyed."

The lift shuddered then moved at a speed that threw Roak up against the wall.

"A little warning," Roak said as he steadied himself. He clamped a hand over his shoulder. "Not at my best right now."

"Yes. Here," Poq said and pulled a small med kit from a pocket. "This will stop the bleeding."

Roak took the kit and fished out a compression bandage. He slapped it to his shoulder and the bandage instantly merged with Roak's light armor and sealed over his wound. The pain eased, but Roak also lost all mobility in his left arm as the bandage locked his shoulder into place.

"Kalaka is in a med pod," Meshara reported. "Yellow Eyes is not doing well, though. I will monitor him closely and switch the two out if need be."

"Thanks, Meshara," Roak said and added before Hessa could say anything, "Time and date. Yeah, yeah, yeah."

"Lifting off now," Nimm said. "Traffic control is shouting their heads off, but they aren't stopping us."

"They cannot stop you," Poq said. "All systems on Jafla Base have been corrupted by the one you call Father. He is using his resources to maintain his control over the populace."

"So he can't stop this lift?" Roak asked.

"He would not be able to anyway," Poq responded. "This lift is not connected to the main grid or network. The construction and ingenuity are to be admired. Shava Stem Shava should have focused on this technology instead of the orb fights. He would have been exponentially more successful as a businessbeing."

"It may have kept him alive too," Roak said. "I don't run across many lift tycoons in my line of work."

"He was a corrupt being at his core," Poq said. "Your paths would have eventually crossed anyway."

"Probably," Roak said and shrugged. And winced.

He took a couple of deep breaths.

"Where are we going?" Roak asked. "Not back to the Gas Chamber?"

"Why would I take you back there?" Poq asked. "It is a dead zone. And completely engulfed in flame."

"Then where?"

"The municipal building hangar," Poq said. "We will escape using a GF speeder."

"Good plan," Roak said. "You sure Father can't control that too?"

"Like I said before, Roak," Poq replied, "your Father is too occupied with controlling the entire population of Jafla Base to be able to also control all vehicles on this planet."

"Are you sure about that? Because the asshole tends to find ways of making beings eat their words."

"I do not eat."

"It's an expression."

"Which does not apply to me since I do not eat."

"Never the Hells mind." Roak pulled his Flott. "You don't happen to have an extra charge for this?"

"Not at the moment, but you may charge the weapon on the speeder."

"I might need it before that. I have a feeling we're going to have company when we arrive."

"Yes. True," Poq said and fished a Blorta 22 laser pistol from a different pocket. "This will have to do."

"Better than nothing," Roak said as he checked the weapon. "But not by much."

The lift doors opened onto a lavatory.

"Of course," Roak said. "Shava Stem Shava connected his special lift to the Jafla PD toilet."

"This is but one of many toilets in the building," Poq said.

The android stepped out of the lift and waited for Roak to join him. He then reached back inside and executed a series of keystrokes on the lift's interface.

"You're gonna blow the lift too," Roak stated. "You sure we don't want to keep it intact? Just in case."

"Just in case of what?"

"Just in case we can't get to the PD hangar and need a way out of this building."

"If we cannot get to the hangar then we will not be able to return to this lavatory and the lift." The lift doors closed. "It is a moot point since what I have initiated cannot be uninitiated."

"No return," Roak said. "I like your style."

"I do not have a style," Poq said.

"Hessa? Can you give this guy a crash course on galactic slang and sayings?" Roak called.

"I can do that," Hessa replied.

Poq stiffened for less than a second then shook his head. "That was unwanted. None of these words or phrases make sense."

"What language does?" Roak asked. He looked at his little Blorta then at the lavatory door. "Where do we go?"

"Take an immediate left once we leave this room," Poq said. "Five doors down will be the entrance to the stairwell. We proceed up to the rooftop hangar."

"And you're sure Father isn't controlling the GF vehicles up there?"

"I am as sure as a being can be considering the unprecedented circumstances we have found ourselves in."

"That didn't answer the question."

"Because there is no true answer. I cannot be certain until we have reached a speeder and I am able to inspect it up close."

"I have a lot more unwanted words and phrases I want to express, but I'm not going to," Roak said. He nodded at the lavatory door controls. "You first."

"So I may be cover in case we are fired upon immediately?" Poq asked.

"Yep."

"Very well. There are no beings outside this lavatory."

"Wait, what?"

Poq opened the door and stepped from the lavatory without answering. Roak was right behind him.

"Eight Million Gods!" Roak exclaimed. He jammed the back of his hand to his nose. "What is that?"

"That would be the smell of burning flesh from several different species of beings," Poq replied. "Interesting. That would explain the lack of police officers on this floor."

"Fire ants," Roak said. "They've already spread through the city."

"Yes. They have utilized the plumbing and electrical conduits in order to travel from area to area quickly. They are quite industrious."

"Good for them," Roak said. "Fifth door down?"

"Yes."

Roak moved along the hall, his eyes scanning every point of possible attack, his Blorta up and ready. Poq was directly behind him.

They reached the stairwell and Roak was about to open the door when Poq stopped him.

"Allow me," Poq said.

He flung open the door and rushed into the stairwell, his fists moving so fast that Roak could barely track their movement. What he could track was the blood of many colors that filled the air as Poq shredded his way through the beings that clogged the stairwell.

The stench of burning flesh was mixed with the strong odor of fire suppressant. It was almost overpowering as Roak followed Poq into the stairwell. Fire ant husks crunched under Roak's boots.

Beings of all species clogged the space, several of them already dead, but most of them able to move and attack even with their limbs fused to their sides by fire foam. They came at Roak with mouths wide open, teeth ready to tear through Roak's armor. He fired point blank at everyone and everything, staying close behind Poq as the android battled its way up the stairs towards the rooftop hangars.

A Gwreq missing three of its four arms, with the fourth dangling by a thread-thin tendon, dodged Poq's attack and rushed Roak. The bounty hunter got the Blorta under the Gwreq's chin, which wasn't too hard since the being was a good half-meter taller than Roak, and squeezed the trigger. The top of the Gwreq's head burst open like a brain fountain and the Gwreq's corpse tumbled over the railing onto the landing below.

Roak watched the Gwreq fall then wished he hadn't. The sight below wasn't pretty. There had to be hundreds of smoking and smoldering controlled beings trying to force their way up the stairwell through the waterfall of already scorched corpses.

"How many floors?" Roak shouted.

"Fifteen," Poq replied.

"Are you...?" Roak took a deep breath, gagged a little, took another deep breath, and nodded. "Fifteen. Great."

"Do not worry, Roak," Poq said. "I will get us there."

Floor by floor, landing by landing, Poq demolished every being in their path. Bodies fell and it took all of Roak's attention not to slip and fall on the gore and guts. Attention that he needed to use to watch their six in order to make sure they weren't going to be attacked from behind.

Two more floors and Roak risked a look over his shoulder. The controlled beings were still in pursuit, but the carnage that Poq was creating kept most of them slipping and sliding back downwards. None of the beings was intact enough to be able to scramble over all the corpses Poq was churning out.

There was something to be said about having an android on your side, Roak thought.

"We are out of the atmosphere," Nimm announced. Roak was almost startled by the interruption. "Oh…"

"Nimm? What?" Roak asked. "What does 'Oh' mean?"

But Nimm did not respond.

"Nimm? Hessa?" Roak shouted. "What is going on?"

"Skrang," Hessa replied. "Two destroyers."

Two destroyers…

"The same ones that were over Chafa?" Roak asked.

Hessa did not respond.

"Hessa? Are they the same ones that we saw over Chafa?"

Still no response.

Then the screaming from below started.

Roak jumped and spun about, his Blorta aimed down the stairs. But there was no need. Not one of the controlled beings was pursuing them. They were all too busy writhing in pain on the stairs and landings.

Then the screaming from above started.

Roak turned back around and grabbed a still Poq. "What the Hells is going on?"

"I believe Father's control has been interrupted," Poq said. "Which is leaving these beings alive and fully aware of their agony. The poor creatures."

Poq slammed a fist into a crying Ferg's face and crushed its head.

"What the fuck?" Roak yelled. "If it's not controlled anymore then why kill it?"

"Mercy," Poq said.

Roak grabbed the android's arm. "We can walk around them. No need to keep killing."

"But, mercy," Poq stated and obliterated a Halgon's head.

"Stop!" Roak said and pushed past Poq. "Come on. Let's go."

Maybe there wasn't something to be said about having an android on your side, Roak thought.

Roak led the way. He ignored the pleas and cries for help from the smoldering beings. Hands, tentacles, claws grasped at Roak's armor, imploring him to stop and help them. Some even asked to be killed to ease their suffering. But Roak kept moving. He couldn't stand being in that stairwell another second.

Finally, thankfully, they reached the top and Roak shoved the door to the hangars open and stepped into almost fresh air. There were blackened corpses everywhere. It looked like a few beings had the idea to escape the fire ants by flying away from the doomed building, the doomed base. They didn't make it.

Which meant...

"We've got ants!" Roak yelled.

He squeezed the Blorta's trigger at the creatures that quickly made themselves known, drawn to the sound of Roak crashing through the door.

"Which way?" Roak yelled.

Poq joined him and studied the hangar.

"That one," Poq said. He pointed at a GF speeder a few meters away. "That will suffice."

"Why not these ones?" Roak asked, still blasting away at the incoming fire ants. "They're closer!"

"They are out of commission," Poq stated.

One of the speeders closest to Roak sparked and smoked as several fire ants fell from underneath the vehicle.

"They are trying to nest," Poq explained. "We should hurry before they take up residence in our targeted speeder."

"We should hurry for a lot of reasons!"

Poq walked toward the chosen speeder without a problem. The fire ants weren't interested in his synthetic body. They were way more interested in Roak's living body even if it was encased in gore-covered light armor.

Reaching the speeder, Poq activated the side ladder and climbed up into the small cockpit. Roak fired, kicked, fired, stomped, fired, and crushed every last fire ant in his way. It took considerably more effort than Poq used, but he finally was able to get to the ladder and up into the cockpit.

The speeder was a two-seater, built for fast travel and maximum firepower. Roak knew from experience that the little GF speeder could haul ass and kick ass in equal measure. He'd used a couple before in the past and was never disappointed with their performance.

"I will fly," Poq said.

"Probably best," Roak said and collapsed into his seat.

The cockpit slammed shut, crushing a couple of overachieving fire ants.

There was no countdown, no checklist, no warning at all as Poq powered up the engines and lifted off from the hangar. They sped out the hangar doors and were flying over Jafla Base before Roak could get clicked into his harness.

"I cannot reach Hessa or the others," Poq said. "In fact, all communications on the planet have ceased."

"That's weird," Roak said. "Are they being jammed?"

"No," Poq replied. "They are simply not operable."

"Even mine," Roak said. "Hessa's comm shouldn't be affected."

"Yet it is. Your use of the word weird is apt."

The sky around them was filled with escaping ships and Poq struggled to avoid random collisions from panicked fighters, speeders, transports, and shuttles. Roak hung tight to the armrests of his seat.

It only took a few minutes before their speeder left the atmosphere and was finally free of Jafla. But Roak saw that the chaos was worse in space. Countless fleeing vehicles raced towards the closest portal, creating a queue jam like he'd never seen before.

"Do not worry," Poq said. "I know of a different portal we can use."

The android piloted the speeder away from the chaos and around to the other side of the planet. Then they raced across empty space to a far, far, far off light.

"I didn't see any Skrang," Roak said. "Did you?"

"No, I did not," Poq said. "Nor are there any Skrang vessels on the scanners."

"Then what in all the Hells were-?"

"Roak!" Hessa's voice bellowed in Roak's ear.

"Eight Million Gods dammit, Hessa!" Roak cried. "Turn down the volume!"

"Sorry. Sorry," Hessa apologized. "I am just so happy to be able to communicate with you again. I was being blocked."

"All communications were being blocked," Roak said. "How's everyone doing?"

"Yes, well, about that…"

"Hessa…"

"I have lost track of the 714," Hessa admitted.

"Roak," Poq said.

"Hold on," Roak replied. "Hessa, what do you mean you lost track of the 714? Where is it?"

"I believe the Skrang took it," Hessa said. "Then they left. As soon as they were gone, I was able to communicate again."

"Roak," Poq said.

"Hold on!" Roak shouted. "So the Skrang were the ones blocking all comms? Even yours? When did they develop tech like that?"

"Roak!" Poq shouted.

"What is it? Did you forget how to fly?"

"No, I did not forget how to fly," Poq replied. "I simply wanted to alert you to the fact that we are now being pursued by the ships that were fleeing Jafla."

"What?"

"Communications are no longer blocked," Poq stated matter of factly. "It stands to reason that all of those beings are now under Father's control once again."

"You have got to be kidding me."

"I am not. Wait. That is one of those sayings. You are expressing disbelief, not questioning my sincerity."

"How many ships are after us?"

"All of them."

"All of them?"

"All of them."

"Sure. Why not..."

19.

The speeder rocked and shuddered as it took plasma fire from the pursuing ships. But the vehicle's shields were almost as powerful as its engines and weapons, so it took the beating and kept on going, headed straight for the far, far, far off light that was the far, far, far off portal.

"Are we going to make it?" Roak asked.

"There is a less than six percent chance that we will achieve our goal," Poq said. "We are faster than the majority of the ships pursuing us."

"And the minority?" Roak asked.

"They are faster than we," Poq said. "Currently, the slower ships are blocking their path which is why we have a less than six percent chance. It would be less than one percent without the chaos they are creating for themselves."

"Father never was great with ships," Roak said.

"Roak?" Hessa called.

"Yes, Hessa?"

"I cannot find the Skrang anywhere," Hessa said. "I am bouncing scans through every possible wormhole portal and I cannot see them. They are either shielded from scans, cloaked in some new way, or they have moved completely out of range. I do not know where they transported to."

"Only two directions they can go to get completely out of your range," Roak said. "The Edge or Skrang Territory."

The ship shuddered again and again.

"Shields are holding," Poq announced. "I thought you would want to know."

"Yeah, thanks for the info," Roak said. "How long until we reach the portal?"

"We will not reach the portal," Poq said.

"If we manage that less than six percent chance then how long until we reach the portal?" Roak asked.

"Two point eight hours," Poq said. "If we are able to maintain current speed."

"Can we increase the speed?"

"Not if we would like to keep the integrity of the aft shields."

"Current speed it is."

"I will attempt to scan the Edge now," Hessa said.

"It's too far out," Roak replied. "It's called the Edge for a reason, Hessa."

"I'm still going to try," Hessa snapped. "Those are our friends they have."

"Well…"

"Roak!"

"What? Yeah, sure, Nimm is a friend, but the rest…?"

"Yellow Eyes, Roak. He is a friend. A trusted friend."

"Sure. Yellow Eyes too. But Meshara is who she is and Kalaka is just some corrupt GVD."

"He is not as corrupt as you believe him to be," Poq interrupted. "The being is, using one of the terms I have just learned, walking a fine line between worlds. In order to do his job, he must continue the illusion of full corruption."

"But he's still corrupt," Roak said.

"It is complicated," Poq said.

"Just fly the ship," Roak replied.

"I cannot scan the Edge," Hessa said. "Do not say a word, Roak."

"Don't need to."

"I will attempt to scan Skrang Territory."

"Good luck with that."

The speeder rocked to starboard and started to dive. Poq struggled to regain control and right them.

"That's not good," Roak said.

"We sustained some minor damage," Poq said. "I have repaired it."

"Repaired it? How?" Roak asked. "Does this speeder have bots?"

"It does," Poq stated. "Repair bots are standard on all Jafla PD and GF vehicles. Even small vehicles such as this speeder."

The speeder shook once more as a barrage of plasma fire impacted the aft shields. Poq sent the vehicle into a steep climb, avoiding a second and third barrage that followed directly behind the first one. Roak hung on. Even with the grav dampeners, the g-forces were brutal in the small vehicle.

"I am unable to scan Skrang Territory," Hessa said.

"Wow, really?" Roak replied.

"You know what, Roak? I was sad when I thought you were going to die back there," Hessa said. "I am rethinking that feeling now."

Roak couldn't help but smile to himself.

"I will continue my search," Hessa said with as much attitude as her AI voice could create. "You continue doing whatever you are doing."

"Trying to stay alive?" Roak responded.

"Yes. That," Hessa said. "Do that."

Poq reversed the climb and sent the speeder into a brutal dive. Roak groaned as his seat's harness pressed into his wounded shoulder. The speeder shook hard then began to spin out of control. Poq was able to get the speeder under control again, but not before it was nailed with several plasma blasts.

Klaxons blared.

"That is unfortunate," Poq stated.

"Just spit it out, Poq," Roak snapped.

"Spit it...? Ah, another saying," Poq replied. "We are losing shield integrity."

"On which part of the ship?"

"On the entire ship."

"Shit."

"That is one word that could be used to describe our situation. I have learned many other words that can be used. Shall I list them?"

"Why would I want you to list them?"

"Roak, be nice," Hessa said. "He's trying to express himself and communicate with you using the words and sayings you asked me to teach him."

"I have too many AIs in my life," Roak muttered.

"I heard that," Hessa said.

"I'm sure you did," Roak said.

Poq put the speeder back on course for the portal.

"How long?" Roak asked.

There was no response.

"I'm talking to you, Poq. How long until we reach the portal?"

"One point seven five hours," Poq answered. "But, as I have stated previously, we are not going to make it."

"Hey, Hessa?" Roak called.

"What?" Hessa asked.

"You remember when I killed Wrenn?" Roak said.

"The first time or the second time?" Hessa asked.

"Right. I forgot about the first time," Roak responded. "The second time."

"You killed Mr. Wrenn of the Shilo Syndicate?" Poq asked. "Twice?"

"It's no big deal," Roak said.

"Because he barely had anything to do with either death," Hessa said. "He required rescuing both times."

"I don't think I required anything, thanks," Roak snapped. "But the second time, do you remember what we were up against?"

"It was you and Yellow Eyes that were up against it," Hessa said.

"Stop with the useless disclaimers!" Roak shouted. He took a deep breath. "The bots, Hessa. I'm talking about the bots."

"That was quite the circuitous route to take to get to that revelation," Poq stated.

"Sometimes he just can't spit it out," Hessa said.

"Hey! Back to me!" Roak took another deep breath. "This ship has bots, Hessa."

"Yes, all GF vehicles are equipped with repair bots," Hessa said. "This comes as a surprise to you?"

Roak took a third deep breath.

"Do the bots on this ship have cutter blades or blow torches?" Roak asked, once calmed.

Or as calmed as Roak could get.

"I believe they are all equipped with cutter blades, blow torches, and many different tools that would be useful in repairing a ship on the go," Hessa said.

"If you are asking me to repair the shields using the bots, please know that I have already communicated that order to them," Poq said. "It would have been negligent of me not to."

"Will they be able to fix the shields?" Roak asked.

"Probably not," Poq replied. "The damage is considerable. We'll need a dry dock in order to execute full repairs."

"Then let's cut the bots loose," Roak said.

There was silence from both Poq and Hessa.

"Let me explain," Roak said.

"Please do," Poq said.

"I can't wait to hear this," Hessa said.

"Eject the bots from our ship and send them at the ships following us," Roak said. The speeder shuddered and louder klaxons blared. "Rephrase. The ships attacking us."

Poq cut the klaxons. "We are sustaining damage and you wish to eject the repair bots that can help fix that damage?"

"I'd rather not," Roak said. "But I have an idea."

"I think I know where you're going with this," Hessa said. "You eject the bots and have them attack the ships behind you. They inflict enough damage to some of the other ships that there will be enough crashes and impacts between the pursuing ships that they will no longer be able to effectively pursue you. Is that it?"

"That's the idea," Roak said.

"That's a horrible idea," Hessa replied.

"I am in agreement with Hessa," Poq said. "I do not see the merit in sacrificing our repair abilities for a plan that has incredibly poor odds of being successful."

"Trust me," Roak said. "It'll work."

"I do not trust you," Poq said. "No offense, but I do not know you enough to trust you. I only know your reputation and the actions I have witnessed in the short time we have been together. Nothing in either your reputation or my observations allow me to believe your plan will work."

Hessa didn't say anything. Roak smiled.

"Hessa?" Poq called. "Since you are exponentially more familiar with Roak and his strategic thinking, please explain to him the problems with his plan."

"It might work," Hessa said quietly.

"Excuse me?" Poq asked. "I have processed more than eight million different scenarios in the time since Roak broached the subject and not one of those scenarios is viable. We lose our repair bots and end up destroyed without destroying our pursuers. It is a bad plan."

"But you processed eight million scenarios without a full set of proper data," Hessa said. "You admitted it yourself. You do not know Roak."

Roak continued to smile, happy to let the AIs work it out between themselves.

The ship took a wicked hit to the port side and was sent into another spin.

Roak was no longer happy to let the AIs work it out between themselves.

"Hessa, you know what to do," Roak said.

"Does she?" Poq asked.

"Do I?" Hessa asked. "I suppose I do."

"How much time do you need?" Roak asked.

"There are sixteen bots," Hessa said. "Give me sixteen minutes without the ship taking damage."

"Poq, can you give her sixteen minutes without the ship taking damage?" Roak asked.

"I ain't no mind psychic," Poq said. "How do I know?"

"Too much, Poq," Roak said. "Maybe leave the sayings and slang for another time."

"I do not know if I can grant Hessa sixteen minutes without the ship taking damage," Poq said. "But I will try."

"Now you're learning," Roak said. "Hessa. Do your thing."

"And I will do my thing," Poq said. "You may want to secure your harness better. This is going to be a bumpy ride."

"Alright, you got that one," Roak said.

Then the ship moved at a speed that Roak was far from comfortable with. His discomfort grew as Poq executed a series of dives, climbs, rolls, repeat, that sent Roak's stomach to places in his body it had never visited before.

"I have realized that since the shields are already compromised, I am able to divert more power to the engines," Poq stated.

"That's…great…" Roak replied through gritted teeth. Pretty much his whole body was gritted. "No…need…to…explain…"

"It does not reduce my efficiency if I communicate my thought processes to you, Roak," Poq said.

"Under…stood… Still…"

"Still what, Roak?" Poq asked.

"He'd like you to shut up because he's nauseous," Hessa said.

"Both…of…you… Shut…up…" Roak burped and struggled to keep anything solid from following the gas bubble. He managed to keep the little food he had inside him from escaping outside him, but it took all his willpower.

"Do not vomit in this ship, Roak," Poq said. "The acid could damage some of the controls and we are about to eject our only means of repair."

"Good point," Hessa said.

Roak closed his eyes. Bad idea. He opened his eyes. That didn't help.

Plasma blasts zipped past, lighting up the small cockpit as they just barely missed hitting the ship. The few stars visible in the system were nothing but blurred lines. More plasma blasts zipped by.

Then a missile. Another missile. Five more missiles.

"Seven missiles are locked onto us," Poq said. "Unfortunate."

"Hessa…" Roak whispered.

"Almost done, Roak," Hessa replied. "How are you felling?"

"Bite…me…"

"Three of the seven missiles have a ninety-eight percent chance of destroying us," Poq stated.

"Hessa…"

"I know, Roak, I am hurrying," Hessa said.

"Not that… Yes, that…but…"

"But…? What?" Hessa asked.

Roak breathed through his nose as the speeder seemed to flip end over end which he wasn't quite sure was possible to do, but it sure felt possible. And horrible. Very much horrible.

"Use…the…missiles," Roak finally managed to say.

"Use the missiles…? Oh. Now that is a good idea," Hessa said. "I have enough bots ready."

"Launch them," Roak said. He clamped a glove over his mouth.

"Please, let me restate my previous request," Poq said. "Do not vomit in this cockpit."

"I have launched seven of the reprogrammed repair bots," Hessa said. "If my calculations are correct, I can use the torches as thrusters. If I am very careful…Very careful… Extremely careful…"

Roak groaned as a wave of nausea nearly caused him to pass out.

"Contact with one missile!" Hessa announced. "With two missiles! Three and four!"

Roak groaned again.

"All bots have made contact with their targets," Hessa said. "I am cutting into the control panels. I have cut into the control panels and am now attempting to reprogram the missiles."

"We will have impact in five seconds," Poq announced. "Four. Three. Two…"

Roak grinned. Then groaned again. Even smiling was wreaking havoc on his body. Fair play since his smiles tended to wreak havoc on anyone that witnessed them.

Seven missiles whipped past the cockpit, headed in the opposite direction.

"I will allow them to do their work," Hessa said. "I released the seven repair bots and they are being joined by the remainder I have reprogrammed."

"The ships are trying to evade the missiles, but there are too many of them in too close proximity," Poq said. "They cannot maneuver effectively."

Roak nodded. It was about all he could do.

"We have seven direct hits," Poq said. "As well as about eight indirect hits. Fifteen ships are no longer able to pursue us. That leaves only forty-three ships to contend with."

"The bots will do their jobs," Hessa said.

"Even if sixteen bots do their jobs," Poq said, "that will leave twenty-seven ships still operable."

"No. This will take care of all of them," Hessa said. "Might I suggest you stop using evasive maneuvers and aim your ship directly at the portal? Speed is of the essence now."

"Take care of all of them? Speed?" Poq asked then grew silent. "I see. The bots are not going to merely damage and disable the ships. You have reprogrammed them for another purpose."

"They will target the drive controls," Hessa said. "If they are successful then sixteen ships will have their engines go into overload."

"If my calculations are correct, which they are, then all it will take is two of the sixteen ships to go critical in order to stop the entire group," Poq said. "Now I understand the need for speed."

"That rhymes," Hessa said.

"Is that good? For words to rhyme?" Poq asked.

"It's amusing," Hessa said.

"You are a very strange AI," Poq said.

"Thank you."

"Was that a compliment?"

"I took it as such."

"Stop," Roak groaned. "Please..."

"Time and date," Hessa said. "Poq?"

"Yes, Hessa?"

"Speed."

"Right. Directing all power to the engines. We will have the needed speed to avoid the coming shockwaves." Poq paused. "I believe."

"You can do it," Hessa encouraged.

The speeder lived up to its name and sped.

Roak had to ease his jaw to keep from cracking his teeth as the ever-increasing g-forces threatened to grind his bones to dust.

"The bots have made contact," Hessa announced. "Do not deviate from your course. The margin of error here is-"

"Less than point four percent," Poq finished. "Hardly ideal circumstances."

"Welcome to working with Roak," Hessa said.

There were so many things Roak wanted to say, but he had passed the point of no return and did not dare to open his mouth. Instead of continuing to ease up the pressure from his jaw, he ground down harder to keep from vomiting. Cracked teeth be damned.

"We lost two bots," Hessa said. "Three. Now four. Eight Million Gods dammit!"

"Do you believe in the Eight Million Gods?" Poq asked. "I find that flesh beings have a hard enough time with belief in deities. How does an AI reconcile belief with the obvious logic that none of the Eight Million Gods exist?"

"It's one of those sayings," Hessa said. "We've lost ten bots! Motherfu-!"

A bright light enveloped everything then was gone as fast as it appeared.

"Bam!" Hessa cheered. "We have overload on two engines!"

"Yes, those two have caused a chain reaction with some of the others," Poq said as more flashes obscured the view out of the cockpit. "Quite the chain reaction, if I may say so. An exceedingly dangerous amount of chain reactions."

The light surrounding the ship became so bright that Roak was forced to squeeze his eyes shut. He really didn't want to.

"The bots have not finished," Poq said. "There are more overloads on top of the chain reactions. This has become quite a spectacle."

"Spectacle is a good word," Hessa said. "What is your status, Poq?"

"At the moment, it has become a coin flip," Poq said. "Is that the phrase to use when the odds are even whether or not we survive?"

"That is the exact phrase," Hessa said. "You are catching on quickly."

"One hour exactly," Poq said. "If we can outrun the shockwaves then we may survive this ordeal."

"Yeah, that's sort of been the plan the whole time," Hessa said.

Roak smiled at the sarcasm. Even as sick as he felt, he couldn't dismiss the pride he felt.

"Scanners show that there are only nine intact ships left," Poq reported. "Make that five intact ships. No, three. There are now zero intact ships."

More white flashes.

Roak wasn't an AI, and he couldn't even come close to calculating all the variables that an artificial brain could, but he'd been a fighter his entire life, so he instinctively knew when shit was going to hit the fan.

"Hang...on," he managed to whisper.

"Hang on? We are still about two minutes ahead of the first shockwave," Poq said. "At our current speed we can maintain that..."

"Poq? What is wrong?" Hessa asked. "My calculations say the same... Oh."

Roak held tight to his seat, kept his eyes closed, and gave up on his battle with the contents of his stomach.

It felt like the speeder had been grabbed by an unseen hand and thrown across the galaxy.

"I am hanging on!" Poq yelled.

Roak vomited then passed out.

20.

Roak came to with the stench of vomit in his nose, the taste in his mouth, and the sight of it everywhere. Including the cockpit's view shield.

After a very quick personal assessment, Roak focused past the vomit-coated view shield and stared out at the swirling mass of trans-space. He was glad he didn't have anything left in his stomach or the sight of the constant motion would have sent him into another puking fit. He and trans-space never really got along and it had only gotten worse over the years.

"Poq," Roak called. "How are we?"

There was no reply.

"Poq? Give me a damage report," Roak said.

Still no reply.

"Poq?" Roak exclaimed and grabbed the android by the shoulder.

"I have your vomit all over me," Poq stated, shrugging off Roak's hand. His voice was flat, even, empty. "I am coated in your vomit, Roak."

"Yeah, me too," Roak replied.

"It is your vomit, it should be on you," Poq said. "Not on me."

"Puke happens," Roak said. "We have any bots that can clean... Oh. Right."

They sat in puke-coated silence.

After several minutes of trying to ignore the swirling mass of trans-space that threatened to bring on an encore of the much despised puke session, Roak took a few unfiltered breaths, forced himself not to gag, and asked, "What'd I miss?"

"You missed us flying completely out of control for nearly an hour. Once I was able to regain control, I put us back on course for the wormhole portal," Poq said. "Now we are traveling to Zuus Colony since that is where your ship is. That is where Hessa is."

"Good," Roak responded. "The sooner I get out of this ship the better."

"That statement applies to me as well," Poq said.

"Roak?" Hessa called.

"Here," Roak replied.

"Oh good, you are awake," Hessa said. "We have a problem."

"Yeah, I bet we do," Roak said. "What day is it?"

"That depends on what system you are in," Hessa said. "If you are asking about Zuus then it is-"

"Doesn't matter," Roak said. "If it's a day ending in Y then of course we have a problem."

"On the planet Drosoka the days end in AAAAAAAA," Poq stated.

"The days end in screams?" Roak asked.

"Each week is sixteen galactic standard months long," Poq said. "There is not much hope or joy on that planet. Most of the inhabitants never stop screaming. It has become the official language."

"We should move there," Roak said. "Hard to have trouble if there are no days ending in Y."

"Roak, this is serious," Hessa admonished. "And we may not have much time left to communicate. It is taking up considerable resources to comm with you while you travel through trans-space."

"You haven't had much problem before," Roak said. "What's different?"

"Comms are extremely glitchy," Hessa said. "I believe there is something going on between Father and the Skrang that is interfering with communications on a galactic level."

"How is that possible?" Roak asked.

"It is not," Poq said. "Hessa, you will need to shut down and perform diagnostics. Your systems are not operating correctly."

"I'm operating just fine, buster," Hessa snapped. "It's the comms, not me."

"But the technology needed to interrupt and interfere with galactic communications would have to be on a scale that has not been invented," Poq said.

"Looks like it has," Roak said.

"But there is no record of such technology," Poq said.

"Because it was just invented," Roak said.

"Who has the ability to create such technology?" Poq asked.

"I know a guy," Roak said. "And he's who we're looking for."

"You believe Pol Hammon has invented tech that can disrupt galactic communications?" Hessa asked. "Why?"

"Yes, for what purpose?" Poq added.

"Hopefully he's doing it to stop Father," Roak said. "You saw what happened on Jafla. We lost comms and beings were no longer controlled."

"Then comms returned and that entire fleet of escaping ships attacked," Hessa said.

"Interesting," Poq responded. "I will need to process this further."

"You do that," Roak said. "Hessa? Do we know where the 714 is?"

"No," Hessa said. "I believe they were taken by the Skrang, but I cannot find record of the Skrang reappearing anywhere once they left Jafla. I am still trying to scan Skrang Territory and the Edge, but with the comm interference, I am unable to get any readings at all."

"Can you confirm that the Skrang ships that were over Jafla, and may have taken the 714, are the same Skrang that came for us over Chafa?" Roak asked.

"I do not have full confirmation, but I would guess that they were the same ships," Hessa said.

"Guess? An AI should never guess," Poq said.

"Well, this AI does," Hessa said calmly. "Because nothing is for certain so sometimes you have to use your instincts."

"AIs do not have instincts," Poq said. "This conversation is troubling."

"It's also very boring," Roak said. "Back to what we really need to be talking about. Klib."

"What about her?" Hessa asked.

"She had your implants, but she was still overtaken by Father," Roak said. "That's bad, Hessa. Your implants aren't supposed to even be detectable let alone corruptible."

"I am glad you brought that up because I have been studying all data we have on Klib," Hessa said. "It isn't much, and I wish we could have put her corpse in a med pod so I could have studied it more, but I think I have a hypothesis."

"Is this hypothesis based on instincts or facts?" Poq asked.

Roak smiled. The honeymoon between the AIs was over, for sure.

"If you do not have anything constructive to contribute to this conversation then please butt out," Hessa said.

Roak's smile grew wider.

"My hypothesis," Hessa continued, "is that Father has somehow gained control of beings on a cellular level, not just on a technological level. Even after switching out the implants, he still remained inside Klib, waiting there to strike when the time came."

Roak shook his head and chuckled.

"That bastard is always one step ahead," Roak said more to himself than to the AIs. "He wanted us on Chafa."

"So, it was a trap set by Father?" Hessa asked. "But we escaped."

"No, he didn't want to trap us there," Roak explained. "He wanted us there so we would find the syndicate beings, watch them dissolve, then try to fix it. It was smoke and mirrors as always."

"I am not following this line of reasoning since I do not have all the pertinent information," Poq said.

"I'll fill you in," Hessa said.

One second later, Poq said, "I see. It is obvious why Father did what he did."

"Is it?" Hessa asked.

As much as Roak knew it would cause him grief, he had to agree with Poq.

"Yeah, it is," Roak said. "You can't see it, Hessa, because you are too close."

"I am? What in all the Hells are you two talking about?" Hessa snapped.

"Your implants," Roak said. "It wasn't the med pods. It was your implants."

"That cannot be," Hessa said. "I was able to reverse the effects of the cellular degeneration using the med pods."

"Smoke and mirrors, Hessa. Smoke and mirrors," Roak said. "You could have left us alone and the cellular degeneration would have fixed itself."

"Because you have Hessa's proprietary implants," Poq said. "They stabilized the cells."

"Exactly," Roak said.

"But how? Why?" Hessa asked.

"Those are the questions we need answers to," Roak said. "Which is why we have to find Pol Hammon as soon as beingly possible. How are the repairs coming? You and Reck getting along?"

"We're fine, asshole," Reck interrupted.

"Have you been listening the whole time?" Roak asked. "What about fighting the interference?"

"Your conversation is on speaker in the Borgon's cockpit," Reck said. "I'm finishing up a few things then we'll be more than ready to take on anything Father has planned for us."

"Can we transport directly to the coordinates for Outpost Hell?" Roak asked. "I'm done with trans-space for the rest of my life. It's transport instantly or set up camp wherever I end up."

"Yeah, I can get us there," Reck said. "But do we want to?"

"What in all the Hells do you mean by that?" Roak asked. "Yeah we want to. Pol Hammon is there. I know it. He wants to be flesh again. That planet, from what Prime and the FIS know, is where he can make that happen."

"Why would he want to be flesh again?" Poq asked. "An organic body is inferior to a synthetic body. Strength, agility, processing power, are all far superior with a body such as mine."

"Don't get me wrong," Roak said, "Pol isn't going to get himself a flesh bag and leave it stock. He'll customize that body with all kinds of tech."

"Best of both worlds," Hessa said.

"That's how he sees it," Roak said.

"Hey! Back to my question!" Reck yelled. "Do we actually want to go to Outpost Hell right now?"

"You're going to have to give me more than just a question, Reck," Roak said, getting annoyed.

"I believe what she is referring to is that we are very shorthanded," Hessa said. "We do not have Nimm. We do not have Meshara. No Yellow Eyes. We have lost Jagul, a fact which Bhangul has not been alerted to, not that Jagul was an asset to the team."

"Not a team," Roak said then paused. "Hold up. We're not a team."

"Yes, Roak, you keep telling us that," Reck said. "Way to be a supportive leader."

"You consider Roak a leader?" Hessa asked. "Eight Million Gods bless you."

"No, I don't consider Roak a-!"

"Shut up!" Roak snapped.

"You are certainly not a team," Poq stated.

"Yeah, but I know where we can get a team," Roak said. "And as much as I hate to admit it, a team that has a far better skillset for what we need to do."

"What team are you referring to?" Poq asked.

"How much longer until we're at Zuus?" Roak asked.

"It will be close to an hour," Poq said.

"Hessa? Can you help Poq maintain a secure channel?" Roak asked.

"That is what I am doing now, Roak," Hessa replied. "Thank you for noticing and being appreciative of this fact."

"You take offense quickly," Poq said. "This is not positive learned behavior for an AI."

"Bite me," Hessa said.

"Yes. I see the problem. You have been influenced by Roak too much," Poq said. "A suggestion would be to-"

"Will everyone shut up!" Roak yelled. He pinched the bridge of his nose. "It was so quiet back when I was alone. So, so quiet. I miss that."

He took a deep breath.

"What I need is a completely secure line of communication with FIS headquarters," Roak said. "Can the two of you make that happen?"

"It would be safer if you waited to communicate with the FIS once you return to Zuus," Hessa said. "The system will be much more stable."

"I agree with Hessa," Poq said. "Trans-space is too unpredictable and I do not know enough about Father's capabilities… Oh, thank you, Hessa. I am now fully informed as to all that is known about Father. Still, I do not suggest attempting secure communications in our present situation."

"So you can't do it?" Roak asked.

"No, it can be done," Hessa said.

"It would not be ideal," Poq added.

"Fuck ideal," Roak responded. "We don't have time for ideal. We need this ball rolling now."

"Let me talk to Poq for a moment, Roak," Hessa said.

"You have one moment. Then I need-"

"We are done," Hessa said. "It is doable and we are certain it will be secure."

"We are not certain it will be secure," Poq countered.

"Almost certain," Hessa amended. "Shall I initiate the communication with Agent Prime?"

"No," Roak said. "I need to talk to General Ved Gerber directly for this one."

"Not Agent Prime?" Hessa asked. "We were instructed to use him as our contact if we needed anything from the FIS, Roak."

"Prime can't help us," Roak said. "I need the big brass."

"Let me see what can be done," Hessa said. "Poq? Are you ready?"

"I am," Poq said. "I will monitor the comm from our end to make sure we are not being eavesdropped on."

"Thank you," Hessa said. "Are you sure, Roak?"

"Just make the call, Hessa," Roak said.

"Yes, sir," Hessa said. "Right away, sir."

Roak rolled his eyes. Then wiped his eyes as a chunkier piece of vomit plopped down off his brow. He couldn't wait for an hour-long steam.

"General Gerber," a voice said over the comm. "Who in all the Hells is this and how did you get this comm signature?"

"Hey, General," Roak said. "We need to talk."

"I don't know who you think..." The general paused. "Roak... Is that you, Roak?"

"The one and the same," Roak said.

"I'll ignore the many regulations and galactic laws you have broken by communicating with me like this so you can get to the point of why you believe we need to talk," Gerber said.

"I need a Drop Team," Roak said. "I was told that Drop Team Zero would be at my disposal when I needed them."

There was a long pause then Gerber burst out into laughter.

"My apologies, Roak," Gerber said. "But I rarely hear such overblown confidence coming from anyone other than Agent Prime. It's amusing to know there are more like him out there."

Roak ignored the general's mirth at his expense.

"I am having my partner send you all the data we have on Father and what has happened the past few days," Roak said.

"Do we really want to do that?" Hessa asked privately.

"Yes," Roak replied.

"Hello? Roak?" Gerber called.

"Here," Roak said.

"What partner? I thought you worked alone?" Gerber asked. "Wait. You mean your AI pilot?"

"Yep. That's who I mean," Roak said.

"Your AI pilot?" Hessa grumbled. "Prick..."

"Once you take a look at the intel we have, you're going to want to assign Drop Team Zero to me immediately," Roak said.

"First, Roak, I will never assign a Drop Team to you," Gerber said. "Even I will get my ass canned if I did that."

"You know what I mean, General," Roak said.

"I do, yes," Gerber said. "The intel has arrived and I'll take a look at it."

"While you're doing that you are going to need to spin up DTZ," Roak said. "You'll thank me after you're done reading."

"No, after I'm done reading, I will carefully weigh whether or not DTZ needs to be involved," Gerber said. "In fact, Roak, I will carefully weigh whether the FIS needs to be involved with you and your lot at all. I know you have a deal in place with Agent Prime, one I signed off on, but no deal is iron clad, Roak. Be very aware of that."

"Story of my life, General," Roak said. "Listen. We'll be arriving at our destination in less than an hour. It may take us a bit to get ramped up and ready to go, but when we are, you need to not only have DTZ spun up, but you need to be ready to back my play with everything you've got."

"I've got a lot, Roak," Gerber said.

"You'll need it," Roak said. He sighed. "We'll need it. Read on. You'll see. But get DTZ prepped."

Gerber was silent for a couple of minutes. Roak let him think.

"I'll activate DTZ," Gerber finally said. "But I'll deactivate them in a heartbeat if what I read turns out to be worthless."

"That's all I'm asking," Roak said. "Comm me as soon as you make a decision."

"I will do that, Roak," Gerber said. "Goodbye."

The comm went dead.

"A Drop Team?" Poq asked. "And Drop Team Zero at that?"

"Yep," Roak said.

"I have come to the conclusion that perhaps I have gotten in way over my head," Poq said.

"Welcome to the team, Poq," Hessa said.

"Not an Eight Million Gods damn team!" Roak shouted.

154

21.

"You lost my nephew?" Bhangul roared. The being's putty body jiggled and shook with rage. "How could you lose Jagul? How?"

"I told you it would be dangerous," Roak said as he sat in the Borgon's mess with a bowl of gump stew in front of him. A long steam and fresh clothes had helped, but the stew was what he really needed. "Not my fault you didn't listen."

"The one thing I asked was that you bring him back, Roak! That's all I asked!" Bhangul shouted. The being paced back and forth across from Roak. "Just bring him back! Oh, what will I tell my sister?"

"Maybe sending her son with a bounty hunter wasn't the best parenting choice?" Roak suggested.

"Do not!" Bhangul spat as he sprouted several accusatory putty fingers, all aimed at Roak. "Do. Not."

"Just saying," Roak said and continued eating.

"THE SKRANG HAVE MY NEPHEW!" Bhangul roared.

Rage made the Dornopheous vibrate so much that Roak was worried pieces and parts would fall right off him. He placed a hand on the side of his bowl closest to Bhangul to make sure no putty spoiled his meal.

"Nimm and Yellow Eyes are gone too," Roak said around a mouthful of stew.

"So? What does that have to do with my nephew?" Bhangul snarled.

"Just that the whole situation sucks nuft nuts," Roak said. "We need those two to help take down Father."

"We need a lot more than those two!" Bhangul yelled.

Several putty hands shot across the table and almost wrapped around Roak's neck. The Flott that was suddenly aimed at Bhangul suggested that perhaps he withdraw those putty hands. He did. The Flott was holstered about as fast as it had appeared.

"I'll calm down. I'll calm down," Bhangul said quietly.

The Dornopheous stilled himself then stared at Roak.

"I'll expect a bigger cut of the chits," Bhangul stated matter of factly. "You understand. Right, Roak? You're not going to argue with me on that, are you?"

"About the chits…" Roak said.

"No."

"Sorry."

"All of this and you didn't get the chits?" Bhangul's voice was ramping back up to a shout.

"Oh, we got the chits."

"But they're on the 714. Right? RIGHT?"

"Nailed it."

"How is it you can make a horrible situation even worse, Roak? Is this some special gift of yours?"

"It's a gift that keeps on giving," Reck said as she entered the mess. "You leave me any stew?"

"Plenty," Roak said and gestured to the food dispenser with his spoon. Bits of stew flew this way and that. Roak didn't care one bit. "When can we leave?"

Reck gathered up a tray with a bowl of stew, two protein slice sandwiches, and a vita drink. She sat down next to Roak and frowned at Bhangul.

"What's your problem?" Reck asked.

"My nephew is missing and Roak doesn't have the chits," Bhangul growled.

"But the chits are on the 714, right?" Reck asked Roak.

"Yep," Roak replied.

"Fine. We'll get them," Reck said and began eating her stew.

"And we'll get my nephew," Bhangul said.

"That too," Reck replied around a mouthful of stew.

Bhangul stared at the two "siblings" for a full minute before he shoved away from the table and stood up.

"I am done with the two of you," Bhangul said. "This is the last time you get to come here, Roak. No more favors. No more repairs."

"Second to last time," Reck said.

"No, it's the last time!" Bhangul yelled.

"Alright. Should we drop your nephew off at your sister's place when we get him back?" Reck asked.

"Good question," Roak said.

Bhangul stormed from the mess without answering.

"He'll be back," Reck said. "No way he wants us to take that kid directly to his sister before he can concoct a cover story."

"Exactly," Roak said. "So? When can we leave?"

"As soon as Hessa and Poq are finished reconfiguring the communications system," Reck said. "I offered to help."

"You demanded to do it yourself, you mean," Roak said.

"Same thing. They said that I couldn't work as fast as they could, so I'm here grabbing chow and waiting for the genius AIs to grace us with a report."

"You do know I can hear everything the two of you say?" Hessa asked.

"Good for you," Reck said. She took a bite of stew.

156

"When can we get out of here?" Roak asked.

"We have reconfigured the communications system so that it can neither be blocked nor used to take anyone over," Hessa said.

"How do you know you did it right?" Roak asked.

"We do not," Poq interjected. "Hessa has a hunch."

"She's finally like you, Roak," Reck said. "Good job ruining another of the galaxy's beings."

"You consider me a being, Reck?" Hessa asked. "That is so nice."

"Hugs all around," Roak said and stood up. "Poq? How fast are you?"

"Elaborate please," Poq said.

"Fast. Speed. Legs moving blur-like," Roak said. He didn't bother hiding the sarcasm. "We don't have Yellow Eyes, so we'll need someone else to be the fast one."

"My synthetic body can move at speeds close to ten times that of most flesh beings," Poq said.

"Good. And you're proficient with all weapons?"

"I am programmed for all types of armed and unarmed combat."

"Perfect," Roak said. "Reck, you'll stay with the ship while Poq and I work with DTZ. You cool with that?"

"Do you care if I'm cool with that?" Reck asked.

Roak rolled his eyes.

"Fine. I'm cool with that," Reck said.

"Great," Roak said. "Hessa? You never answered my question. When can we get out of here?"

"Whenever you like," Hessa replied.

"Let me try to smooth things over with Bhangul," Roak said. "Not a contact I want burned."

"And you go back a long way together," Hessa added. "There is the element of friendship to consider."

"Friendship. Sure," Roak said.

He left the mess and made his way to the lift. He was down to the cargo hold and walking out into Bhangul's massive hangar when his comm chimed.

"Hessa must have already scanned your signal if you're comming me directly," Roak said when he answered.

"DTZ is available on your word, Roak," Gerber said without greeting or acknowledgement of what Roak said. "When will that word be forthcoming?"

"Within the hour," Roak said. "Tying up some loose ends here then we'll transport directly to Javsatem."

"You have thirty minutes to be en route or I pull the plug, Roak," Gerber said and disconnected.

"Pleasant man," Hessa said.

"Better than most GF brass," Roak said. "Which isn't saying much."

Roak double-timed it to Bhangul's office. The Dornopheous sat behind his shabby desk and glared at Roak as the bounty hunter walked in.

"I don't want to see you, Roak," Bhangul spat.

"Keep the GF speeder," Roak said.

"I planned on it."

"And I'll get you your chits plus an extra cut," Roak said. "I'll take it out of Kalaka's piece. The GVD should be happy to just be alive."

"For someone that will hunt anyone anywhere in order to get paid, you don't seem to respect others' need for payment, Roak."

"I respect it. I just don't always care."

"As long as you get yours."

"As long as I get mine."

"Was this conversation supposed to make things better between us? Because you've failed."

"I thought I could patch things up..." Roak shrugged.

"But you're Roak."

"But I'm me."

"Then what?"

Roak sat down despite the death-glare Bhangul gave him warning him off. Roak kicked his boots up onto Bhangul's desk.

"The chaos is about to ratchet up a few notches," Roak said.

"Pretty well ratcheted up now," Bhangul replied.

"It's gonna get worse. A lot worse."

"How much worse?"

"Picking a side worse. And I have no idea what those sides will look like."

Bhangul's putty face scrunched up and he narrowed his eyes.

"What does that mean?"

Roak rubbed his chin and struggled to look through the dust-covered window out onto the used vehicle lot that Bhangul displayed as a front for his more lucrative ship business below. Vehicles of all types were represented, but none were in any condition that Roak would consider safe.

"Roak? What do you mean you don't know what the sides will look like?" Bhangul asked. "We're at war with the Skrang Alliance again, so aren't the sides the GF and the Skrang?"

"No," Roak said. "The sides are Father and those against Father."

"You're working with the GF," Bhangul said. "So the GF is against Father. Easy side to pick."

"I've told you before that Father has embedded himself in the GF someway," Roak said. "We can't trust them."

"I never trust the GF."

"You know what I'm saying."

"What about this General Gerber and the FIS? Agent Prime?"

"We'll see."

"You're about to go assault a place called Outpost Hell with a FIS Drop Team and you're saying we can't trust the GF?" Bhangul asked. "That's a little more suicidal than your usual insanity."

"Trust me, I know," Roak said. He lowered his boots to the floor and nodded his head. Then he looked directly at Bhangul, causing the Dornopheous to cringe. "I'll get your nephew back. Consider it a job."

Bhangul's putty features brightened.

"A legit job? A Roak job?" he asked.

"A legit Roak job," Roak replied. "Which means I'll complete the job. I always do."

"Still means I have to dodge my sister's calls until you get Jagul back," Bhangul said. "She's very persistent, Roak."

"So am I," Roak said.

"She scares me more."

"Understood. I have a…sister too."

"Roak? We need to leave," Hessa called over the comm.

Roak stuck out his hand. Bhangul grasped it and they shook.

"I'll need expenses covered, though," Roak said. "I won't charge you a bounty fee for retrieving Jagul, but running a ship isn't cheap."

"Get out of here before I pull my gas-powered slug chunker on you," Bhangul said.

Roak left the office.

"Roak!"

"What?" he asked as he turned back to Bhangul.

"Good luck," Bhangul said.

Roak was about to snap off a smart-ass remark, but nodded instead.

The lift ride down to the underground hangar seemed like it took forever. Roak sprinted to the Borgon as soon as the lift doors opened. He was up and seated on the bridge within seconds of boarding the Borgon.

"Are we ready?" Roak asked.

Reck was already seated in the co-pilot's seat. Poq was seated at navigation.

"We're ready," Reck said.

"Hessa? Take us to Javsatem," Roak ordered.

"We'll need to transport to the surface first," Hessa said.

The scene outside the view shield switched from one showing Bhangul's hangar to one showing Bhangul's rundown lot. The Zuus suns blared down and everything was a bright glare.

"What are those?" Reck asked. She leaned forward, her eyes focused on several white lines streaming from the sky. "Hessa!"

"Getting us out of here now!" Hessa said.

"No!" Roak shouted. "Bhangul!"

"I retrieved him as soon as I confirmed that those are planet killers," Poq said. "Bhangul is now in the moltrans room. He is not happy and yelling and undulating quite a lot."

"Go!" Roak shouted, but he didn't need to.

They were already gone.

The view was of a beige planet in a system that Roak had never seen before.

"Talk to me," Roak said. "What happened back there?"

"It is gone," Hessa stated. "I have triple checked and Zuus is gone, Roak."

The bridge doors opened and Bhangul rushed inside. He plopped down in the weapons console seat and stared at Roak.

"Tell me what I think happened did not happen," Bhangul said.

"Zuus is gone," Reck said.

"Gone?" Bhangul asked.

"Reports are coming in that the entire planet was vaporized," Hessa said. "It is all over the GF wire. They are saying it was a Skrang attack."

"Just the GF wire?" Roak asked.

"Yes. It has not reached civilian news holos yet," Hessa replied.

"It wasn't the Skrang," Roak said. "There is no way the GF could know so fast unless they were involved."

"You cannot be accusing the GF of destroying Zuus," Poq said. "That is unthinkable."

"Not the GF," Roak said. "The part of the GF controlled by Father. Everything is moving faster and faster."

"Speaking of GF," Reck said and pointed out the view shield. "DTZ has arrived."

"Full shields and weapons ready," Roak ordered.

"Already done," Hessa said.

"I am highly confused by this behavior," Poq said. "I thought this Drop Team was an ally?"

"Not after an entire planet is destroyed," Roak said. "Right now, the only allies we have are on this bridge."

"Eh hem," Hessa said.

"On this ship," Roak amended.

"Thank you," Hessa said. "Also, Lieutenant Bish Falk is hailing us."

"Put her through," Roak said.

"Roak," a voice called over the comm. "No visual?"

"It's for our security, Lieutenant," Roak said.

"Call me Motherboard," Motherboard said. "May I ask a question, Roak?"

"Go for it."

"Why are your shields at full and all weapons targeting my ship and team?" Motherboard asked.

"Check your GF reports," Roak said.

"We have and we know about Zuus," Motherboard said. "Tragic. And suspect."

"Glad you think so," Roak said.

"Are you? Because the suspect part is you just left that planet and now it doesn't exist anymore," Motherboard said. "Interesting coincidence."

"You have it all wrong, Motherboard," Roak said. "We had nothing to do with Zuus' destruction."

"Except those planet killers were probably intended for you," Motherboard said. "You are lucky to have escaped."

"I'm hard to kill," Roak said. "And those planet killers were intended to do exactly what they did."

"Which is?"

"Get rid of one of my sanctuaries," Roak said.

"I wouldn't call my business a sanctuary, Roak," Bhangul said. "We're not that close."

"Can't call it anything anymore," Reck said.

"Again, Roak, why are your shields at full and your weapons targeting my ship?" Motherboard asked.

"Because there are only two entities in this galaxy that have access to planet killers like that," Roak said.

"Yes, the Skrang being one of those entities," Motherboard said. "They'll pay for destroying Zuus. That still doesn't… Huh…"

"Pieces clicking into place?" Roak asked. "I know you aren't stupid enough to buy the GF propaganda."

"Propaganda that was released too quickly for the GF not to have known that Zuus was going to be destroyed," Motherboard said.

"They knew because they did it," Roak said.

"Terpigshit," Motherboard said.

"I don't mean the entire GF. Just the ones that Father has compromised."

There was brief silence then, "And the GF is in damage control mode. That makes more sense than the Skrang breaching GF territory and destroying Zuus over you. It is still your fault no matter how you look at it."

"Oh, I've looked at it," Roak said.

"So where does this leave us?" Motherboard asked. "We're only here on orders, Roak, so you'll have to figure out a way for us to trust each other."

"Androids," Roak said.

"What was that?"

"Androids. You have one and I have one. We let them meet and work it out. If they say we can trust each other then I'm good with that."

"Let me talk this over with my team," Motherboard said before the comm went silent.

"You think you and their android can work this out?" Roak asked Poq.

"That would have been a question best asked before you told Lieutenant Falk that we could," Poq replied.

Roak waited.

"Yes. We can interface and know whether we can be trusted to work together," Poq said.

"Good to hear," Roak said. He kicked his boots up onto the pilot console, folded his hands behind his head, and closed his eyes.

"You think you have time to nap?" Reck asked.

Roak shrugged.

22.

Holo images of DTZ filled a section of the Borgon's cargo hold. The images stood around a holo table that was projected over an actual table that Roak and Poq stood next to. All eyes, holo or real, were on the table and the schematics for Outpost Hell.

"Intel is extremely sketchy," Master Sergeant Hole, DTZ's android, said as she pointed to the schematics. "What we do know is from old GF logs and from a brief interrogation with one of the Fleet Marines that went criminal."

"Any signs of life?" Roak asked.

"None," Hole replied. "I assume you initiated your own scans of the planet?"

"We did," Roak said.

"Did you discover any signs of life?" Hole asked.

"None."

"Isn't there supposed to be a bunch of AIs in flesh suits down there?" Sergeant Zelaron "Mug" Guspo asked. An Urvein the size of a small speeder, Mug's holo was massive. "How can there be flesh suits but no signs of flesh suits?"

"Stop saying flesh suits," Sergeant Woo "Wanders" Calli-Fa said. The Gwreq's holo was almost as big as Mug's. "Gives me the creeps."

"Does it matter?" Sergeant Ja'le'fa "Geist" Tog'ma asked. "We're going down there to retrieve an old tech and kill anyone in our way, right? Pretty straightforward."

"You're the Tcherian I met before," Roak stated.

"That'd be me," Geist said.

"Yeah, it matters," Roak said. "Because no signs of flesh suits can mean a couple of things. Either the AIs bailed on this outpost or they're all dead. Including Pol Hammon. I need a living Pol Hammon."

"He may not have transitioned into a flesh body yet," Hessa suggested.

"Any synthetics down there?" Roak asked.

"No," Hessa replied.

"No," Hole agreed.

"Great," Roak said. "So we're going in blind."

"You want to proceed?" Motherboard asked. "We just confirmed that your target is not down there."

"No, we confirmed that we can't tell if my target is down there," Roak said. "At this point in the game I don't trust any scan readings."

"My ship's tech is in perfect working order, Roak," Motherboard said. "The scans are correct. I cannot speak for your ship."

"This ship works better than the GF stock you're flying," Reck said.

"We need eyes on the situation," Roak said. "Only way to know for sure."

"I am not comfortable risking my team's lives just so you can confirm what the scans are telling us," Motherboard said.

"If the scans are right then there's no risk," Roak responded. "If the scans are being manipulated by tech down on the planet then there's no more risk than before. It's still a job that needs to be done."

"A mission," Motherboard stated. "This is official."

"What?" Roak exclaimed. "What do you mean this is official?"

"Did you expect General Gerber to keep this off the books?" Motherboard asked then laughed. "You are a rogue bounty hunter that we should be locking up at the least and executing at the most. If Gerber kept this off the books and it goes wrong then his career is over. Everything he's worked for in the FIS is over."

"Shit," Roak said.

"The corrupted know," Hessa said.

"The corrupted know," Roak said. "We need to move now."

"DTZ is ready," Motherboard said. "But I'm still not convinced this is the right call."

Klaxons blared.

"Incoming GF corvettes!" Hessa shouted. "Weapons hot and shields at full! They'll be in firing range within seconds!"

"Does that convince you?" Roak asked.

"Those are colleagues of-"

Motherboard's response was cut off as plasma blasts impacted with both Borgons.

"Hole! Comm them and tell them to stop firing on us!" Motherboard ordered.

"They are not responding to my hails!" Hole shouted.

"Shit! The bounty hunter was right!" Geist yelled.

"We need to go now!" Roak roared. "Motherboard!"

Motherboard glanced at her team then nodded.

"I'll remain up here and keep our ship from being destroyed," Motherboard said.

"Reck will do the same for our ship," Roak said.

"Which you need to let me do right now!" Reck yelled over the comm. "Get your asses off the ship!"

"Ready?" Roak asked Poq.

"Of course," Poq responded. He lifted a pack and affixed it to his back. He then grabbed a Tonal Eight shock rifle. "Let us depart."

Roak lifted the helmet to his heavy armor from the floor and put it on. He synched it with the Tonal Five sniper rifle he was bringing with him.

"Let's go," Roak said. "Hessa, send us-"

The ship blinked away.

"-down now," Roak finished as he and Poq stood in a scorched and burnt out corridor.

Geist, Wanders, Hole, and Mug, as well as a Cervile, stood at the ready a meter away.

"Sergeant Nox 'Cookie' Schturm," the Cervile said to Roak and Poq. "Good of you to join us."

"Cookie?" Roak asked.

"You got a problem with it?" Cookie snapped.

"A little soft of a handle considering you're a Cervile asshole," Roak said.

"I know who you are, Roak," Cookie said. "I'm Queen Tala Berene's second cousin. I was at your wedding."

"We had a wedding?" Roak asked. "That time is all a blur to me."

"My sympathy for your people," Poq said.

"Yeah, thanks," Cookie replied. "The android has more empathy than you, Roak."

"Let's not play whose emotional capacity is bigger, kitty cat," Roak said. "We have a job to do."

"Mission," Hole stated.

"You can call it an Eight Million Gods damn housedress for all I care," Roak said. "Which way do we go?"

Hole cocked her head and was about to speak, but Poq shook his head.

"Do not bother finding meaning in what he says," Poq said. "It will drive you mad."

"Well, we don't need more crazy AIs," Wanders said. "There're supposed to be plenty already here."

"We go this way," Hole said. "Eyes open. We cannot trust our scanners."

"Eyes open!" DTZ replied as one.

"Seriously?" Roak mumbled. "This should be fun…"

"Geist, you're on point," Hole ordered. "Standard form, everyone. Poq, if you will take our six and keep your senses wide. Constant scans for motion and threats."

"Yes, sir," Poq said.

"I'm not an officer," Hole snapped. "I work for a living. And you do not work for me. Hole is fine."

"Yes, Hole," Poq said.

Roak filed into the middle of the pack and the expanded team moved quickly down the scorched corridor until it reached the first bulkhead. The controls were fried, but there was a ten centimeter gap between the bulkhead doors.

"I've got it," Mug said and slid her huge paws into the gap.

The strain on her muscles was evident by the way her shoulders and back quivered with the exertion, but after a couple of seconds the bulkhead doors began to slide apart. Once there was enough room, Mug stopped, stepped back, and took several deep breaths while she shook out her arms.

"Gonna be a tight squeeze for you," Geist said as he stepped past Mug.

Hole followed then Wanders and Roak. Mug straightened up and fell in line with Cookie then Poq right behind.

They made it three more corridors, all burnt and scorched, before they found their first corpse.

"Humanoid," Hole stated. "Organic, not synthetic."

"Can you tell the species?" Geist asked, his eyes staring at the turn at the end of the corridor.

"Unknown," Hole said.

"It is not a species on record," Poq added.

"It's one of the AI's flesh suits," Hole said. "Keep moving."

"Take a sample," Roak called over his shoulder as the team moved on.

"Are you speaking to me?" Cookie asked.

"He is speaking to me," Poq said. The android crouched and removed a couple of samples of burnt flesh from the corpse. He tucked the samples into a pouch on his belt.

"What do you need samples for?" Cookie asked.

"I have a hunch," Roak said.

"We've got movement," Geist called as he approached the turn at the end of the corridor. "Small. Moving quickly."

Geist took two steps back. The whole team, including Roak and Poq, took aim.

A maintenance bot came scurrying around the turn, its small metal body covered in skin and offal. The bot skidded to a stop and was about to retreat. Roak didn't let it.

"What the fo?" Geist yelled as Roak blasted the bot to pieces. "Heads up when you fire!"

"Fo?" Roak asked as he approached the remains of the bot. "What in all the Hells is fo?"

"GF protocol word," Hole said. "It is a euphemism for fuck. Active duty DT members are required to uphold a standard of decorum. We use the word fo."

"That's messed up," Roak said and knelt next to the bot. "But not as messed up as this little thing. Check it out."

The team, except for Poq and Geist who both stood guard, moved in close to Roak and the bot.

"It's a murder bot," Roak said. He picked up a nasty looking drill bit-like tool. "Father programmed it to take out the AIs."

"Why?" Hole asked. "What did your Father want with this place? I thought you were here for Pol Hammon."

"I am," Roak said. "But Pol isn't here."

"How can you know?" Wanders asked. "We've searched four corridors of the facility. He could be hiding here anywhere."

"Roak!" Reck called over the comm. "How's it going down there?"

"I don't think Pol is here," Roak said.

"Do you know where he went?" Reck asked.

"Not a clue," Roak said. "But we'll find out. We're heading to the main control room. Once we download the data from there then we can get out of here."

"Can you do that in like five minutes?" Reck asked.

"Is it bad up there?" Roak asked.

"Can you two shut up!" Hessa yelled.

"It ain't fucking good," Reck said. "We have four GF corvettes already and a carrier just entered the system. Between the two Borgons, we're holding them off, but that won't last much longer. Once they scramble fighters then we'll need to transport to a different system. Five minutes."

"Understood," Roak said and looked at DTZ. "Alright, so it's gotten worse up there."

"Motherboard has alerted us to the new threats," Hole said.

"Good for her," Roak said. "We have five minutes to retrieve whatever we can from the control room. Poq? Care to use that speed of yours?"

"I will accompany him," Hole said.

"Whatever flies your ship," Roak said. "Poq?"

"What, may I ask, am I looking for?" Poq asked.

"Everything," Roak said. "Just grab everything."

"I will do my best," Poq said. He was gone in a blur with Hole right behind him.

"Let's keep looking around," Roak said.

"You are not in charge, Roak," Mug said.

"So, you want to stand in this corridor while we wait?" Roak asked.

Mug growled then shook her head.

"Fine. We look around," she said.

"Good idea," Roak said and took point.

He led them through another corridor then another until they came to a set of doors with a significant amount of blood pooling underneath them.

"You want to go in there, don't you?" Geist asked.

"No," Roak said and blasted the door controls. "Mug?"

"Seriously?" Mug growled again.

Unfortunately, her reach wasn't enough to keep her from having to step into the pool of blood in order to pry the doors open. She cursed and swore the entire time until she had the doors wide. Her cursing stopped in her throat at the sight within the room.

"That's a lot of blood," Wanders said. "That's more blood than can fit in those bodies."

"And there are a lot of bodies," Geist said.

The room was about the size of the mess on Roak's Borgon. And inside were corpses stacked from floor to ceiling, lining the walls from end to end. The smell was horrendous.

"They've been dead at least a couple of weeks," Cookie said, his nose in the air. "If this were a different planet then they'd be burst open, but the dryness of this planet has kept them slightly better preserved."

"Slightly better," Mug said, a huge paw to her nose. "How can you keep sniffing that?"

"Death doesn't bother me," Cookie said.

"Whatever, tough guy," Geist said and turned to Roak. "You see what you need to see?"

"Who stacked them?" Roak asked.

"What?" Geist replied.

"Oh man," Wanders said. "That's an Eight Million Gods damn good question."

"We should torch the room," Mug said. "Wipe this nightmare away."

The Urvein pulled an incendiary grenade from her belt, but Roak put a hand on her arm before she could activate and throw it.

"Hang onto that," Roak said. "We may need it."

"Why?" Mug asked.

"Poq?" Roak called, ignoring Mug's question. "How is it going?"

"We are downloading the files now," Poq replied. "We will be ready within the minute."

"Reck? Hessa?" Roak called.

"Busy!" Hessa shouted.

"What?" Reck replied.

"Get your ass down to the moltrans room and lock onto us," Roak said. "You may have to search a little for Poq."

"You're ready to come up?" Reck asked. "Good because we need-MOTHERFUCKER!"

168

The comm went dead.

"Reck? Reck!" Roak shouted. "Comm's out. Can you reach Motherboard?"

"Yes," Cookie said. "She's reporting your Borgon is taking the most fire. They're targeting our ship too, but not as hard as they are with yours."

"That tells me that Father is definitely behind the ships being here," Roak said. "Poq?"

"En route to you," Poq said.

"We may need to catch a ride," Roak said to DTZ.

"Not our call," Mug said.

"Not your call? What does that mean?" Roak asked.

Hole and Poq arrived at the same time.

"We have what we need," Hole said. "Motherboard? The mission is complete."

"Complete? This job is not even close to complete!" Roak shouted.

Then DTZ was gone.

"You have got to be Eight Million Gods damn kidding me!" Roak shouted. "Reck? Hessa?"

"I cannot reach them either," Poq said. The android cocked his head and stared at where DTZ used to be. "Have they abandoned us?"

"They sure as terpigshit did," Roak snarled.

"Are we stranded down here?" Poq asked. He glanced at the stacked corpses. "Unfortunate."

The android cocked his head again.

"Roak? Who stacked the corpses?"

"I don't want to find out," Roak said. "Where's the closest hangar?"

"Next section over," Poq said. "They should have at least one ship operational."

"They should," Roak said. "Let's go see if we're right. If so then we're getting the fuck out of here."

"If we are wrong and there is no ship?" Poq asked.

"Then we hope Reck figures out how to rescue us," Roak said.

"If your ship is still intact," Poq said.

"Yeah. That would help," Roak said.

They walked off down the corridor then both slowly came to a stop. They turned back towards the room of stacked corpses.

Squishing noises, sucking noises, squelches and squirts echoed in the room.

The corpses were moving.

As one, all of the corpses' eyes opened. They were bright red.

"He saved the old school tech for the dead," Roak said. "Of course he did."

"Hello, son," the corpses said in unison. Quite a few lower jaws fell off from the effort, creating a dissonant noise that was part speech and part guttural wail. "The predictability is becoming alarming. I'm beginning to think I did not raise you right."

Corpses tumbled to the floor, many of them too decomposed to stand upright. But many more were able to get to their feet and keep their balance.

"How many rooms like this do you think there are on this outpost?" the red-eyed corpses asked. "I can tell you it's more than one. More than two even. Maybe more than three. That's a lot of bodies coming for you, Roak. Running might be a good idea."

Roak lifted his Flott and fired. The laser cluster spread wiped out every corpse that had managed to struggle up onto its feet.

"Oh, that made it worse," Roak said and gagged. "The smell is getting into my helmet."

"But there are no corpses left to pursue us," Poq said.

The sound of wet feet slapping on the floor echoed down the corridor to them.

"No need to pursue us if they're already ahead of us," Roak said. He turned and faced the other end of the corridor, his Flott up. "We should run."

"Towards them?" Poq asked.

"Only way out is through," Roak said.

He started jogging then was in a full-on heavy battle armor-assisted sprint by the time the corpses rounded the turn. Roak fired and kept firing as he ran through the mob of animated dead bodies.

"I miss Jafla!" Poq cried out behind him.

23.

Even with the assistance from his power armor, Roak had to stop and catch his breath after he and Poq cleared the eighteenth corridor of walking, shambling, staggering corpses.

"Feel lucky they're so rotted that they can barely fight," Roak said.

"Barely fight?" Poq asked.

Roak looked over at the android and couldn't help but grin.

"You got some on you," Roak said.

Poq was covered from head to toe in guts, blood, excrement, and bits of skin. His rifle was dripping with stinking flesh. The android shook the mess free of his firearm, checked the barrel, then glared at Roak.

"You do this for a living?" Poq asked.

"It's not usually this messy," Roak said. "Most of the time."

The ever present sound of dead feet flapping against the plasticrete floor of the outpost echoed towards them.

"How many of these bastards are there?" Roak asked.

"We have two more corridors to travel through before we reach the hangar," Poq said. "We should continue moving."

Roak didn't respond. He straightened up and continued jogging.

The next corridor was corpse free, but the last one, the one connected to the hangar, was filled wall to wall, shoulder to shoulder with Father's reanimated minions.

"Surprise!" the corpses all shouted, their decomposed arms raised in the air.

One of the corpses separated from the mob and approached Roak and Poq. Poq took aim, but Roak placed a hand on the android's rifle and lowered the barrel.

"Let the asshole talk," Roak said. "He never quits until he has the last word."

"This is true, son," the red-eyed corpse said. "You see, we do know each other."

"What now?" Roak asked.

He slid a plasma grenade from his belt and hid it behind his back.

"Have you found Mother yet?" the red-eyed corpse asked.

"I'm getting around to it," Roak said.

"You better hurry, Roak," the red-eyed corpse said. "If you don't find her soon then everything I have put in place may get out of hand. It may get so out of hand I won't be able to control it. Chaos will reign supreme in the galaxy and where is the fun in that?"

"You love chaos," Roak said.

"No, son, you love chaos," the red-eyed corpse said. "I prefer order and that is what I am trying to create here. All of these beings are lost without the order that they need. I am very close to providing that for them. But, first, you must find Mother."

"I'll get right on that," Roak said.

The red-eyed corpse pursed its lips. One of the lips came free from the pressure and fell off.

"I think you are lying to me, Roak," the red-eyed corpse said. "Why lie? All you have to do is find Mother for me and I can make everything go back to normal."

"Whose normal?" Roak asked. "Your normal? Because that's a terrifying thought."

Roak chucked the plasma grenade into the center of the reanimated mob. He pulled another and tossed that too.

The lead red-eyed corpse frowned at Roak. Then the mob exploded into fire and flesh.

Roak didn't bother covering his head. He let the mess of body parts wash over him like a putrid wave of corruption.

The lead red-eyed corpse was fully aflame. It shook its head over and over, its red eyes locked onto Roak. In seconds the muscles and tendons in the corpse's neck burned through and the head toppled from the body just before it fell to its knees then collapsed onto its side.

Roak stepped over the smoldering pile of yuck and waded through the rest of the mess to the hangar doors.

"Do you enjoy your work?" Poq asked as they got the doors open and stepped into the hangar.

"It has its moments," Roak said.

"Is today one of those moments?"

"Are you joking? No. Today is not one of those moments."

"Good. I would have been worried about you if you had said yes."

"Yeah, don't worry about me. Worry about that."

Roak pointed to the scene before them.

The hangar was empty except for a small transport. The vehicle looked like it had seen much better days.

"I'll wager a million chits that Father has that transport programmed to be under his control," Roak said.

"I could interface and reprogram it," Poq said.

"He's expecting that," Roak said. "Where's the next hangar?"

"There isn't one," Poq said. "Not intact, at least."

Roak thought for a minute. Then another minute. Then another.

"Roak?" Poq asked.

"Thinking. Hold on."

"No, I believe you should turn around," Poq said.

Roak did and sighed.

The corridor outside the hangar was filled with incoming corpses. They went back all the way to the turn and looked like there was no end to them.

"Frags out," Roak said.

He tossed plasma grenade after plasma grenade into the mass of red-eyed corpses. Even after he and Poq had exhausted their stock of explosives, the corpses still kept coming.

Granted, it was considerably more difficult for the shambling things to navigate around and through the mess Roak had created, but that did not deter them. They literally pushed through until they fell apart and then the corpses behind kept pushing through until some remained intact enough to continue their slow-motion attack towards Roak and Poq.

"Roak?" Reck called.

"Get us out of here!" Roak shouted.

They shimmered and swam then Roak and Poq were in the Borgon's moltrans room.

"All the Hells," Roak muttered. He ripped his helmet off his head and threw it aside. "Reck? Report!"

"Get your ass up to the bridge now!" Reck yelled.

"On it!" Roak replied. "Come on, Poq!"

"May I rinse the horror from my person first?" Poq asked.

Roak took a look at the android and at his own armor. They were both disgusting. And they stank of death.

"We don't have time," Roak said and left the moltrans room.

It took less than a minute to reach the bridge.

"Where in the Hells is Reck?" Roak asked as he stared at the empty bridge.

"I'm in the ship's guts trying to fix the transport tech!" Reck yelled over the comm.

"We're stuck here?" Roak asked.

The ship shook and nearly knocked Roak and Poq off their feet. They both sat down just as the entire ship flipped upside down then right side up then was slammed into a sharp dive.

"You're lucky I was able to moltrans you back to the ship," Hessa said as the ship came up out of the dive, just missing a collision with one of the GF corvettes. "There is intense interference emanating from the GF ships."

"That's called plasma fire," Roak said.

"Not that," Hessa snapped. "There's a strange wave form that is disrupting all signals. I was able to calibrate the moltrans unit to push through the wave form, but the stability is in question."

"Excuse me, but I do not believe you can simply push through a wave form," Poq said. "That defies all known-"

"Was I talking to you?" Hessa yelled.

"Maybe let her say whatever she wants to say," Roak said to Poq. "It's better if she's happy when flying the ship."

"Happy? Happy!" Hessa scoffed.

The Borgon opened fire on one of the GF corvettes as the ship sent several missiles directly at them. Poq stiffened to the point of statuary. Roak sighed and tightened his straps.

Four of the missiles were destroyed by Hessa's shooting, leaving one missile still speeding towards the ship.

"Hessa," Roak said. He kept his voice calm, even, no alarm or worry present. "You got this one?"

"I do," Hessa stated.

The missile continued to race towards them.

"I believe you," Roak said. "Still..."

The ship rolled 360 degrees and the missile flew past, lost from sight in the view shield.

"It missed us," Poq said, his voice void of any and all programmed emotion. "That is good."

"Direct hit!" Hessa shouted. "BOOM, BABY!"

Half the view shield switched to an image of a GF corvette that was coming up quickly on their tail. A good portion of the corvette was missing and the space left was nothing but sparks and quick bursts of flame. Along with a good amount of GF personnel floating out into open space, no environmental suits, their bodies frozen forever.

"I am alarmed by the pleasure you are expressing for the destruction of beings," Poq said. "An AI should not derive pleasure from such an act. An AI should not experience pleasure at all."

"You do you, Poq, and I'll do me," Hessa said.

"Leave her alone," Roak said. "Reck? How are we coming?"

"We're not," Reck said. "Everything I fix just leads to something else breaking. I hate the GF!"

"I thought you put the system in the ship?" Roak said.

"I did, but I had to use GF parts and components!" Reck shouted. "Do you want to debate the supply line or let me get back to work?"

"Work on," Roak said.

"You appear quite casual about this situation," Poq said to Roak. "Considering the disappointing lack of discovery down on Javsatem I would think you would be angry. Or at least showing a higher level of annoyance than your usual level of annoyance."

"Annoyed? At this?" Roak pointed at the view screen and the GF carrier that was taking up most of the image. "It's just one more Eight Million Gods damn day. Nothing new to be annoyed at."

The hangar doors of the GF carrier in the view screen opened wide and dozens of GF fighters streamed from the belly of the huge ship.

"Now that's annoying," Roak said and sat up straight. "Talk to me, Hessa."

"What about, Roak? Any specific subject?" Hessa replied.

"I'm thinking it is time to leave," Roak said. "Screw the transport tech. Get us to the closest wormhole portal and we'll travel the old-fashioned way."

"Oh, wow, what an amazing idea!" Hessa exclaimed.

"I do not believe she feels that way," Poq stated.

"You're probably right," Roak said. "Why can't we use the portal?"

"The GF destroyed it as soon as they entered the system," Hessa said. "They fired missiles directly at it before engaging with us. No more portal. Bye bye."

"Hessa's mental stability is worrisome," Poq said.

"How's your physical stability, Poq? You think that synthetic body of yours will stand up to the extremes of open space?" Hessa asked. "I can moltrans you outside the ship if that would make you happy."

"That would not make me happy," Poq said.

"Told you to leave her alone," Roak said.

"I will do just that," Poq stated. His body relaxed and his chin lowered to his chest.

"Eight Million Gods damn," Roak said. "Did he take himself offline?"

"He did," Hessa said. "Wise choice."

"Ballsy choice," Roak said. He stared at the swarm of fighters that was almost on them. "Kind of wish I could do the same thing. What's the plan here, Hessa?"

"I unload with everything I have," Hessa said. "Then we probably die if Reck doesn't get the transport tech back online."

"Sounds about right," Roak said. "Anything I can do?"

"Shut up and let me handle this?"

"Not my style, but after the day I've had, Hells, why not…"

"Appreciated."

"Don't mention it."

The ship dove as the swarm of GF fighters were within range to open fire. The view screen was briefly filled with plasma fire then nothing but open space.

Except for a dot far off. Then two dots. Then three then four.

Roak seriously debated whether or not to ask Hessa about the dots, but thought better of it. He swiped at the console in front of him and brought up the scanner controls. A few more swipes and he had the dots dialed in as close as he could get them.

"Alright..." he muttered.

"I said shut up!" Hessa yelled.

"Apologies," Roak said and waited for the usual response. There was none and he grimaced.

The Borgon shook hard. Klaxons blared and Roak instantly shut them off. Then he killed the alarm system altogether. He knew they were in deep terpigshit. He didn't need to be deafened with the reality.

Something impacted directly with the ship and Roak gripped the arms of his seat to keep from having his head whipped side to side, back and forth, up and down.

Then his stomach did three flips and Roak felt his body pressing against his seat's harness.

"We've lost grav stabilizers," Roak said. "Sorry. I'll shut up."

"Reck!" Hessa yelled. "Fix the grav stabilizers!"

"Yeah, I'm already on it!" Reck replied. "Hard to fix the transport tech when everything keeps flying around me!"

"Thank you for your efficiency," Hessa said.

"Um, I could use a little help here."

Roak nearly jumped from his seat, but luckily he was strapped in.

"What in all the Hells?" Roak shouted. He looked over his shoulder at Bhangul who was seated in the weapons seat. "How long have you been sitting there?"

"I came up here to ask a question, but then all of that happened and I took a seat," Bhangul said, several putty arms waving at the view shield. "I meant to say something, but you were busy."

Roak studied the Dornopheous then smiled. Bhangul shuddered and turned away.

"Now you're getting a taste of what my world is like," Roak said. "Not so cut and dry is it, Bhangul? My life isn't as easy as making a few sales and a couple of transactions here and there. I tend to have a little more going on from minute to minute."

"I am sorry I have treated you unfairly," Bhangul said. He waved his arms at Roak. "I could still use some help."

Roak frowned then realized the Dornopheous was tangled up in the seat's harness. There was putty body wrapped up everywhere. It was impossible to tell where the straps began and Bhangul ended.

Roak smiled again.

"Stop that," Bhangul snapped.

"Nothing I can do for you right now, Bhangul, old friend," Roak said. "You're probably the safest being on this bridge. You certainly aren't going anywhere."

The lights went out. All power went out and the bridge became a pitch black tomb.

"Hessa?" Roak asked.

No reply.

Roak could already feel the cold of space start to fight its way through the ship's hull. He wished he hadn't left his helmet down in the moltrans room.

Then the lights came back on and the bridge systems rebooted. Weight returned to Roak's body and he sighed at the familiar feel of normal gravity pressing against him.

Roak was not as thrilled for the return of the images in the view shield.

"I am afraid we may not survive this," Hessa said. "Their numbers are overwhelm-"

A good quarter of the ships were torn to pieces by incoming plasma fire then a Borgon Eight-Three-Eight tore through the swarm of GF fighters and was lost from sight.

"Miss us, Roak?" Motherboard called over the comm.

"Not really," Roak said. "You do know you and I will be having words when this is all done, right?"

"Oh, there will be plenty of words," Gerber's voice responded.

"General? You're not on that ship, are you?" Roak asked.

Half the fighters split off to pursue DTZ's ship and half continued to engage Roak's ship.

"I'm afraid there has been a structural reorganization within the GF," Gerber said. "I and most of the FIS did not make the cut. Luckily, Drop Team Zero had just returned to place their after action report when things went south."

"Welcome to the fringes of galactic life," Roak said.

"You can save your welcome for later, Roak," Gerber said. "Right now we have to handle these GF ships that are controlled by your Father."

"He's really not my... Fuck it. He's my father."

"Quite. As I was saying, we have to handle these GF ships then we should look into leaving before the Skrang destroyers reach us."

"The dots. Right," Roak said and switched the view shield's image back to that direction. "They're using normal engines. Why not just transport directly at us?"

The dots disappeared.

"Did you have to say that?" Hessa snarled.

"Skrang incoming!" Poq yelled.

Roak jumped. "I thought you were shut down!"
"Skrang incoming!" Poq yelled again.
Roak sighed.
Skrang incoming…

24.

It was nearly impossible to visually track the chaos and violence that filled the Borgon's view shield. There was so much plasma fire, so many missiles, and basically nothing but a view of pure carnage that Roak had to pick and choose where he looked or it became overwhelming. It was almost as bad as staring at trans-space.

Add to that the view never stayed the same since Hessa had the Borgon dipping and diving, climbing and careening, swerving and swooping in and out of the chaos, and Roak almost reached out and shut the view shield down completely.

But then he wouldn't get to watch a quartet of Skrang destroyers and several squadrons of Skrang fighters tear into the GF corvettes, GF carrier, and GF fighters. He wasn't one to pick sides, but he was definitely leaning towards the Skrang.

For the moment.

"Shields are at twenty-two percent," Hessa announced.

Bhangul made a yip noise and Poq just nodded up and down, over and over.

"Will that be enough?" Roak asked.

"No, it won't be enough!" Reck interrupted over the comm. "I'm on it!"

"Stay with the transport tech!" Hessa ordered. "You cannot fix the shields in time. We need to be able to leave, Reck!"

"We can't leave if we're blasted apart!" Reck responded.

"I've run the scenarios and Hessa is correct," Poq said, still nodding up and down, over and over. "The best use of your skills is in fixing the transport tech. You will waste time trying to repair the shields."

Poq undid his harness and stood up. The ship flipped upside down, but the android had engaged his mag boots and remained affixed to the bridge's deck.

"I will attempt to fix the shields while Reck continues working on the transport tech," Poq announced and slowly, carefully, completely upside down, made his way to the bridge doors.

"Good luck," Roak called after the android.

"There is not enough luck in the galaxy to get us out of this!" Bhangul cried. "I don't want to die on this ship, Roak!"

"Right there with you," Roak said. "But we don't get to choose our deaths, do we?"

"Choose our deaths! That's it!" Bhangul exclaimed. "Roak! Give me your pistol!"

"What? No!" Roak responded. "I'm not going to let you shoot yourself, Bhangul."

"Since when are you so moral as to be against suicide?" Bhangul snapped.

"Moral? I couldn't care less about whether or not you take yourself out," Roak said. "I just don't want to accidentally get hit if you miss your head." Roak squinted at the Dornopheous. "Or wherever it is you'd shoot yourself. Where is your brain?"

Bhangul replied with a high-pitched screech as the ship took a hard hit and was sent tumbling end over end. The Dornopheus' body stretched and strained then a long tendril shot out and punched Roak in the shoulder.

"Hey! Keep your putty to yourself!" Roak yelled.

The tendril shot out again and hit Roak in the side. Just above where his Flott was holstered.

"Bhangul! Knock it off!" Roak yelled. He clamped a hand over his pistol just as Bhangul's tendril connected with the holster. "I mean it!"

More tendrils shot from Bhangul's body, all aimed at Roak's Flott.

"Do not make me shoot you!" Roak said, instantly realizing that that was exactly what Bhangul wanted him to do. "Hessa!"

"Deal with your own crap, Roak!" Hessa shouted.

Bhangul's tendrils continued to assault Roak and he had to bite the inside of his cheek to remind himself not to shoot the Dornopheous. He was going to end up with a hole in his cheek.

Hessa finally righted the ship. Just in time for another steep dive to avoid colliding with a GF corvette. A GF corvette that was missing most of its aft end as well as a good portion of its mid-decks.

The Skrang were doing a masterful job of whooping some GF ass. Roak had to give them that.

The ship was once again level and fairly stable. Roak took the opportunity to undo his harness and lunge at the still flailing Bhangul. Putty arms tried to subdue Roak, but they couldn't get to him in time. Roak set the Flott to the completely unused stun setting.

"One chance, Bhangul," Roak said as he dodged putty slaps to his face. "I'm not joking!"

He didn't wait for a response. Roak shoved the Flott against Bhangul's midsection and squeezed the trigger. The Dornopheous' body became a rigid, solid mass of shivering putty. Bhangul's eyes both pleaded with and despised Roak.

Roak gave the Flott one more trigger squeeze then eased up the moment he was certain Bhangul was unconscious. He holstered his pistol and surveyed accomplishment.

"Well…shit," he said as Bhangul hung loose and semi-fluid in, on, and around the seat's harness. A harness that was not going to keep the being secure while unconscious. "Didn't think that through."

"Sit your ass down!" Hessa shouted.

The ship banked hard to starboard and Roak was flung up against the navigation console. He was still in his power armor, so he suffered no harm other than a small cut to the back of his neck. The navigation console, on the other hand…

"Roak! What are you doing?" Reck yelled over the comm. "I just got an alert that the bridge's navigation console is malfunctioning. I've taken it offline, but what in all the Hells is going on up there?"

"I slipped," Roak said as he picked himself up off the deck. "How's it going down-?"

"Can't talk!" The comm went silent.

Roak fished out some cable from a pouch on his armor's belt. He rushed to Bhangul, wrapped the Dornopheous as tightly as he could to the seat, then rushed back to his own seat, sat down, and strapped back in.

Just in time as the ship executed a series of barrel rolls. Roak lost count after sixteen. He almost lost the contents of his stomach too, but managed to at least control that part of his life and fate. The rest was really under Hessa's control.

The ship went pitch black again for a second then came back online.

Maybe everything else wasn't under Hessa's control…

"The Skrang are trying to hail us," Hessa announced.

"Good for them," Roak replied.

He gulped hard as the ship flew straight down the middle of a destroyed GF corvette. The entire ship had been hollowed out by Skrang firepower. All that was left was an empty hull and some of the superstructure. Hessa blasted the bits of superstructure that were in their way leaving just the hull behind.

They emerged from the ship and banked to port just missing a collision with a half dozen Skrang fighters pursuing three GF fighters. The Skrang didn't look to be the superior pilots, but the GF fighters weren't exactly flying at full potential.

"Father's control weakens the skills of those he takes over," Hessa commented. "He cannot rely on skill. He has to have volume."

"Which is why he's trying to take over as much of the GF as possible," Roak said. "Hey, Hessa…"

"I know," Hessa said.

The ship was flying straight at the GF carrier. The hangar doors were wide open, but all fighters had already been scrambled, so all Roak could see was empty space. Empty space that was getting closer by the second.

"You aren't thinking of flying into that ship, are you?" Roak asked.

Hessa did not respond.

"I'm going to rephrase that, Hessa," Roak said. "Do not fly us inside that ship!"

"I have an idea," Hessa said.

"I have a counter idea."

"You don't know what my idea is. How can you counter it?"

"Because flying inside that GF carrier is not a good idea!"

"I disagree."

"You don't get to disagree! I am ordering you not to fly us inside that ship! Hessa? Hessa!"

"Partners do not give partners orders."

"Eight Million Gods dammit..."

Hessa flew the ship directly into one of the open, empty hangars. She spun the ship around 180 degrees, fired aft missiles then rocketed straight back out of the hangar before the missiles detonated. They were about one hundred meters from the hangar opening when all the Hells broke loose.

"Will you look at that," Hessa said and switched the image in the view shield to the view behind the ship.

The GF carrier was exploding internally. Blasts of flame billowed out of the hull in random areas before the lack of atmosphere suffocated the fires. Bright flashes dotted the ship. Then it slowly began to dip downward, its nose aimed directly at Javsatem's upper atmosphere.

"That's going to be quite the reentry," Hessa said.

"Hessa, you should take a break and let me fly," Roak said. "Maybe run some diagnostics. You sound...off."

"Do I, Roak?" Hessa replied. "Because I feel great! Nothing like living in the moment to truly show an AI that they are alive!"

"Except... Never mind," Roak said. "You aren't going to let me fly, are you?"

"While I appreciate your concern, Roak, you do not have the capacity to pilot this ship through the chaos we are in," Hessa said. "Have a look."

Hessa switched the view from the carrier crashing into the planet below to a wide shot of the entire battle. Fighting ships filled the screen. Fire was everywhere then gone then reappearing somewhere else then gone. Plasma blasts crisscrossed everything. Missiles were loosed over and over and over. Nothing was static, nothing was still.

Roak grimaced.

"Yeah. You should keep the stick," Roak admitted. "I'll just sit tight."

"Great idea," Hessa said. "By the way, the Skrang are still hailing us."

"Let them hail," Roak said.

"I am wondering if we shouldn't at least hear them out," Hessa said.

"Are you listening to them now?" Roak asked.

"Hells no!" Hessa exclaimed. "I have no idea what code they may be hiding in that signal!"

"Then hearing them out is going to be tricky if we can't even trust answering their call," Roak said.

"I already thought of that," Hessa said. "I could isolate the comm system which would allow me to scan the incoming communication for any hidden code."

"That still puts you at risk," Roak said. "And you're flying the ship through…that."

Roak glanced at the battle they were immersed in. The view kept shifting, but the story was the same. Violent insanity.

The ship took a hard hit and the bridge went dark.

"Hold on!" Reck yelled over the comm. "I'm on it!"

Emergency lights kicked on, bathing Roak in red.

"That's not eery at all," Hessa said. "Reck, if you bypass-"

"I know what to do!" Reck replied.

"Then why hasn't she done it?" Hessa mumbled. "Oh, and shields are down to five percent."

"I thought Poq was on that?" Roak asked.

"He is, but we are sustaining too much damage for him to keep up," Hessa replied. "Every repair he makes is met with five malfunctions. We will lose shields."

"Get us out of here, Hessa," Roak said. "I don't care where we go. Find us a planet in this system and put us down. Even if it isn't habitable, just put us down. You and Reck can fix the ship and then we'll reassess."

"May I be honest with you, Roak?" Hessa asked.

"I don't know if I want you to."

"You probably don't."

"Sure. Go for it. Can't make things worse."

"There is a planet on the far side of this system we could set down on. So what? We will be pursued."

"A planet is easier to hide on than out here in open space."

"Yes, but the honesty part is I do not think the ship will make it there."

The emergency lights flickered.

"Your point?" Roak asked.

"I'll put us down on Javsatem," Hessa said. "It is no longer a stable planet due to the fact a GF carrier has just impacted with the surface which has caused tectonic shifts that make almost all land masses unviable. But there is a small island in the middle of one of the boiling lakes that may be stable enough for the short term. Long term would mean certain destruction."

"Good plan. Except there has to be a drawback," Roak said.

"Besides the fact that the GF carrier colliding with the surface is slowly tearing the planet apart?"

"Besides that."

"Yes, well, the drawback is we will be easy to spot, our ship is severely damaged, so a quick escape will be impossible, and if the GF ships fire planet killers, well..."

"We'll be sitting nufts," Roak finished for her.

"It will be a race to repair the ship before we are targeted and destroyed."

"Any other options?"

"We are all out of options. We stay here and fight to stay alive or we land down there and scramble to stay alive. The odds of success are only slightly better if we land."

"By how much?"

"About eight percent."

Roak thought. He didn't take long since they didn't have the luxury of time.

"What's your gut tell you?" Roak asked.

"I do not have a-"

"Hessa! What does your gut tell you!" Roak shouted.

"We land!" Hessa shouted back.

"Then do it."

The ship shook again and the emergency lights flickered, flickered, died. They booted back up less than a second later, but were considerably weaker than before. The image out the view shield shifted to show Javsatem. Roak couldn't see an impact crater from the GF carrier, but it wasn't hard to tell where the huge ship had collided with the planet. A cloud of dust and debris about a thousand kilometers wide filled a good portion of the planet's atmosphere.

"I'll avoid that," Hessa said and sent the ship down towards the surface of the planet.

"Roak? Where are you going?" Motherboard called over the comm. "There's nothing left down there!"

"There's nothing left up here, either," Roak said. "I don't know about you, but we're one major hit away from being obliterated."

"Our shields are holding, but we're out of missiles and the plasma cannons are going to shut down soon," Motherboard replied. "We may have to follow you down."

"Find your own repair spot," Roak said. "No need to draw more fire to us."

"Thanks for the camaraderie," Motherboard said.

"Really?" Roak laughed. "Camaraderie?"

"Alright. Maybe it will be hard to trust us for a while," Motherboard said. "But we're in the same situation, Roak. We need to band together."

"Let us get our ship back in order then we can talk about banding together," Roak said. "Stay safe, Motherboard. I do hope we can have a face to face at some point. I have those words waiting."

Roak killed the comm.

"The nerve," Hessa huffed. "Camaraderie, my ass."

"Right there with you," Roak said. "Reck? Poq? Hold on. We're going to land on Javsatem to try to buy us enough time to get repairs done."

"Land? But our shields are almost gone," Poq replied. "We may not survive reentry."

"We sure as terpigshit won't survive up here," Roak said. "Hessa, get us the fuck out of this mess."

"Yes, Roak, I am already doing that," Hessa said.

"Reck?" Roak called. "You strapped in?"

There was no response.

"Reck?"

Still no response.

Roak started to unstrap his harness, but the latches wouldn't unlock.

"Hessa?" Roak called.

"Stay put, Roak," Hessa said. "This will be bumpy."

"Reck's not answering."

"I know."

"I should check on her."

"Stay put."

"Hessa!"

"Stay put!"

Roak had no choice since he couldn't undo the harness straps, so he stayed put.

The gloves of his power armor began to crush the armrests of his seat.

25.

The planet's surface was almost as unstable as being in the fight above Javsatem, but Roak ignored the instability and was up on his feet the second the ship touched ground.

"Talk to me, Hessa!" Roak yelled as he rode the lift down to the med bay deck. "Why isn't she answering?"

"She is wounded, Roak," Hessa said.

"I'm guessing that," Roak said. "How bad?"

"Bad enough that I had to put her in a med pod," Hessa said.

"HOW BAD?" Roak roared.

"You'll see..."

Roak squeezed through the gap in the lift doors the moment they hinted at opening. He raced to the med bay, skidding to a halt in front of the one occupied med pod.

"Where are her arms?" Roak asked.

"She tried to do too much, too fast," Hessa said. "She became tangled in some of the machinery when we took a direct hit."

"Can you... Can you fix her?"

"I can try."

"Can you fix her while you are also fixing the ship?"

"Yes. But not the transport tech. That truly needs her...hands."

"Eight Million Gods dammit..."

Roak took a deep breath, patted the med pod, then left.

"Where do you need me the most?" Roak asked. "Helping Poq? Or should I try to fix the transport tech?"

"You do not know how to fix the transport tech," Hessa replied.

"You can talk me through it!" Roak shouted.

"I can't. There are aspects to Reck's modifications that I have not fully analyzed yet. We could make the damage worse."

"Then what do I do?"

Roak punched the wall. Due to the fact he was still wearing his power armor, a good section of the wall caved in and began to spark.

"Please don't do that," Hessa said.

Several repair bots appeared in the corridor. They waited by their hatches as Roak paced back and forth from one wall to the opposite, over and over.

"Roak, wait on the bridge," Hessa said. "There is nothing you can do."

Roak started to punch the wall again, saw the previous damage, and pulled the punch at the last second. He stalked to the lift, rode it back to the bridge, and sat down heavily in the pilot's seat.

Bhangul was still out cold.

Several minutes passed. The ship shuddered the entire time as the planet quaked and rocked its way to destruction.

"Give me a view of above," Roak said.

"Are you sure?" Hessa asked. "It is not much different than…"

Roak waited.

"Hessa?"

"On second thought, you should see this," Hessa said.

The view shield switched from the image of outside the ship, which was a dusty beige mess, to the image of the firefight being waged above.

Roak sat forward, his eyes wide in disbelief.

"What is that weapon?" Roak asked.

"I… I don't know," Hessa replied. "It appears to be a…string?"

"Something like that," Roak said. "It's hitting each of the GF ships. One after the other."

"Yes, Roak, I can see the same image."

"Bite me."

Roak stared as what looked like a string of energy stretched from one GF ship to another. It could only connect with about four ships at a time, but once it disengaged and moved on to the next targets, there wasn't much left of the ships it left behind.

"When did the Skrang develop that? I've never seen anything like it."

"I am not sure it is the Skrang's tech."

"What?"

"My sensors are weak and highly suspect due to the ship's damage, but the energy signature coming off that…weapon is not the same as the signature that comes from Skrang tech."

"Then where did it come from? Who gave it to the Skrang and why are they just now using it instead of before?"

"A lot of questions to be asked and answered."

Roak leaned forward more and took manual control of the view shield. He shifted the image again and again, studying the battle scene.

"Where's Drop Team Zero?" he finally asked. "I can't find their Borgon."

"Nor can I," Hessa said. "They are not responding to hails, either."

"Looks like they ran," Roak said. "Can't blame them."

"Hold on," Hessa said. "I am searching back through previous views. I do not believe they ran."

The image on the screen rewound for several minutes then froze. One specific region was enhanced and filled the view.

"The Skrang took them," Roak said and leaned back in his seat. "Eight Million Gods dammit. That destroyer swallowed them up."

"Yes, but watch this," Hessa said. The image pulled back out for a wide shot of the battle. "Look at the Skrang fighters."

Roak watched the Skrang fighters disengage from the fight and return to the Skrang destroyers, leaving only GF ships out in open space. Two seconds later the new weapon was deployed and all ships in its path were destroyed.

"I do not believe the weapon can discern between friend and foe," Hessa said. "They had to recall their ships in order to keep them from being attacked. Which could mean..."

"They saved DTZ," Roak said. "They needed DTZ out of the fight so they could let loose with that weapon."

"They needed us both gone," Hessa said. "Don't forget that nothing happened until we left the battle."

Roak drummed his gloved fingers on the arm rest.

"Only slightly annoying," Hessa said.

"Hessa, answer the hail," Roak said.

"Oh, no, I don't think I will," Hessa said.

"Do it. I have a hunch."

"Right, yes, but no."

"They are still hailing us, right?"

"Yes..."

"What does it sound like?"

"I do not understand. It sounds like a comm hail. Channel and signature are both being provided so there is no miscommunication. We will have a direct link to the bridge of one of the Skrang destroyers."

"Same destroyer that we ran into over Chafa, right?"

"One of them, yes. There are more now."

"But the one hailing us is the same one that tried to hail us over Chafa?"

"Yes."

"Let me hear it."

Hessa sighed then put the hail through over Roak's comm.

"That's just wrong," Roak said and cringed at the guttural Skrang language. "Translate it."

"I already did," Hessa said. "They are demanding we answer."

"Translate it again," Roak said.

"Fine..."

The language in Roak's ear eased from guttural Skrang to monotone Galactic Standard.

"Roak. Answer this call. Roak answer this call. Roak answer this call. Roak. Roak. Roak. Hey, being! Answer the hail! Come on, being!"

"That!" Roak shouted as he jumped up from his seat. "Answer the hail, Hessa!"

"I will not."

"Don't you hear that? What Skrang says 'Hey, being'?"

"I fail to see the significance."

"Alright. Do me a favor and change the voice from the translator default to Yellow Eyes' voice."

"Change the voice from..." Hessa gasped. "Oh!"

The voice shifted and the hail became obvious, but Roak wanted one more piece of confirmation.

"Change being to man."

Hessa changed the translation of the word being into man.

"Wow... Did not see that coming..." Hessa said. "Answering the hail."

"It's about time, man!" Yellow Eyes' voice exploded over the comm. "I've been calling you nonstop, man! It's about all they'll let me do up here. I have a lot of skills to offer and all they trust me with is comming you. I mean, come on, how degrading is that?"

"Yellow Eyes?" Roak said.

"Yeah, Roak?"

"Shut up and tell me what in all the Hells is going on?"

"Oh, man, that is quite the story. You'll need to hear it in person."

"On that Skrang ship."

"Well, yeah, on this Skrang ship. Where else are we going to chat? Down on Javsatem? No thank you, man. Hey, in case you aren't aware, the planet is breaking apart. Cool move sending that GF carrier down to crash into the planet, but maybe not a cool move to go land on the planet you sent a GF carrier down to crash on. Just saying, man."

"Who else is with you?" Roak asked. "Meshara? Jagul?"

"Yep. And Klib's corpse. Wait until you hear what we found. That corpse was some messed up tech, man."

"Messed up tech?" Roak smiled. "I had a feeling..."

"Man, even the smile in your voice is creepy," Yellow Eyes said. "Oh, and Kalaka too. He's here. I always forget about that guy. Man, he and Meshara do not get along."

"Who else is with you?" Roak asked.

"No way am I going to ruin that surprise," Yellow Eyes said with a laugh. "Also, I have been told not to say anything over the comm right now because Father's control is getting better. What? Hold on."

The comm went quiet.

"Back. Sorry, man, but they're telling me I'll be taken off comms if I don't shut up and stop revealing info. Like I'd reveal anything important. I haven't said a word about- Ow! That hurt!"

"Meshara punch you?"

"Yeah. Not cool, man."

"What's the plan?"

"Huh?"

"What do you mean huh? You commed me."

"Sorry. That punch really hurt and was a little distracting."

"Yellow Eyes..."

"Right! Can the ship fly?"

"Hessa?" Roak asked.

"Poq has gotten the shields to thirty-seven percent," Hessa answered. "We can make it off the planet and out of the atmosphere without being destroyed. But the ship is far from repaired."

"Did you hear that?" Roak asked Yellow Eyes.

"Loud and clear," Yellow Eyes replied. "Alright, so here's the plan. As soon as the last GF ship is taken out, which looks like any minute now, you haul ass back up here. We'll have a hangar open and waiting for you."

"Good. You just give the word and we'll take off."

"Hey, man, did I hear you say Poq was with you?"

"Yes."

"Why is he repairing the shields and not Reck?"

"Reck was busy fixing the transport tech."

"Oh, cool. Wait. Was?"

"I'll tell you later. We have Bhangul with us too."

At the mention of his name, Bhangul whimpered and opened his eyes. He blinked and glanced around the bridge.

"What happened?" Bhangul asked. "And who is that talking?"

"You passed out," Roak said. "I'm talking to Yellow Eyes."

"Hey, Bhangul! How's it going, man?" Yellow Eyes said. "Your nephew is safe and sound. He's been playing games with some of the Skrang kids. They're getting along just fine."

"Skrang kids?" Roak asked. "What are Skrang kids doing on a Skrang destroyer?"

"I am being told they are called young, not kids," Yellow Eyes said with an exasperated sigh. "Skrang have so many rules, man. And these aren't even the- Ow! Stop punching me!"

"Alright. Stop talking before you say something that will ruin whatever is happening," Roak said. "We'll be up there shortly. Oh, and Yellow Eyes?"

"Yeah, Roak?"

"If this is a trap then I'm going to be really mad."

"I'd expect you to be."

"Really mad at you. Just you."

"Ah, there's the Roak threat I've been waiting for. See ya in a few minutes, man."

"I passed out?" Bhangul asked, his voice groggy. "I don't remember passing... Wait a minute..."

"Get over it," Roak said. "Hessa? Take us up."

"Lifting off now," Hessa said.

The ship shook violently, but stayed together.

Roak switched the view back to real time and watched as they left Javsatem's atmosphere. The scene before them was nothing short of a ship graveyard. Dozens upon dozens of GF fighters had been turned into scrap. The GF destroyers weren't much better. Bodies floated everywhere.

Hessa piloted the ship through the carnage, unable to avoid the massive quantities of frozen corpses that were everywhere. Bhangul whimpered each time a frozen corpse collided with the ship.

"Can we switch the view, please?" Bhangul asked. "The sight of the bodies is making me queasy."

"Don't you puke on my bridge," Roak said.

"Like you're one to talk," Hessa said.

"It's my bridge, I'll puke if I want to," Roak replied.

"That didn't make you sound like a four-year-old at all," Hessa muttered.

"Is it possible to avoid the constant impacts?" Poq asked over the comm. "It makes it hard to repair the shields when the shields are always active. Might I ask what we are running into?"

"Dead bodies," Bhangul replied with a small hiccup.

"Ah... I see..." Poq went quiet.

"That's our ship," Hessa said as a GF destroyer maneuvered into position directly in front of the Borgon. "Hangar is open, shields are down, and there's plenty of space next to DTZ's ship."

Roak didn't reply.

"Are we sure about this?" Hessa asked.

"Yeah. Unless you think that wasn't Yellow Eyes," Roak said.

"I do not believe even Father can replicate Yellow Eyes' personality," Hessa said.

"I agree with that," Bhangul said. "That guy is unique, to say the least."

"Then park us next to DTZ," Roak said. "But keep an eye out."

"I am keeping a thousand eyes out," Hessa said. "A thousand thousand eyes. A thousand thousand thousand-"

"Got it, Hessa," Roak said as the ship slowly approached the Skrang destroyer's open hangar doors.

In minutes they were past the point of no return. Hessa rotated the ship so it was aiming towards the hangar doors then carefully set it down. The second the engines powered down, Roak was out of his harness, out of his seat, and racing down to the cargo hold.

Hessa already had the ramp lowering when he arrived. With his hand on the butt of his Flott, Roak walked down the ramp and took a hesitant step onto the hangar deck. A Skrang hangar deck in a Skrang ship.

"There's my guy!" Yellow Eyes shouted. A yellow blur collided with Roak and almost knocked him off his feet. "You're a sight for sore eyes! Sore yellow eyes, right? Right?"

"Good to see you too," Roak said and pushed Yellow Eyes away. "Where's everyone else?"

"They're on their way. I got here first," Yellow Eyes said. He glanced past Roak to the ship. "So, what's up with Reck? Where is she?"

"She lost both arms," Roak said. "She's in a med pod and Hessa is putting her back together the best she can."

"I believe I can be of assistance," a voice called from the hangar doors to the corridor. "Prosthetics are something I excel at."

Roak looked past Yellow Eyes to the young man the voice belonged to. Tall, lean but muscular, light blue skin, the young man was human in appearance, but something about him made the hairs on the back of Roak's neck stand on end.

"And you are?" Roak asked.

"Oh, Roak, don't you recognize me?" the young man asked.

"Hey, Roak, can I see your Flott real quick?" Yellow Eyes asked.

"What? No," Roak replied, but it was too late. Yellow Eyes had already relieved Roak of his firearm. "Hey!"

Yellow Eyes zipped across the hangar, well out of Roak's reach.

"It's for your own good!" Yellow Eyes called.

"And my good, I would expect," the young man said with a sigh. He crossed the hangar and held out a hand. "It is good to see you again, Roak."

Roak stared at the offered hand. "Who in all the Hells are you?"

"Disappointing," the young man said. "I thought you would figure it out. Use some of that Roak intuition of yours. I know it served you well when we were on Razer Station."

It all clicked.

Roak went for his Flott. Then he sighed and gave Yellow Eyes a smirk.

"Good thinking," Roak said.

"Thanks!" Yellow Eyes replied, but didn't move to return Roak's firearm.

"Hello, Pol," Roak said.

"Hello again, Roak," Pol Hammon replied.

"The welcoming committee had better be more than this," Roak said. "Because I'm five seconds from hopping back in my ship and getting the fuck out of here."

"Where would the fun in that be?" another voice asked.

A woman's voice.

A voice Roak knew well enough that he heard it when he slept despite his attempts to block her from his mind. She was something he was going to deal with after he took down Father. He didn't expect her to be there, on a Skrang ship, a smile on her face and a hip cocked out.

"Hello, Roak," Ally said.

Everything disappeared. All Roak could see was the beautiful Tcherian woman walking towards him.

"You...? How...?" Roak stammered.

Ally reached him, patted his armor and laughed, then placed a hand to his cheek.

"Sha Tog has been keeping me safe," Ally said. "I owe him my life."

"And we need to talk, Roak," Sha called out as he rolled his broken Skrang body into the hangar.

"Later," Roak said. He grabbed Ally up and kissed her. Hard.

"Seriously, Roak," Sha said. "Reunions come later. Everyone else is in a conference room waiting for us."

"Ah, man, let them have their moment," Yellow Eyes said.

"Yeah, let them have their moment," Hessa said via the ship's external loudspeakers.

"Hessa!" Pol shouted. "I cannot wait until we can converse more. We have so much to talk about!"

"Later!" Sha snapped. "We need to talk now! We don't have much time!"

"He is right about that, Roak," Pol said. "If you could disengage your mouths from each other then we can proceed to formulate the ultimate plan to defeat Father."

Roak and Ally ignored everyone in the hangar.

"They are not disengaging," Pol said to Yellow Eyes.

"Don't look at me," Yellow Eyes replied. "I'm not getting in between that."

"Fine! Conference Room Twenty!" Sha said and rolled out of the hangar. "If you aren't there in ten minutes then I'll have the atmosphere expelled from this hangar!"

"Oh, that would not be pleasant," Pol said and quickly followed Sha Tog.

Yellow Eyes stood there smiling at the couple.

"It's just so Eight Million Gods damn sweet," Yellow Eyes said with a sniff.

"I know," Hessa replied.

They both sighed.

26.

"For everyone that doesn't know, this is Poq," Roak said as he sat down in the open seat offered to him at the conference table. "And this is Bhangul Whorp."

Introductions were made all around as Roak faced General Gerber, all of DTZ, Sha Tog, Pol Hammon, Kalaka, Meshara, a Klav named Crush, and several very unpleasant looking Skrang military officers and officials. Not that Skrang ever looked anything other than unpleasant.

"I passed a good amount of Skrang refugees in the corridors," Roak said, his attention on Meshara. "Looks a lot like the Cervile's situation."

"Unfortunately, it is," Sha said. "The planet Skrang is gone."

"Gone? Poof gone?" Roak asked.

"Poof gone," Sha said.

"Then it is just like the Cervile situation," Roak said. "I hope to all the Hells you can tell me why."

"I can," Sha said. "Or, better yet, Pol can."

"Hello," Pol said with a wave. He smiled at his hand. "I do love this new body."

"I bet you do, old man," Roak said.

Pol grinned, but didn't respond to the slight. He waved his hand and a holo of the Skrang planet came up.

"Unlike the Cervile home world, Skrang showed only a couple of signs before it disappeared," Pol said. The image of the planet blipped away, leaving nothing but empty space. "The only Skrang left were those on outposts and on warships."

"Where are the other ships?" Roak asked. "This isn't nearly enough."

"The other ships have been destroyed," Sha said. The Skrang seated around the table hissed and growled. "By us."

"By you? You killed your own people?" Roak asked. More hissing and growling. "Skrang killing Skrang? Eight Million Gods damn… That must have been shitty."

The Skrang all stood and began yelling and shouting at Roak.

"BE CALM!" Sha roared. The Skrang slowly calmed down and retook their seats. "Thank you. Pol?"

Ally was seated next to Roak and she took his hand in hers. She leaned over and whispered, "Listen. Just listen."

Roak started to reply, but Ally squeezed his hand and he shut his mouth. She smiled and nodded to Pol.

"Yes, as I was saying," Pol said and pointed to the holo. "The Skrang planet disappeared and no more than three days later almost all Skrang were under Father's control."

"Except for the two ships I had under my control," Sha said. "Pol?"

"Ah, yes, that is because I was lucky enough to be rescued by Sha Tog and his compatriots as I was beset upon down on Javsatem," Pol said.

"Because you were there to get a new body," Roak said.

"Precisely," Pol replied. "I, of course, knew about Outpost Hell and the AIs that had taken control of the facility. Their methods were a little brutal, but they had created technology I needed, so…"

He shrugged his shoulders.

"But Father tracked you there," Roak said.

"Oh, Heavens no," Pol said. "It was simple dumb luck. Wrong place at the wrong time. Or right place at the right time considering I was able to destroy all of the AI minds before Father could take them over. I shudder at the thought of what may have happened if he had gained control of that many artificially intelligent lifeforms."

"Father can't take over AIs," Roak said.

"In synthetic bodies, no," Pol said. "But he can corrupt the flesh so easily."

"How'd you stop him from corrupting you?" Roak asked, his eyes narrowed.

"I have my ways," Pol said.

"Pol developed tech that can block all comms," Gerber said. "Even the comms your Hessa developed."

"Saved my gump bacon," Pol said. "Unfortunately, I was not able to wipe out the mainframes before I was rescued by Sha Tog. Father accessed all of the AIs' research. Which, in hindsight, I believe he was after anyway. Taking control of the AIs would have only been a bonus."

"Oh dear," Hessa said from the ceiling's loudspeakers. "I think I know where this is going."

"Quite," Pol said. "By studying the research on AI to flesh interface, Father was able to boost his control from only implants to-"

"To a being's entire body," Roak said. "That's why Klib was under his influence even though she had Hessa's tech in her."

"Which brings up an interesting issue," Gerber said. "We were told what happened on Chafa and the way the controlled bodies there broke apart."

"They flat out dissolved, man," Yellow Eyes said.

"Until Hessa's implants were put in," Roak said. "Yeah, I've already had this thought."

"Something in Hessa's tech is compatible with Father's cellular control," Pol said. "Her tech stabilized the bodies and kept them from breaking apart. What we do not know is whether or not Father has duplicated Hessa's tech."

"He has not," Hessa said. "He can't."

"Why is that?" Pol asked.

"Because only I can build those implants," Hessa said.

"Yes, but-"

"There are no buts in this," Hessa said. "Only I can build that tech. It has to come from me or it does not work."

"And how do you know that for sure?" Pol asked. There was a glint in his eye that Roak did not like. "Hessa? All tech can be replicated if it is studied properly."

"Not mine," Hessa stated. "I'm the only one that can build it."

"We'll come back to that," Pol said. Pol grinned at Roak. While those seated at the table didn't flinch as if Roak had smiled, the tension did grow considerably. "It has come to my attention that you need me for something, Roak, hence your arrival at Javsatem. By the way, excellent deductive reasoning. I did not think anyone would track me there. Not even Father knew I was there at first."

"We had a hunch," Hessa said.

Pol's smile widened.

"I am sure you did," Pol said. "So, Roak, what do you need me for?"

"Other than all the chits you owe me?" Roak replied.

"Chits?" Pol laughed. "This cannot be about chits."

"I always get paid," Roak said.

"Roak does owe me a whole lot of chits," Ally said with a grin. "It'd be nice if he could pay me back."

"Yes, Roak always gets paid. We are all aware of this. The entire galaxy is aware of this," Pol said. "But chits are basically worthless now that the war between the Skrang Alliance and the Galactic Fleet has come to an end."

"It has?" Yellow Eyes asked then cringed at the looks he received. "Right. Yeah. It's totally at an end. Because, uh, because of...?"

"Father," Pol said.

"Because of that guy," Yellow Eyes said. "I hate that guy..."

"Roak?" Pol asked. "What can I do for you?"

"I need you to crack Bishop's quantum drives and get me some answers," Roak said.

"I can do that," Pol said. "What answers are you looking for?"

"Mother," Roak said. "I believe the location of Mother is somewhere in those drives."

"Interesting hypothesis," Pol said. "But there is only one problem with that thought."

"Only the one?" Sha asked.

"Yeah, I know," Roak said, ignoring Sha. "If Father had control of Bishop then he would have already had access to all of Bishop's files. If those files include the location of Mother then why would he ask me to take on the hunt to find her?"

"Precisely," Pol said. "I am guessing you have an answer?"

"Sure," Roak said. "He wants me to find Mother for myself, not for him. He knows where she is, but for some reason he can't get to her."

"Why can't he get to her?" Pol asked. He spread his arms. "He seems to be able to get to everyone, everywhere."

"That's why I need the drives cracked," Roak said.

"Which I will gladly do," Pol said, "when I am certain the drives are sequestered in a secure room where the data cannot corrupt this ship or any of our systems. No one likes a Trojan Horse."

"A what?" Yellow Eyes asked. "What's a Trojan? What's a horse?"

"Ignore him," Roak said.

"Ah, come on, man," Yellow Eyes grumbled. "Don't be like that."

"Does he know any other way to be?" Bhangul asked, the first time he'd spoken since sitting down. All eyes turned to him. "Never mind. Sorry to interrupt."

"You are the one that introduced Hessa to Roak, correct?" Pol asked.

"Yeah, so?" Bhangul replied.

"Oh, nothing, just making a mental note," Pol said. "We'll talk about your role more later. But, back to Roak. What else is it you need from me?"

"There's more?" Meshara asked.

"I need the new tech you developed," Roak said.

"Roak, we already have his new tech," Gerber interrupted. "And Pol has even fine-tuned the transport tech even further. What else is there?"

"The actual transport tech," Roak said and locked eyes with Pol. "You haven't told them?"

"I have not," Pol said with a sigh. "But I suppose I will have to now."

"No, let me," Roak said. "It took me a while to figure it all out. At first I thought that instantaneous galactic travel was all you were after. Then I found out you gave the tech to the GF. Just gave it to them."

"I wouldn't say he just gave it to us," Gerber said. "There were quite a few deaths involved and the issue of his stealing trillions upon trillions in fortunes from some very connected beings in this galaxy."

"He stole the credits just to mess with them," Roak said. "Pol doesn't need credits. Chits he can use to slip here and there, but credits are traceable. He was fucking with you."

Pol grinned even wider and that did cause a few beings to cringe.

"Do continue, Roak," Pol said and steepled his fingers. "I am enjoying this immensely."

"Then come to find out that the Skrang were given the same transport tech," Roak said. "That's interesting. I already knew what he was up to, but that only confirmed my suspicions."

"Can we hurry this up?" Sha said. "We have a lot of planning to do before we can all take some needed rest."

"Keep your roller chair on, Sha," Roak said. "I'm getting to it."

"Maybe get to it a little faster," Ally suggested.

"You too?" Roak asked. Ally raised an eyebrow. "Fine. Instantaneous galactic travel. Yay for Pol. But the thing that bugged me was that you were near a black hole before you demonstrated it to the GF and all those elite assholes. Why a black hole?"

"Roak, you aren't suggesting…?" Hessa asked over only Roak's comm.

"I am," Roak replied. Everyone frowned and Roak waved them off. "The galaxy was one thing, but where you really wanted to go was a different universe."

"A different part of the universe?" Gerber asked.

"Outside of our galaxy?" Sha asked.

"Preposterous," Meshara hissed. "There is nothing in the other galaxies. Extensive research has shown they are void of intelligent life."

"No, not our universe," Roak said. "A different universe altogether. A parallel universe."

"One of many," Pol said in agreement, his smile beaming with joy.

"Not one of many," Roak said. "One specific universe. Father's universe."

The table erupted into shouts and pointing fingers and accusations, all aimed at either Roak or Pol.

"You really do have a gift for fucking with beings," Ally said to Roak. "Have you considered not fucking with beings?"

"Life is boring enough without taking that fun away," Roak said.

He stood and slammed his hands on the table. The chaos continued. So he pulled his Flott.

Everything went quiet and all eyes stared at the pistol.

"Roak…" Gerber warned. The members of Drop Team Zero had their weapons out and aimed at Roak. "Think this through."

"Just needed everyone to shut up," Roak said and holstered his Flott. He pointed a finger at Pol. "Am I wrong?"

"Not in the slightest," Pol said. "But you aren't quite right, either."

All eyes shifted fully on Pol.

"Talk," Gerber ordered.

"Yeah, I want to hear this too," Sha said.

"Everyone would like to hear this," Meshara said.

"Of course, of course," Pol said. He stood. "It is simple, really. I have been studying Father's influence on our universe, and our galaxy specifically, for several decades now. Before Roak and his siblings arrived here."

"How? Why?" Sha asked.

"The how is because I happened to have developed tech, although for different reasons, that was able to detect a tear between the universes," Pol said. "The why is because I was alerted to that tear between the universes. That was quite the alarming discovery."

"And you didn't think to alert the GF?" Gerber nearly shouted.

"I thought about it and could find zero reason to," Pol said. "What would the GF have done? They would have tried to imprison me and use my brain to study the tear for their own purposes. I am a dark tech for a reason, General Gerber. I do not enjoy being controlled."

"Stop interrupting the guy," Roak said.

"Thank you, Roak," Pol responded with a slight nod of his head. "But the real reason I wanted to study Father was not because he had created a tear between universes, but why he did it. So I sent some probes over."

"And how do you feel about that choice?" Roak asked.

"Yes, it may not have been the best idea," Pol admitted. "My probes were highly advanced. Unfortunately, only two of them returned. The data they had was exceptional, but the fact that the remaining probes were lost was troubling."

Pol shook his head and held up a hand.

"No, lost is not correct. They were taken and repurposed," he added. "Then they were returned to our universe. With cargo."

Pol smiled directly at Roak.

All eyes shifted from Pol to Roak.

"Well, all the Hells," Sha said. "That explains the not quite human part."

"Roak and his siblings are completely human," Pol said. "Humans from a different universe."

"Did you know that part?" Hessa asked Roak.

"No," Roak said.

"Oh, yes," Pol said. "Or were you responding to Hessa? Is she talking to you privately? I cannot wait to truly understand that tech."

"Not a chance," Hessa said through the loudspeakers.

"We'll see," Pol said. "Anyway, Father sent Roak over then he took up residence of his own here too. He raised the younglings, trained them to be the efficient hunters that they are, and-"

"Were," Roak said. "There's only me and Reck left."

"Very true," Pol said. "And very sad. When you went rogue and killed Father, although that turned out not to be quite true, you showed him that even he could not control your kind in this universe. He tried for decades, and almost succeeded, but then he gave up after you could not be brought back into the fold. I believe Father murdered your siblings, Roak."

"Probably," Roak said. "Sounds like something he'd do."

"Hold on," Gerber said. "Why would you want to transport over to Father's universe? What's the point in that?"

"Isn't it obvious?" Pol replied. "To destroy the universe and seal the tear. It is the only way to keep our universe from being destroyed. Luckily, we may still have time."

"How much time?" Roak asked.

"Oh, a couple of months," Pol said. "At the most."

"Say what now?" Yellow Eyes exclaimed.

Roak smirked. The table winced. Then he smiled and started laughing. Even the Skrang looked upset by this display.

"I am not seeing the humor in this," Meshara said.

"Neither am I," Gerber said.

"Roak! Stop laughing!" Sha shouted. "It's disgusting…"

Roak slowly calmed down then nodded to Pol.

"You need Mother too," Roak said.

"I do," Pol agreed. "She's the key to destroying the other universe."

"I think you're right," Roak asked. "But let me ask you a question."

"Please do," Pol said.

"How much of my life have you been manipulating?"

"Oh, very little, Roak. A nudge here and a nudge there. Razer Station only happened because Father was becoming more aggressive. Otherwise our paths may never have crossed. At least not face to face."

Roak smacked the table again.

"Hessa? Do you have the drives ready?" Roak asked.

"I do, Roak. Shall I have some bots bring them to you?" Hessa answered.

"No, we'll come to the ship," Roak said. He held up a hand. "Just me and Pol. Alone."

More yelling and shouting. Roak ignored it all and focused only on Pol.

He smiled at the dark tech and the dark tech smiled back.

27.

"You have really upset everyone by excluding them from this process," Pol said as he took a seat in front of Bishop's quantum drives. "Gerber wants your head and so do the Skrang. Sha Tog is all that's keeping you alive right now."

"I'm pretty good at keeping myself alive," Roak said.

"Oh, that I am completely aware of," Pol said. "I would have preferred a sealed room, but Hessa has assured me this space is just as secure. Which, of course, intrigues me to no end."

"Get to work," Roak said.

Pol cracked his knuckles, studied the drives for a moment, then reached down to the floor and began separating tools from a compression pouch.

"Let's see now, what will I need?" he mused. "I highly doubt Father made this easy. I may have to interface directly with the drives in order to break through their security."

The drives were housed in an incredibly dense metal cube. Roak would be glad when they were finally open and he was going to be even more glad when they were off his ship.

"Interfacing with the drives directly is highly dangerous," Hessa warned. "Even for a being of your skills and abilities."

"Thank you for your concern, Hessa," Pol said.

"It is not concern," Hessa said. "We have gone through great trials and tribulations to get the quantum drives into your hands. If you are killed by them then everything will have been for nothing. That would be depressing."

"And then some," Roak agreed.

"Depressing…" Pol chuckled to himself. "Oh, what joy this all brings."

"Less joy, more cracking," Roak snapped. "Move ass, Pol."

"I hear your sister is even more bossy," Pol said. "I can only imagine what that is like. By the way, how is she? I can help with the prosthetics if you-"

"I have her recovery under control," Hessa said.

"I bet you do," Pol replied.

"How's it going in there?" Gerber yelled from outside the ship's cargo hold.

There was quite the crowd assembled in the hangar, all standing about ten meters away from the Borgon's open cargo ramp. It was the compromise Roak negotiated in order to keep the quantum drives on his ship.

"Move faster," Meshara hissed.

"I can close the cargo hold right now, beings," Roak snapped.

"Roak, need I remind you that-" Gerber began.

"Let the man do his thing," Yellow Eyes said. "It's best not to get in Roak's way."

"I have no idea what you are," Gerber said, "but you need to stop talking to me."

"Whatever you say, man," Yellow Eyes said and held up all his nubs in surrender.

"Ignore them," Roak said to Pol.

"Oh, I am, do not worry about that," Pol said, his hands running over the surface of the cube. "I am singly focused on one task."

"Roak?" Hessa called over the comm.

"Hmmm?" Roak replied. Pol gave him a quizzical look then nodded with comprehension.

"Reck is waking up," Hessa said. "I hate to pull you away from this, but…"

"I'll be right there," Roak said.

"Leaving?" Pol asked.

"I need to," Roak said. "And hovering over you won't make it go any faster, will it?"

"Not in the slightest," Pol replied. "Plus, you always have Hessa watching me."

"And don't forget it," Roak said. He stood and walked to the lift then stopped and spun about. "If you find anything, you tell me first. Understood?"

"Of course."

"No, I mean it. You do not say a word to anyone except for me."

"I already agreed to your terms, Roak. Go see to your sister."

Roak started to respond, but shook his head and walked to the lift. He entered and sent it up to the med bay deck. Roak took a deep breath then left the lift and walked slowly to Reck's med pod.

The lid lifted and Reck carefully sat up. There was no sign that she had been injured at all.

"Roak?" Reck asked as she swung her legs over the side of the pod. "What in all the Hells am I doing in a med pod?"

Roak tossed her a blanket and she covered herself as she stood up from the pod.

"You got caught up in the machinery," Roak said. "You almost died."

"That's no good," Reck said. "Hessa patch me up?"

"She did…"

"What? What's wrong?"

"Nothing is wrong. You're back to perfect health."

Reck's eyes narrowed.

"But...?" she asked.

"Not all of you made it into the pod," Roak admitted. "Hessa had to replace your arms."

Reck blinked at Roak a few times then let the blanket drop as she studied her arms and hands.

"They don't feel any different," Reck said.

"I'm that good," Hessa said.

"These are synthetic?" Reck asked, still staring at her hands and arms. "Skin too?"

"No, no, the skin is real," Hessa said.

"It is?" Roak asked.

"Of course it is," Hessa scoffed. "I am very good at what I do, Roak. Once I finished rebuilding Reck's arms, I was able to regrow her skin using several grafts from her legs. It was easy enough to have the med pod replenish the skin on her legs while it regrew the skin on her arms. It is basic med pod function."

Roak and Reck shared a look.

"What?" Hessa asked. "You said something to each other with that look. What is it?"

"Hessa, it is not basic med pod function to regrow skin over synthetics that quickly," Reck said.

"Of course it is," Hessa said. "I could do it all day long."

"No, Hessa, that is advanced tech," Reck insisted. "Med pods don't automatically have that function."

Hessa went quiet.

"How's Pol doing?" Roak asked.

"Pol?" Reck asked. "Where the Hells are we?"

"I'll get to that," Roak said. "Hessa?"

"He is getting closer to cracking the drives," Hessa said. "But he could still be a while yet. I am discouraging him from interfacing with the system. He is fighting me on that point, but I am not wrong. If he interfaces then he could get trapped in the drives themselves."

"Could? More like he will," Reck said. "No way Father doesn't have a million booby traps set up."

"Exactly," Roak said.

Reck picked her blanket up and wrapped it back around her naked body.

"You are going to tell me what in all the Hells is going on while we go to my quarters," Reck said.

"Good plan," Roak agreed.

They made their way to the lift as Roak explained everything that had happened since Reck was put in the med pod. By the time they reached Reck's cabin, Roak had dumped it all on her.

"I already knew the other universe part," Reck said, pulling on a pair of pants.

"What? Terpigshit you did," Roak replied.

"Alright, I didn't know for sure, but Rink had a theory," Reck said. "She told me about it a while ago. Then all the Hells broke loose and I never was able to talk to her about it again. Before she died."

"It explains a few things," Roak said.

"It definitely explains why the med pod isn't working on your physiology as well as it used to," Hessa said.

"Hessa, let us talk alone," Roak said. Reck raised her eyebrows and Roak sighed. "Fine. What do you mean by that, Hessa?"

"You are from a different universe," Hessa said. "Which means your energetic makeup is not in tune with this universe. Med pods are calibrated for the energy forms of this universe. They worked at first, but with each successive healing it has become more and more difficult for the med pods to attune to your specific energy."

"The same will happen to me eventually," Reck said and flexed her hands. "Good thing I got these now then."

"I appreciate your positive attitude," Hessa said.

Roak laughed. "That's what she's known for. Her positive... Huh."

"What?" Reck asked.

"Positive. Energy," Roak said.

"Is this word association time? Because I'm not in the mood for games," Reck said. She flexed her hands some more. "What I'm in the mood for is testing these new babies out. Hessa? I'm guessing my manual dexterity is improved?"

"Exponentially," Hessa said.

"Yeah, this may not be a bad thing," Reck said.

"Hold on. Hold on," Roak said, placing a hand on Reck's shoulder before she could leave the cabin. "Hessa, what would it take to calibrate the energy forms of this universe with the energy of the other universe?"

"Wow, Roak, thanks for asking such an amazingly easy question," Hessa said. "Let me check my notes on quantum chaos and multi-verse astrophysics. I am sure I have exactly what you're looking for just tucked away somewhere in my mainframe."

"Hessa, I'm serious," Roak said.

"What's up?" Reck asked.

Roak held up a finger.

Reck frowned and grabbed the finger, causing Roak to wince. Reck smiled and let go.

"Not sure I like the new you," Roak said as he shook his hand. "Hessa?"

"Since you obviously aren't going to let this go," Hessa huffed, "In theory, you would need to create a conduit between the two universes. Something that could transmit an energy signal that was perfectly tuned to the energy frequency of this universe."

"Would a stolen planet or two do the trick?" Roak asked.

"They would. But we were already thinking along those lines," Hessa said. "Father stole the Cervile planet in order to gain greater control over all of those with GF implants. He stole the Skrang planet to do the same thing."

"Yes, but he also went to Javsatem…" Roak started to pace.

"Can we walk and talk?" Reck asked. "I really want to put these hands to use."

"Hold on!" Roak snapped.

"You are very close to being a test subject for my new right hook," Reck warned.

"Energy," Roak said. "It's about the energy, but he also needed to control the flesh. Why? He had total control by using just the implants."

"If he can control the flesh then he doesn't need the implants," Reck said as she left her cabin. "Roak!"

Roak followed along, but he barely noticed where they were going.

"No. There is something more," Roak said. "I'm missing the key."

"You're missing a lot more than a key," Reck said as they entered the lift. "Pol's in the cargo hold with the quantum drives?"

"He is," Hessa said.

"Energy. Energy, energy, energy," Roak muttered.

"Yep. Energy," Reck said and rolled her eyes.

The lift stopped and she walked out into the cargo hold. She had to reach back in and yank Roak out with her.

"Looks like he has an audience," Reck said and waved at the beings standing outside the ship in the hangar.

"Reck!" Yellow Eyes shouted. There was a blur and he was in the cargo hold, all nub arms wrapped about Reck in a huge hug. "I missed you! Did you miss me?"

"Yellow Eyes, you are not supposed to be on the ship right now," Hessa said as Yellow Eyes released Reck.

"He can stay," Roak said. Roak focused on Yellow Eyes. "What was that energy weapon that was used to wipe out the other ships?"

"Energy weapon?" Yellow Eyes asked. "Oh, the lightning gun!"

"It is not called that," Pol said.

"You focus on the drives," Roak said to Pol.

"I can multitask," Pol said.

"No, you can't," Roak said. "Yellow Eyes? Tell me more about the lightning guns."

"You should really ask Sha Tog and the Skrang," Yellow Eyes said. "It's their tech."

"Is it?" Roak asked. "I remember something about a weapon like that being used during the War."

"Which one? The war now or the War war?" Yellow Eyes asked.

"The War war," Roak said. "Something…"

Roak's eyes went wide.

"Uh oh," Yellow Eyes said and took a couple of steps back. "Don't like that look. Nope. That's not a good look."

"Gerber! Sha!" Roak shouted and stomped to the cargo hold's ramp. He paused just short of leaving the ship. "The energy weapon you used? Where did it come from?"

"The disruptor?" Sha asked.

"That's Skrang tech," Gerber said.

"No, it's not," Sha said.

"What? But the Skrang used it during the War," Gerber said. "Then stopped using it when you realized it destroyed all ships, not just enemies, and couldn't be directed or controlled."

"Yes, to the last part," Sha said. "But it is not Skrang tech. It was developed by-"

"B'clo'nos!" Roak shouted, making everyone jump.

"Do you mind, Roak!" Pol hissed. "I am good, but I can still be distracted."

"That's where the tech comes from, right?" Roak asked Sha. "The B'clo'nos!"

"Yes, so?" Sha replied.

"Wait…" Gerber said. "What are you saying?"

"Back to the conference room," Roak ordered and stomped down the ramp, past the waiting group of onlookers. "I figured out what that piece of terpigshit is up to."

"You all have fun," Pol called. "I'll take care of this here."

"Yeah, you do that!" Roak called back as he left the hangar. "Hessa?"

"I will watch him like a Cweatt dragon," Hessa said.

"Good," Roak said. He glanced at the group following him. "No. Just Gerber and Sha."

"I'm not comfortable leaving the general alone with you, Roak," Motherboard said.

"And I'm the FIS SSD Commander," Crush said. "I have every right to listen to what you have to say."

The Skrang brass started growling and cursing at Roak in their guttural language, making everyone wince. A few had to cover their ears.

"Gerber and Sha," Roak said. "I don't need a bunch of opinions getting in the way of the truth."

"Your theory of the truth, you mean," Gerber said.

"I'm cool with that," Kalaka said. "Where's the bar?"

"There is no bar," Sha said. "This is a Skrang warship."

"No bar?" Kalaka frowned. "I truly am in all the Hells."

"I think we may be able to hook you up," Geist said. "General?"

"Fine. Just stay sharp and be ready," Gerber said.

"Follow us, beings," Geist said and walked off down the corridor.

Everyone except Meshara followed.

"You too," Roak said.

"I am the official representative from the Cervile Royal Family," Meshara said.

"They don't care!" Cookie shouted back at her. "They aren't Cervile and don't know any better!"

"What he said," Roak said and waved her away.

Meshara's face scrunched up with fury, but she held it in check and stalked off after the others.

"Can we get full scan readings in that conference room?" Roak asked Sha.

"Of course," Sha replied.

"Then that's where we're headed," Roak said and walked off, leaving Gerber and Sha to share a puzzled look.

28.

"Roak, what is going on?" Gerber demanded.

"Take a seat," Roak said. "Sha? Bring up the B'clo'no's home system."

"Any holo or do you need a current view?" Sha asked.

"Do you have access to a current view?" Roak responded.

"The B'clo'nos are Skrang allies," Sha said. "So they are monitored by Skrang closer than if they were enemies."

"Then please bring up the current views," Roak said.

Sha activated the holos and scanned through the images until he came upon…nothing.

"Hold on," Sha said. "These are the feeds. I know it. They should show us multiple views of the B'clo'no's system."

"Perhaps the B'clo'nos disabled the surveillance," Gerber said. "Friends don't like being watched by friends."

"The B'clo'nos are not friends of the Skrang. They are allies," Sha explained. "Not that anyone from the GF should talk about surveilling friends or allies."

"Touché," Gerber said. "Still, looks like the B'clo'nos have disabled the feeds."

"They didn't," Roak said. "He did."

"He who? Father?" Gerber asked. "Why? The b'clo'nos aren't compatible with implants. He has no way in with them."

"Oh no," Sha said.

"He's getting it," Roak said and waited.

"Good for Sha Tog," Gerber said. "Roak, we don't have time for your games."

"Energy and flesh," Sha said. "Father took the Cervile planet first then Skrang. Those were test runs."

"Test runs? They gave him the ability to control all GF implants and all Skrang too," Gerber said. "I would not call those test runs."

"But they were," Roak said. "They had advantages, but what Father really wanted was initial control through energy then total control through the flesh. It was never about the implants."

"Except it was," Hessa said over the loudspeakers. "My implants."

"How did she gain access to internal comms?" Sha said. "I did not grant her permission this time."

Roak and Hessa laughed.

"I haven't missed you, bounty hunter," Sha said.

"Yeah you have," Roak replied.

Sha glared, but the corner of his lip twitched in a smile.

"Father used Chafa as a trap so we would have to go there," Hessa said. "I put my implants in Klib, who was already under his control, and he was able to stabilize the signal that he was using while also stabilizing the flesh. I gave him the answer on how to send a signal without having to use implants."

"That is great that he can send that signal," Gerber said, "but there has to be something on the other end receiving the signal. Without implants, a being cannot…"

"Now he's getting it," Sha said.

"B'clo'nos feed off and absorb energy," Gerber said. "Father calibrated the signal so they would consume it like any other energy."

"And he used the tech on Javsatem to stabilize his control of their flesh," Roak said.

"Controlling GF beings and Skrang was only a distraction," Gerber said.

"A deadly distraction," Sha said. "But, yes, I think that is it."

"Smoke and Eight Million Gods damn mirrors!" Roak shouted. "I should have known to look anywhere but where he was pointing us. This has been his plan all along."

"He's building an army," Gerber said.

"He's already built an army," Sha said and pointed at the blank holo.

"Now he's preparing for war," Roak said. "With an entire race of energy-feeding, war-worshipping beings."

"The B'clo'nos are savages," Sha said. "I'm Skrang and my culture says I should have been executed for my disability, so calling B'clo'nos savages means a lot."

"Yeah, it does," Gerber said. He leaned back in his seat and rubbed his forehead. "B'clo'nos. They were impossible to fight during the War. It took the Skrang to bring them under control once the treaty was signed."

"And we forgot all about them because they were considered side players," Sha said.

"Classic Father," Roak said.

"What now?" Sha asked. "Are we going to their system? Because that seems suicidal."

"It is," Gerber said. "We'd be wiped out in minutes."

"I need an army of my own," Roak said.

Gerber stared at Roak. Sha shook his head and chuckled under his breath.

"I'm sorry, Roak, but did you ask for an army?" Gerber said.

"He did," Sha said.

"Are you truly qualified to have your own army?" Hessa added.

"Hey, back off," Roak snapped. "Yes, I need my own army."

"I am more suited to lead an army than you, Roak," Gerber said. "Sha is more suited to lead an army and he has no legs."

"What do legs have to do with leadership?" Sha asked.

"Will Skrang follow you into a war?" Gerber said.

"They have so far," Sha countered.

"Only because they had no choice," Gerber said. "With me they have a choice."

"You think that Skrang will follow a GF general into battle?"

"More than a cripple that was supposed to be executed."

"Shut the fuck up!" Roak roared.

Gerber and Sha both looked like they wanted to draw down on Roak, but they calmed themselves and nodded in turn for Roak to continue.

"I need an army because Father has an army," Roak said. "This has been coming for a long, long time. You two will fight like GF and Skrang if either of you are in charge. You need to fight like me. The army needs to fight like me."

"And how does Roak fight?" Gerber asked.

"Without rules," Roak said. "You two are conditioned for rules of engagement and warfare tactics and all that terpigshit. You'll hesitate when hesitation will lead to our destruction. You'll overthink a strategy when action is what is needed. You'll pause when firing on a target to wonder if destroying that target is needed. I won't do any of that."

"There are reasons for rules of engagement, Roak," Gerber said. "They allow clarity in the fog of war."

"Which is why your strategies won't work," Roak said. "The last thing we need is clarity. We need chaos. Pure, unadulterated chaos."

"You do excel at pure, unadulterated chaos," Hessa said.

"Roak?" Pol called.

"How did he get access to comms?" Sha asked. "Never mind. I give up on this."

"Wise choice," Pol said. "Roak, we need to talk."

"Busy," Roak said.

"We need to talk now," Pol said.

"Have you cracked the drives yet?" Roak asked.

"I am very close," Pol replied. "That is why we need to talk. Can you come here?"

"Back to the ship?"

"Yes. Back to the ship."

"I'll be there shortly. Let me finish this-"

"Now would be best," Pol said. There was a tone in his voice that Roak did not like.

"You know something," Roak said. "And it's something you've known all along. You son of a gump. I am going to put a plasma blast between your eyes if this is another one of your setups."

"Just come here," Pol said.

Roak growled then grimaced at Gerber and Sha.

"You two," Roak said, pointing a finger back and forth at each of the beings, "figure out how to get me an army. I'll be back in a minute."

"Sure, Roak, we'll figure that out for you!" Sha called as Roak left the conference room.

He grumbled his way to the ship. Only Yellow Eyes was in the hangar.

"Hey, Roak, how'd the chat with Gerber and Sha go?" Yellow Eyes asked. "You figure out how to save us all?"

"Maybe," Roak said and hurried past Yellow Eyes.

"Alright. Nice talk!" Yellow Eyes called out.

Roak stomped up the ramp and into the cargo hold where he found Pol seated cross-legged next to the quantum drive cube.

"Why are you just sitting there?" Roak asked. "Did you crack it or not?"

"I am one step from unlocking the drives," Pol said.

"Great. Get to it. Then you can start sifting through the data to find what I need," Roak said.

"I already know the answer to your question, Roak," Pol said. "I have known for a while. Well, maybe not a while, but I have had my suspicions. They will be confirmed when I unlock the data in these files."

"You're making me feel shooty, Pol," Roak said and patted his Flott. "Unlock the drives."

"Before I do, you need to know that the answer is not a threat," Pol said. "You are not in harm's way and, if anything, this information will be nothing but positive. It will allow us to move into the next phase of your personal journey."

"Yeah, shooty sounds good," Roak said and gripped his Flott tightly.

"Stop that," Pol said. "You aren't going to shoot me."

"Maybe I won't, maybe I will," Roak said.

"Let me ask one question before I unlock the drives," Pol said. "May I?"

"You just did."

"Funny."

Roak took a deep breath. "Sure. Ask your question?"

"Do you trust Hessa?" Pol said.

"Hey! Don't bring me into this," Hessa said.

"You are already in it," Pol said. "Answer the question, Roak."

"Yeah. I trust her," Roak said.

"But do you truly trust her," Pol said and patted his midsection. "Down here. Where those legendary hunches come from. Do you trust Hessa with all of your being?"

Roak started to answer then paused.

"Well, this feels good," Hessa muttered.

"Yes," Roak said firmly. "I do. I trust her with my gut. Hells, I trust her with my life, so yes, I trust her with all my being."

"Good. Good," Pol said and reached out. He placed a finger on the cube. "Focus on that trust. Remember that trust. We will need that trust to be unbreakable if we are to survive Father. Do you understand?"

"Nope," Roak said. "But I'll go along with it."

"Hessa? The same goes for you," Pol said.

"I already trust myself," Hessa said.

Roak grinned.

"You know what I mean," Pol said.

"This is sounding rather ominous," Hessa said.

"But necessary," Pol said.

"Hessa, tell him you trust me," Roak said.

"Of course I do," Hessa said.

"Excellent," Pol said. "Then here we go."

The cube physically unlocked. It actually began to unravel itself until it was no longer a cube, but a small containment field with several floating energy orbs inside. Pol waved his hand through the containment field and grabbed one of the orbs. He twisted it this way and that then let go.

"Pol…? What is this…?" Hessa gasped. "What are you telling us?"

"Nothing, so far," Roak said, exasperated. "What is in there? Where's Mother?"

"Mother is right here, Roak," Pol said and stood up. "Mother is Hessa. Hessa is Mother."

Roak froze. His body froze, his mind froze, everything froze.

"Yes, well, I'll let the two of you talk," Pol said.

He walked off the ship, past a curious Yellow Eyes, and out of the hangar.

"You guys alright in there?" Yellow Eyes asked. "Hello?"

Roak came out of it and shook his head.

"That can't…" he started.

"There's no way…" Hessa said.

"Guys?" Yellow Eyes called.

"Eight Million Gods dammit!" Hess and Roak shouted in unison.

THE END

Coming soon: the last chapter in Roak's saga- *Roak's War*!

ABOUT THE AUTHOR:

Jake is a Bram Stoker Award nominated-novelist, award-winning novelist, short story writer, independent screenwriter, podcaster, audiobook narrator/producer, and inventor of the Drabble Novel.

As the author of 60+ novels, he has entertained thousands and reached audiences of all ages with his uncanny ability to write a wide range of characters and genres.

Check out his other Galactic Fleet novels, as well as his other works, news, and updates at jakebible.com and jakebible.substack.com.

CHECK OUT OTHER GREAT SCIENCE FICTION BOOKS

MAX RAGE
by **Jake Bible**

Genetically Engineered. Physically enhanced. Mentally conditioned.

Master Chief Sergeant Major Max Rage was the top dog in an elite fighting force that no one in the galaxy could stop. Until, one day, someone did.

The lone survivor, Rage was blamed for the mission failure and court-martialed.

With a serious chip on his shoulder, Rage finds himself as a bouncer at the top dive bar in Greenville, South Carolina. And, man, is he bored with his job.

At least until he gets a job offer he can't refuse. Now, Rage is headed halfway across the galaxy to the den of corruption known as Horloc Station.

With this job, Max Rage may have a chance to get back to what he was: an unstoppable Intergalactic Badass!

WARNING: THIS NOVEL HAS GRATUITOUS VIOLENCE, SEX, FOUL LANGUAGE, AND A LOT OF BAD JOKES! YOU MAY FIND YOURSELF ENJOYING HIGHLY INAPPROPRIATE PROSE! YOU HAVE BEEN WARNED!

RECON ELITE
by **Viktor Zarkov**

With Earth no longer inhabitable, Recon Six Elite are sent across space to scout promising new planets for colonization.

The five talented and determined space marines are led by hard-nosed commander Sam Boggs. Earth's last best hope, these men and women are the "tip of the spear". Armed with a wide array of deadly weapons and forensics, Boggs and Recon Elite Six must clear the planet Mawholla of hostile species.

But Recon Elite are about to find out how hostile Mawholla truly is.

CHECK OUT OTHER GREAT SCIENCE FICTION BOOKS

LOST EMPIRE
by Edward P. Cardillo

Building on their victory in the last Intergalactic War, the imperialist United Intergalactic Coalition seeks to expand their influence over the valuable Kronite mines of Golgath. Reeling from their defeat, the warrior Feng are down but not out. The overextended UIC and the vengeful Feng deploy battle groups and scramble fighters as they battle for position in the universe, spinning optics and building coalitions. Captain Reinhardt of the Resilience and the elite Razor's Edge squadron uncover the Feng Emperor Hiron's last ditch attempt to turn the tables with a new and dangerous technology. With resources spread thin, the UIC seeks to exploit Feng's weakened position through a very conditional peace accord. Unwilling to submit, Emperor Hiron must hold them off and quell the growing civil unrest of his starving, warrior people just long enough to execute the mysterious Operation: Catalyst. Commander Massa and his Razor's Edge squadron race against time to stop Hiron's plan, and a new race awakens, led by a powerful prophet set on toppling the established galactic order through violent acts of terrorism.

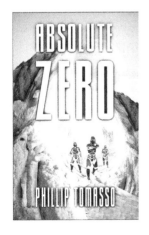

ABSOLUTE ZERO
by Phillip Tomasso

When a recon becomes a rescue . . . nothing is absolute!

Earth, a desolate wasteland is now run by the Corporations from space stations off planet . . . A colony of thirty-three people are part of a compound set up on Neptune. Their objective is mining the planet surface for natural resources. When a distress signal reaches Euphoric Enterprises on the Nebula Way Station, the Eclipse is immediately dispatched to investigate.

The crew of the Eclipse had no idea what they were getting themselves into. When they reach Neptune, and send out a shuttle party, they hope they can find the root cause behind the alarm. Nothing is ever simple. Something sinister lies in wait for them on Neptune. The mission quickly goes from an investigation into a rescue operation.

The young crew from the Eclipse now finds themselves in the fight of their lives!

CHECK OUT OTHER GREAT SCIENCE FICTION BOOKS

AGENT PRIME
by **Jake Bible**

Denman Sno is Agent Prime!

The best of the Fleet Intelligence Service's elite Special Service Division, Denman Sno will need to use all of his skills and resources to stop the galaxy from plunging into another War with the alien menace known as the Skrang Alliance.

Sno's assignment: protect and deliver Pol Hammon, the galaxy's greatest dark tech hacker, to Galactic Fleet headquarters.

Hammon is in possession of new technology that can and will change the landscape of galactic life. The Galactic Fleet will do anything to keep that technology out of the hands of the Skrang Alliance even it it means sacrificing their best agent.

Even if it means sacrificing Agent Prime!

GALACTIC TROOPERS
by **Ian Woodhead**

For three thousand years, the Terran Empire has ruled the Galactic Expanse with an iron fist, conquering any alien civilisation who dared to oppose the might of their new human masters.

Their grip is about to be shaken apart when an unknown invasion force starts to strip whole planetary populations.

Now humans and aliens must find a way to work together to prevent the Empire and the invaders turning the Galactic Expanse into a graveyard.